The death of a beautiful, young patient was the worst thing Sarabeth Love could imagine — until she was accused of her murder...

"I had become a doctor to change people's lives, and that's what I was doing. I was full of myself, full of pride and pleasure at the life I had chosen. I was fighting a network of old boys who were sometimes wrong in their ideas and I was helping women like Hollis Taft Brewster stand up for themselves and define the course of their lives. Somehow I sensed that Hollis hadn't just given birth to Kristin — but to a new future for herself. And how could I know that night, when I thought that changing the world was so easy, that the world had decided, that very night, to change me?"

— DR. SARABETH LOVE

THE WHOLE TRUTH

BY JANICE KAPLAN

THE WHOLE TRUTH

JANICE KAPLAN

B

BERKLEY BOOKS, NEW YORK

THE WHOLE TRUTH

A Berkley Book / published by arrangement with
the author

PRINTING HISTORY
Berkley edition / January 1997

The Putnam Berkley World Wide Web site address is
http://www.berkley.com/berkley

ISBN: 0-425-15603-6

BERKLEY®
Berkley Books are published by The Berkley Publishing Group,
200 Madison Avenue, New York, New York 10016.
BERKLEY and the "B" design
are trademarks belonging to Berkley Publishing Corporation.

PRINTED IN THE UNITED STATES OF AMERICA

10 9 8 7 6 5 4 3 2 1

THE
WHOLE
TRUTH

*I*T WAS A MURDER INDICTMENT.

I stared at it for several minutes, flipping the pages, before I understood that. And when I did, I tried to hand it back to the clerk who had delivered it, a shabby man in a gray suit and frayed tie.

"You've made a mistake. This isn't for me."

"You're Sarabeth Love?"

"Yes."

"Then it's for you."

"But it's not." I looked at the clipboard he held, with names and addresses, and the bag of documents slung over his shoulder. "Maybe you've given me the wrong one."

I held it out again, but he wouldn't touch it. His job was to deliver, and that's what he had done. Usually he delivered divorce papers from the courts, and for a brief moment I was convinced that was what he had meant to give me. But Paco and I weren't even married.

"Everything's right, ma'am. I'm sorry." And he

turned and fled back to the beat-up Chevy he had left double-parked on the street, as if afraid of me, the murderer.

I felt a numbness overtaking me, and I could barely move from the stoop. Doctors didn't kill people, they saved them. I was a doctor, so this was all wrong. I stared again at the complaint, but the words swirled before my eyes, only the name of the victim jumping out at me like a serpent. She wasn't a victim, she was my friend; I hadn't killed her, I had tried to save her. Yes, I had seen blood spilling out, but that was about life, not death. The blood of death had come later and I didn't know about that. I had been as shocked as anyone.

Somehow I got back inside, and stood as if paralyzed, trying to decide what to do. I needed to call someone, but who? Nobody could know about this. Not the doctors, not my parents, not even Paco. My lawyer was supposed to fight this in secret because it couldn't be true, but now this indictment was burning in my hands. And it had to be a mistake. I wasn't a murderer, but good God, how was it that she was dead?

one

LIFE BEFORE

I

CALL ME AMBITIOUS. On a snowy New Year's Day, Dr. John Franklin invited me into the wood-paneled study of his posh townhouse and asked if I wanted to join his ritzy Beacon Hill medical practice. I said yes before he could blink. He handed me a cup of eggnog, poured from a Lalique crystal punch bowl, and said the starting salary would be $80,000 and they'd like me to start immediately. This time I took a sip of the eggnog before I spoke. Maybe I should have smelled something fishy right then, but I didn't. The only thing that struck me as fishy was the caviar displayed on a plate in front of me with a dribble of onion and some grated egg. I stared at the caviar for a moment while images of debts from college and medical school danced in my head and I said, "Start immediately? Why not sooner?"

Dr. Franklin smiled. His year-round tan had been revitalized by a Christmas ski trip to Aspen, and he looked healthy and fit. His whole style, from his tasseled loafers to his silver-gray hair, suggested a movie star rather than a doctor. The fireplace behind us was crackling with a fire so hot I could feel my face flushing, but Dr. Franklin was wearing three layers of clothes—a white turtleneck that set off his tan, a yellow cashmere sweater that looked so soft I wanted to stroke it, and a nubbly tweed jacket in pale shades of gray, complemented by gray twill trousers. He was the ultimate prep-school boy grown up—the type who had to dress in layers because he had so many clothes he wouldn't get to wear them all otherwise.

He dabbed some caviar onto a bread round and said, "I take that as an acceptance?"

"Yes."

"Well, good." His offer was better than his conversation, but he sat down next to me on the sofa, took a bite from the caviar, and asked, "When do you take your obstetrics and gynecology boards?"

Everybody else in the department called it ob-gyn, but John Franklin had his own style, and I had to get used to that fast.

"The next time they're given," I said. "I think it's July."

Dr. Franklin seemed to think about that for a moment. "Aren't you done with your residency before that?"

"Next month," I said proudly. As usual, I was finishing well before everyone else.

"Fine. If you can join us next month—and we could use you then—we'll give you some time off in the late spring to study for the boards. You'll need to pass the first time around."

"Of course. It won't be a problem."

"I know." He looked me straight in the eye and some

of the smoothness was gone from his voice. "I'm making you this offer because I expect a lot out of you. I hope you don't mind my bringing up something so serious at a party. Dr. Pierce and I decided yesterday to invite you to join our practice and when I saw you today, I couldn't wait any longer to ask."

He was lying, and I knew it but I also didn't care. In all the months we had worked together at the hospital, Dr. Franklin had never had me to his home before, and the invitation to his New Year's brunch had been unexpected. Now I understood. I wasn't exactly his type for socializing, but if he was hiring me, he had to introduce me to his golfing buddies. Which would explain why he'd put his arm around me when I arrived and dragged me over to a group of slick-looking men, saying, "Meet Sarabeth Love. Number one in her class at Radcliffe. Number one at Harvard Medical School. Plus the best resident I ever met."

I recognized some of them from the hospital—Physicians & Surgeons, or P&S, where I'd been an intern, resident, and chief resident. The doctors were a tight clique of high-priced practitioners who weren't too worried about the changing health-care plans in the country because their rich patients would find a way to get to them one way or another. But I was worried.

"Dr. Franklin, I'd be very interested in joining your practice," I said, trying to sound professional now. "Maybe we could sit down later this week to talk about details?"

He looked surprised. "Such as what?"

"The terms of our agreement," I said. "Scheduling, benefits, office practices, all that."

"Frankly, Sarabeth, I can take care of all that right now." He stood up and poured himself a glass of Perrier Jouet, then positioned himself in front of me. "I've been in this practice for twenty-five years, and Dr. Pierce has been with me for fifteen. Things are changing in medicine, and we understand that. We're not worried about our financial situation being affected"—he coughed slightly—"but we both want to slow down a little bit. That means taking fewer night calls and delivering fewer babies on weekends. You'll be there to fill in for us. Ditto on our vacations. As you know, ours is an extremely busy practice, and we don't expect anything to change that. You'll have plenty to do just handling our overflow. We don't want you associating with any other groups. Right now we've made deals with Oxford and Brewster Managed Care." They were two of the bigger medical insurers that had taken over where outfits like Blue Cross and Blue Shield had failed or become too expensive. "Because we've joined up with them, we expect to see a lot more patients who aren't our—well, usual style. Eventually you'll be able to help us expand our patient base."

I nodded, reading between the lines. Right now they were comfortable, but they were also smart enough to understand that medicine was changing and they'd better do something to protect themselves. Every rich Wasp socialite on Beacon Hill already went to Franklin and Pierce to have her baby, but as medicine changed, the practice needed to make some concessions to the real world. The very thought of managed care probably made them queasy. But to be a doctor in Boston there was no other choice.

Hiring me meant taking a huge gamble on brains instead of breeding. My background was Catholic parochial school, not Waspy prep school, and my mother hung lace curtains instead of hanging out at the Junior League. But I was smarter than most and worked harder than anybody, which made me difficult to ignore. I'd made a mark during my residency by becoming expert in some of the whiz-bang techniques of nineties medicine. I'd assisted in dozens of in vitro fertilizations. I'd tried fetal surgery and amniocentesis and was so good at chorionic villus sampling, which told about a baby's health very early in pregnancy, that some of the other doctors had asked me to do the procedure on their wives. I had a flair for moving tiny needles in risky places. In an earlier generation, I would have made great needle-point pillows.

Dr. Franklin had more to say. "We're not offering you a partnership right now, and we won't even begin to discuss that for at least two years. You'll be on call twenty-four hours a day, of course. Unless we're on vacation, you'll have off every third weekend. We provide you medical benefits through an arrangement with Brewster Managed Care. You know the salary. Any further questions?"

"Yes," I said. "Hospital privileges."

"You'll need them." He smiled. "We're happy for you to bring some innovations to the practice, but we still deliver babies in the hospital."

"How do I get them?"

"Just apply. Dr. Ardsley's secretary has the forms."

Dr. Archibald Ardsley was the chairman of our department at the hospital. He was aloof, overbearing, and reportedly brilliant, though I'd never seen anything to make me think he was doing much more than living off past reputation. He was more feared than admired by men and more hated than feared by women. Residents arriving at the hospital, as I had a few years ago, were generally advised to work hard on the floors, be prepared for attending rounds, and avoid confrontations with Dr. Ardsley. So far, I'd managed that.

"There aren't many women physicians in the ob-gyn department," I said carefully.

"You're already in the department."

"I'm chief resident," I said, stating the obvious. "As far as I know, Dr. Ardsley has refused privileges to a dozen women who've applied."

"That's all nonsense. They weren't qualified and you are. I hate it when women who aren't up to snuff blame their failings on sex."

The whole comment was so politically incorrect that I didn't even bother to tell him he meant gender, not sex. I could think of plenty of women, former classmates of mine at Radcliffe, who would have run screaming out of the room by now and called a press conference to charge that the gynecologists in Boston were guilty of sexual discrimination, sexual harassment, and being plain old creeps. They'd probably be right. But I wanted a good job. I needed a good job. And the hell with political correctness. So I said, "What happens if Dr. Ardsley doesn't think I'm qualified?"

Dr. Franklin looked at me impatiently, and I realized that I'd missed something. "Gus and I were roommates at Princeton and Yale Medical School."

"Gus?"

"Dr. Ardsley."

I should have known. One of those cute nicknames prep-schoolers always have for each other. At least it was better than Archibald.

"Anyway, we're old friends," Dr. Franklin said. "If I'm hiring you, there won't be any issue about privileges."

I nodded mutely, suddenly understanding the power of the old-boy network. On any other day, I would have railed against it, but today I could only realize in awe that I was about to be a part of it.

"Now, if we're all set, shall we go back into the party? My wife must be wondering what happened to me."

I followed Dr. Franklin back into his living room, which was overflowing with holiday cheer. A crystal chandelier caught the sunlight from the huge windows and splayed rainbows all over the well-polished floors. Blond women in velvet headbands were clustered around a punch bowl and men in Ralph Lauren sweaters picked tiny hors d'oeuvres off the trays and paused in front of the television to check out the scores on the Bowl games. Most of them looked as if they'd stepped out of an advertisement for expensive Scotch. I heard two women behind me squealing when they discovered they were wearing the same dress—a camel's hair number with a short camel-and-gray jacket—and they immediately compared notes on what they'd ordered from Donna Karan for the spring. They talked about the designer as if she were an old friend and exclaimed over her spring collection, which they both agreed was much better than Calvin Klein's. Without even looking, I knew that nobody else in the room would be dressed in my outfit—a long navy skirt, a flowing white blouse with a cotton lace sweater, and flat shoes. My thick auburn hair floated down my back in a tumble of mostly untamed curls. I'd adopted this style during college and didn't pay any attention when designer skirts turned short and tight. Mincing through the hospital would never be for me. Now, long skirts and lace shirts were becoming fashionable again, but that certainly wasn't my fault.

Dr. Franklin's townhouse was so big that the television blaring at one end of the living room was no distraction to the tuxedoed musician at the far end, who was playing pleasant background music on the baby grand. He was just launching into "White Christmas" when my live-in love, Paco, caught my eye and waved to me. I sighed in involuntary relief, realizing that I'd half expected to see him huddled in a corner, ignored by one and all once I disappeared with Dr. Franklin. If I felt out of place here, I expected Paco to feel like a Martian dropped on a desert island. But instead, he was holding court with several attentive women—his tight blue jeans and long hair obviously not upsetting them.

I joined them just as one of the women leaned very close to Paco and whispered, "Now, tell me again about your art show." She had pulled a Gucci notebook out of her purse and stood with gold pen poised.

"It opens February fifteenth at the Massol Gallery on Newbury Street. Actually, it's a group show. Three artists."

The woman scribbled down the information, then cooed, "One of my favorite galleries. I did tell you I'm a decorator, didn't I?"

"I believe so. I hope you'll come by with some clients." He smiled ingratiatingly at her, and I felt my stomach churn. First I'd worried about my artist-boyfriend not fitting in. Now I had to worry about his running off with some doctor's wife.

The decorator put away her notebook and said, "I'll be there, Paco."

I slipped my hand under his arm, and she stared at me. "Hi," I said. "I'm Dr. Sarabeth Love."

"Nice to meet you." She snapped her handbag shut and the group of women around Paco seemed to melt away. I stared after her, wondering if the interlocking C's on the purse indicated a genuine Chanel or just a good imitation. In this crowd, it had to be real, but I couldn't imagine it. Given what I was making as a resident, one Chanel handbag equaled two weeks salary.

Paco, unaware of the attention he had attracted, was equally unaware when it ended. He squeezed my hand and gazed at me with the deep blue eyes that had won my heart in the first place.

"So, what happened with Dr. Franklin? Did he make a pass at you?"

"Better than that. He offered me a job."

"Smart man. And you said . . ."

"Yes—what else would I say? He started off with the salary, which is eighty thousand a year. That's the good news. The bad news is that I'm expected to work all the time. They're tired of delivering babies, and I'm not. So as near as I can tell, they take vacations and I wear a beeper."

"Who's they?"

"Franklin and Pierce."

"Sounds like a gourmet food shop."

"I think that's S. S. Pierce. And it's probably out of business by now."

"My mother used to shop there."

"So did mine, which has nothing to do with the doctors. Doctors Franklin and Pierce have been partners for a long time, and they're not looking for a partner—they're looking for a slave. I've agreed to sell myself into two years of bondage."

"With a hundred sixty thousand dollars at the end. That's not bad, sweetie."

"I know. Better than I could do at an HMO or HIP or as an academic genius staying at the hospital." For the first time, I allowed myself a grin. "Next year we can have a party like this."

"If we'd want one."

"Which we wouldn't."

"Right." We exchanged an understanding look; Paco turned away and dug the toe of his moccasin into the Oriental carpet, so I quickly added, "Of course, by next year you'll have sold so many paintings that what I'm making will seem like a joke. All those decorators will be hanging on to you even more than they are now. I'll have to fight to keep you with me."

"I like you poor, and I'm sure I'll like you rich," Paco said, smiling that comforting smile of his, and I immediately felt better.

"We won't be anything like rich, but at least I can pay off some of my loans. Between college and medical school debts, bondage is about all I can expect."

Paco looked around the room. "Are you going to be comfortable with these people?"

"Probably not. But I don't think the deal is to socialize with them, it's to be their doctor. And if Dr. Franklin had wanted a friend, he would have picked one of the handsome rich-boy doctors from Yale. Instead, he's got me, and I'm not going to ask why."

It was too bad that I didn't.

I started my life as a Beacon Hill doctor at 8 A.M. on the coldest day of the year, and as I walked into the office, I heard Dr. Franklin telling one of his nurses about the trip he was planning to the Caribbean island of Turquoise. The nurse—shapely, blond, and adoring— was standing very close to him and turned around startled when she realized someone had come in. She was wearing sensible nurse's shoes and white stockings, but her very short white dress clung seductively to her curvaceous breasts and slim hips. Fighting for attention was her blond hair—thick and silky and tumbling gracefully over her creamy-complexioned skin.

"Do you have an appointment?" she asked.

"I don't need one." I shook some of the snow off my coat. "I'm Dr. Sarabeth Love."

The nurse looked at Dr. Franklin, reluctant to say anything until she knew how he planned to treat me.

"Welcome, Sarabeth. Glad you're here." He extended his hand and seemed excessively jolly. Not bothering to move away from the nurse, he added, "Meet Juliette Martin—one of the best nurses in Boston, and we've got her. Actually, she's got us. It's really Juliette who runs this office."

"Hi, Juliette."

"Hello." She offered a wan version of a smile, and

turned back to Dr. Franklin. "Should I show Sarabeth her office?"

"Good idea. And then I'll meet you in mine for just a minute, please."

I followed Juliette down the hall, and she gestured to a small consultation room with a large desk and an X-ray stand. "Here you are. This will be yours. I'll find you again in a few minutes."

As I took off my coat, I heard her scurrying down the hall, and the door to another consultation room closed firmly.

I wandered around the room, noting that not a lot of decisions had been left to me. A neat brass plaque on the door said DR. SARABETH LOVE. The desk was outfitted with a green leather blotter and matching desk accessories, and several textbooks on obstetrics already filled the single bookshelf. A small couch, upholstered in a dark green-and-blue tartan plaid faced my desk, and two tasteful flower prints took up the wall above it. The facing wall held three empty frames, obviously awaiting my diplomas from Radcliffe, Harvard Medical School, and P&S residency.

I opened the large tote bag I always carry—this one a gift for donating fifteen dollars to the public television station in Boston—and dug around for the one picture I had brought from home. It had managed to wedge its way to the bottom of the bag, beneath my stethoscope, rumpled white coat, and makeup case, but when I finally pulled it out, Paco's sexy smile glimmered at me. He was sitting under a tree with a curly-haired three-year-old—my sister's daughter, Betsy—in his lap. She was wearing tiny denim overalls, a pink T-shirt, and a wily smile. A poster child for the Gap. I liked looking at Paco and Betsy while I worked—they were as close as I was going to get right now to a traditional family. The real thing would come later, I was sure, but who had time at this point? I'd had Betsy's baby picture at the clinic when I was a resident, and seeing it always seemed to make pregnant women relax. They could draw whatever conclusions they wanted.

"Nice picture. Is it your daughter?"

I spun around and saw Nurse Juliette standing at the door.

"That's Betsy. She's three. And Paco."

"Cute." She looked at me dubiously, then said, "Dr. Franklin would like to see you."

"Sure." We went to Dr. Franklin's consultation room, which was about four times the size of mine but decorated in the same patrician style—lots of wood and dark plaids. His room had a hunting theme, and several English prints of fox-hunting scenes decorated the walls. Was this what he selected to make his female patients feel comfortable—hounds chewing on bloodied foxes?

He was on the phone when I came in, but hung up almost immediately. "You chose an excellent day to start, Sarabeth. That was the labor nurse at the hospital. One of my patients was just admitted. Mona Simpkin. I promised her that I'd try to be over in time for the delivery, but my office hours are packed this morning. I'd hate to have to cancel them. Dr. Pierce can't do it because he's in surgery. Forty-two-year old woman with cervical cancer." He shook his head. "A life and death day, I'm afraid."

"You'd like me to go check on her?"

He nodded. "It's a first baby, so I'm sure she'll be hours. I'll try to get over there this afternoon."

"I'll go over right away."

"Good. Be careful getting there; it's slippery out. Where are you parked?"

"I'm not parked. I took the subway over here."

He looked at me as if I were speaking a foreign language. "How were you planning to get to the hospital?"

"Subway, again. It's only two stops."

"Oh, for heaven's sakes, don't do that. Juliette, show her how to call a taxi on our account, please." Then turning back to me, he said, "Before you head out, let me mention that I'm planning a little vacation for the week after next. First I have a three-day conference that Juliette will also be attending"—he looked meaningfully at her—"then my wife and I will spend four days in the Caribbean. I'm telling the girls up front to book me as usual for that week, and you'll take over. Sound acceptable?"

"Of course." I smiled cheerfully, nauseated by my own I-can-do-anything spirit, but figuring that was one of the reasons he'd hired me. I resisted mentioning that this one little speech of his had offended me on at least three counts, starting with his virtual announcement that he was having an affair with Juliette, moving quickly to the fact that he was keeping Juliette in line by also vacationing with his wife, and topping off this display of misogyny by referring to the nurses and receptionists in the office as girls. I gritted my teeth and smiled some more.

Back at the front desk, I met some of the "girls" who were drifting in. Office hours didn't actually start until

8:30, but they all seemed to have plenty to do. I picked out two who looked like nurses—both were young and efficient, wearing white pants and lab coats that masked most of their curves. An older, matronly woman dressed in a gray wool skirt and blouse, her grayish-blond hair tied in a bun, seemed to be the receptionist. The nameplate on her desk said Delores Patino and she'd probably been with Dr. Franklin since the day he opened his practice and maintained secret fantasies of being his office wife. That role, however, had clearly gone to Juliette.

While I tried to get my bearings, Juliette opened a Rolodex and copied down a phone number. "That's the taxi company. Dr. Pierce is usually in surgery for such a long time that he's too tired afterwards to drive. The account number is HP460. Just tell them that and they'll have a car here right away."

With the car service, I was at the hospital in no time, and ignoring the elevators, raced up five flights of stairs to the obstetrical floor. I saw Mona Simpkin's name on the chalkboard at the nurses' station next to Labor Room 2 and headed down the hall into a scene of total chaos. Close to a dozen people were jammed into the tiny labor room, with others rushing in and out. I felt myself gearing into emergency mode, but an instant later, as I elbowed my way into the room, I sensed this wasn't a typical emergency. The very pregnant patient was lying in a heap in the middle of the labor bed, sobbing, but instead of administering to her, everyone in the room seemed to be screaming at each other. There was no lifesaving equipment in evidence—just three nurses standing in a row like the Three Furies—one clutching an IV pole, another an enema bag, and the third a

wrapped kit of sharp needles. They were glaring at the
sobbing patient, but standing two paces away from her
bed. Kneeling at the head of the bed was a doctor I
recognized as the chief resident in psychiatry, Dave
Schwartz, and next to him was a psychiatric resident
holding an unopened syringe. The chief resident seemed
to be imploring the woman to do something, but she
kept wailing and shaking her head. In the opposite corner of the room, a handsome, broad-shouldered man was
arguing with three obstetrical residents, who seemed to
be holding him hostage. He pretended to be listening to
them, but kept sending panicked glances to the woman
on the bed, who was clearly his wife.

Two days earlier, the obstetrical residents had been
my peers, but today I was a private doctor, an attending
physician, and this was my patient. So in the loudest
possible voice, I called out, "What's going on here?"

If I'd expected the furor to immediately stop as attention turned to me, I was mistaken. Nobody gave me a
glance. I stormed over to the residents, grabbed one
firmly by the arm, and said, "Jay, what the hell is happening?"

He turned briefly from the cornered husband and said,
"You know this woman?"

"She's my patient. Actually, she's Dr. Franklin's patient, but he can't get here until later. Now tell me in
two sentences what's going on."

Jay looked around the room, as if he couldn't possibly
distill the chaos into two sentences. He was saved from
trying by the head nurse on the floor, a tough, mean-
spirited woman named Blanche Dolton, who regularly
insisted that her word was law. She was standing inches

away from Jay, screaming at the top of her lungs, but somehow she'd heard my question, and now she spun around and declared, "The problem is that we have a hysterical woman here. She's making impossible demands and refusing all hospital procedures, and we won't stand for it."

"Nurse Dolton called me when Mrs. Simpkin started causing problems for the nurses," Jay said. "She also called Dave Schwartz, who's been trying to reason with her."

"All I wanted was for him to sedate her," Nurse Dolton said bitterly. "I don't think there's time for psychotherapy here. In fact, there's not time for any of this nonsense, given how irresponsible the patient has been."

The husband, in the corner, snapped, "She wasn't irresponsible, and we've been through this. Now you're just trying to torment her."

"We are not," said Nurse Dolton, her voice rising to a fevered pitch again. "We're just doing what's required."

I looked at Jay, who said, "Mrs. Simpkin's labor has progressed very rapidly. My guess is that she was in labor all night and didn't realize it. She got to the hospital about an hour ago and is already six centimeters dilated. We tried to move quickly, but when the nurses came in to prep her, she got extremely upset."

The picture was becoming clear to me. I started to push my way over to the bed, thought better of it, and went back to the husband. The last thing Mona Simpkin needed was one more doctor trying to talk to her in the midst of this madness.

"Mr. Simpkin, I'm Dr. Sarabeth Love. I work with

Dr. Franklin. He'll be over in a little while, but in the meantime, I'm in charge of the case. I'd like to get this situation back in hand, and I need you to trust me if we're going to help your wife.''

"Gladly.'' He nodded, needing someone to trust, and I was probably the first person this morning who wasn't trying to boss him around.

"Thank you.'' I turned to Nurse Dolton. ''Please clear the room for me of everyone except Mrs. Simpkin and her husband.''

"What?''

Nurse Dolton was so infuriated that I thought she'd haul off and hit me, but I just repeated the request. The nurse was bigger, angrier, older and louder, but I was the doctor, and I wasn't giving an inch. The nurse knew how to follow orders, and within two minutes she shepherded everyone out and slammed the door. The noisy chaos of the room dissolved into silence, broken only by Mona Simpkin's panting sobs.

Her husband raced over to her, shooting me a panicked look. I sat down on the bed and put my hand on her back.

"Mona, I'm Sarabeth Love. Dr. Franklin will be over shortly, but meanwhile I'm here. I'm sorry for what just happened, but let's forget about it. You're here to have a baby. That's what matters right now. Your baby. And you.''

Some of the sobbing slowed down, but she still couldn't catch her breath.

"Did you take Lamaze classes?''

The husband nodded.

"Good. I assume you're her coach. Get her breathing regularly."

For a moment he tensed up, as if he couldn't remember anything, but then he took his wife's hands and started breathing with her. I watched them for a minute. If she was six centimeters dilated, the labor pains were hurting now. Between the pain and hospital-induced hysteria, she was hyperventilating. I opened my tote bag, found the brown paper bag with my lunch, dumped out the apple and sandwich, and took the slightly crumpled paper bag over to Mona.

"Let's try some high-tech medicine," I said. "Breathe in and out in the paper bag. You have too much oxygen circulating right now. If you breathe back some of your own carbon dioxide, you'll restore the balance and feel better."

The simple explanation convinced her. Her husband held the bag, and she continued her Lamaze breathing into it. In two minutes her breathing was regular again, and she seemed in control.

"Magic," said her husband, handing the bag back.

"Having babies isn't really that hard," I said, smiling. "Otherwise people would have quit a long time ago."

"I don't want any medication," Mona said, her voice edging onto tears again. "And Dr. Franklin said I could try doing without it."

"Of course you can. And you're doing great."

"Then why was everyone coming at me with needles?"

"Hospital procedures," I said. "Some of it looked scarier than it really is. Look, I'm sure the last thing you really feel like is being examined, but how about if I take a quick check to see how you're doing? Then I can decide how to proceed.''

She nodded, and as promised I was quick.

"Already eight centimeters, and almost fully effaced," I said, pulling off my gloves. "I don't think it will be too much longer." She gasped as a pain hit her, and I waited until it subsided. I'd never gone against hospital procedure before, but I understood her resistance. Being attacked with needles to start an IV when you were having labor pains every two minutes seemed almost too much to bear.

"Listen, I'm going to stay here with you for a while. If I'm here, we don't need the labor nurse, and we can dispense with the usual rituals. The only thing that I would like is for you to have an external fetal monitor. You don't have to stay strapped to it. Let's just put it on for a few contractions, make sure all is well, and then we're done."

Mona looked over at her husband, clearly too exhausted to make any decisions now, and he said quickly, "That sounds fine." I didn't want to leave the room, so I pressed the white call button next to the bed, wondering how long it would take a nurse to respond. Almost immediately Nurse Dolton flung open the door.

"We're going to do a brief external monitoring," I said, before she had a chance to ask anything, "so would you be good enough to bring in the equipment we need?"

"Certainly." She stalked out the door and, returning moments later, marched over to the bed. I intercepted her and took the equipment from her hands. "Thanks, Miss Dolton. I'll handle it myself."

"As you like. Should I send in the labor nurse to start an IV, or will you take care of the rest of the prepping, too?" She looked as if she wanted to spit at me, but kept herself under control.

"Actually we're fine here, thanks."

The head nurse gathered herself up to her full height and prepared for the final punch. "Dr. Love, I should warn you that it's my job to report any deliberate flouting of hospital policy. If the patient isn't prepped, I intend to report it to Dr. Ardsley."

"Report whatever you like, Nurse Dolton," I said calmly. "Just please make sure you get your facts right. Now, if you'd be kind enough to keep everyone out of this room unless specifically called, I'd appreciate it."

For the second time that morning, Nurse Dolton slammed the door as she left. I slipped the fetal monitor over Mona's belly and we all watched the small screen where the baby's heartbeat was translated to a simple jagged line. Mona had a contraction that left her crying out, but the regular line didn't change. After several more contractions, I was convinced that everything was fine. I gave Mona some ice chips and tried to cheer her up. Her contractions were getting worse, and she squeezed her husband's hand and concentrated on her breathing.

"You don't have to lie in bed," I told her. "Sometimes you feel better if you walk around or get on all fours."

She didn't get up, but she curled onto her side and immediately seemed to feel more comfortable. I began chatting with her husband, who said his name was Rick.

"I remember a Rick Simpkin who played for the New

England Patriots a few years ago,'' I said.

"Are you a sports fan?"

"Always have been. My dad loved the Boston teams."

Rick smiled abashedly. "You must be a really big fan to remember me. I only played two years."

"Running back, wasn't it?"

"Boy, you're good." He grinned. "I like to think it was all practice for catching this little baby. You don't think I'll fumble, do you?"

"Not a chance."

On the bed, Mona groaned, and Rick leaned over to massage her back.

"Don't touch me," she pleaded.

"There can be too much sensory overload," I told Rick, who looked stung by his wife's rejection. "Don't take it personally."

In a few minutes the contractions were so severe that Mona was crying out in pain at each one. It was going to be a very short labor—which usually meant a very painful one. I used the telephone at her bedside to call Dr. Franklin and tell him that the baby would probably arrive before lunch.

"Well, I won't," he said. "Even if I leave right now, it's snowing so hard that it will take me a while to get to the hospital."

"Snowing?" The labor room had no windows, and time—hours, days, seasons—could pass unnoticed. When you were in labor, it always seemed like the middle of the night. I thought of all the hours I'd logged in the hospital, not knowing if it was winter or summer, night or day. "Hold on. I'll give you Mr. Simpkin."

I handed the phone to Rick so that Dr. Franklin could explain the situation himself. He didn't seem at all perturbed. "Dr. Love has been wonderful," I heard Rick say. "We'll be fine."

The moment he hung up, Mona cried out, "I can't take it anymore. I'm being ripped apart! I'm going to die!"

I checked her. "You're not going to die. You're going to have a baby. Let's get you to the delivery room."

I called for some help, but Mona began weeping again. "Don't let them near me! Stay with me, Dr. Love, please!"

I calmed her down, and walked next to her as she was wheeled to the delivery room. Changing into surgical scrubs without leaving her side was going to be tricky, but Rick and I managed to switch off getting changed without leaving her alone. She was screaming on the delivery table when I got in to the room. Again, I shoved everyone else aside and stood very close to her. "Just ignore everything and push," I whispered.

She gave an impressive snort, accompanied by a blast of muscle power, and I saw the baby's head appear.

"It's almost here!" I told her. "You're just crowning."

Rick seemed torn between standing at his wife's head and comforting her and rushing to the other end where all the action was. He helped her through two more pushes and I said, "I'm going to do an episiotomy now," but she was sufficiently numbed that she didn't even seem to feel the sharp edge of the scalpel. Moments later the baby wriggled out and gave a healthy holler and Rick cried out, "It's a girl!" Mona murmured, "Let me see her,'' and I snipped the umbilical cord to let them be together.

I heard their murmurings and kisses and soft sobs of ''Look at her!'' but my eyes were on the blood pouring out with the afterbirth, as if all the life that had been inside Mona could not help spilling into the world: baby, placenta, lifeblood.

Holding her baby, Mona began to shiver and then whimpered softly, ''I'm cold.'' The nurse went to cover her with a sheet, but I said, ''Hold on, please,'' and a moment later asked with all the calmness I could muster that the nurse escort Rick and the baby away from the table.

''I-I w-want them t-to st-tay with m-me,'' cried Mona, unable to control her shaking.

I had been honest all along, and I wasn't going to stop now. ''There's some unusual bleeding here, so let me take care of it. Your husband can get to know the baby in the room right outside.''

Rick, with the firm hand of the nurse on his elbow, had moved away from his wife over to the pediatric resident, who suctioned the baby's mouth, gave it an Apgar score of nine, and dropped the silver nitrate into its eyes. Normally he would have handed the baby back to the father then, but from the bustling around the delivery table, he knew something was wrong, and wanted to make sure the baby—his charge—wasn't affected.

For some reason, I flashed to the first day of medical school when a professor had tossed a test tube full of blood onto a clean white sheet, and the class had collectively gasped. ''Looks like bloody murder, but really it's an inconsequential amount of blood,'' the professor had told us. ''Don't ever be deceived.''

Looking now, I tried to make a rational judgment. How much blood was it? And where was it coming from? The blood gushed with great gusto now, pooling at Mona's thighs.

''Uterine rupture?'' asked the nurse.

''Possible, but I don't think so.'' I was palpating Mona's still-bulging stomach, exploring the potential sources of disaster. Then I spoke to my patient. ''I know this is scary, but stay calm. You're going to be all right. Am I hurting you doing this?''

''N-not really,'' she said. ''J-just a lot of pulling and t-tugging.''

''Good.'' Labor had been so quick that she was probably still numb from the rapid dilation and forceful delivery.

''Do you need some backup help?'' the nurse asked.

''Call in anesthesia, please. I think I've found it. Cervical laceration and a torn vessel. May be extending quite deep—possibly to the parametrium. We need to begin suturing immediately and I'll start an IV.''

''I'll tell anesthesia to start it as soon as someone arrives.''

''No, I'll do it right now.''

The nurse looked surprised, but brought me the equipment, and Mona asked, ''What's happening?''

''There's a tear, but we're going to repair it.''

''I thought you did an episiotomy.''

''I did, and that's fine. But this tear is much farther up—inside the birth canal, on the cervix. I'd like to give you some morphine so you can relax through the procedure. Otherwise there might be considerable discomfort. We didn't start an IV before, but I have to do it now.''

Mona was openly weeping now. ''But I wanted a natural childbirth. You said we could.''

I squeezed her arm. ''And you did it. The baby is fine. She wasn't exposed to any anesthesia. You were terrific, in fact. This wasn't your fault. Just one of those things that happens.''

I slipped the intravenous needle into a vein on Mona's left arm quickly—and fairly painlessly, I must say. I thought of all the older attendings who hated to get their hands dirty with anything technical and wondered if in a few years I'd be arrogant and rusty, too. I hoped not.

''Pump five milligrams of morphine into the IV and prepare for the suturing,'' I told the nurse.

In a moment, with the morphine pumping into her veins, Mona took a deep breath, and wiped her eyes. Then she said, ''Dr. Love, you'll do this, won't you? Nobody else?''

''Yes, I'll do it.''

There's nothing like spurting blood to focus your attention, and our preparations were quick. I talked the nurse through the procedure so she could get ready. ''We need to begin the suturing above the apex of the wound, which is hidden by blood right now. I'll need forceps. Continuous suturing will be the quickest way to get around the torn vessel.''

I worked intently, calling for equipment, moving the needle around the wound and manipulating the bloody tissue. Nobody in the room spoke of anything except the situation at hand. Finally, after forty-five minutes, the bleeding had stopped, and the laceration was delicately closed.

"I think we're okay," I said.

I took a deep breath and tried to release some of the tension that had built up in my shoulders. One of the nurses said, "Nice job" as she swung the table of surgical equipment away, and another just pulled off her gloves and walked out of the room. We were finished.

Moving around the table, I patted the now-groggy Mona's hand. "You're okay," I said softly. "Nothing to worry about. Now let's get you and that baby together."

II

SINCE I WAS already at the hospital, I rounded on the rest of Dr. Franklin's patients, had a quick lunch, and wrote up some medical records. Before leaving, I checked on Mona, who looked wan but was nursing her baby. Amazing how fast you could forget the pain of eight pounds and seven ounces ripping—quite literally—through your body. The IV I had hooked up was still in place, now dripping antibiotics into her bloodstream. Mona begged me to get rid of it, but the messy tear I'd repaired was a prime target for infection, and I said no. I half expected a battle, but she just shrugged and turned her attention back to the baby.

I was just about to head back to the Beacon Hill office when I thought I heard my name on the overhead page. Since the public address system sounded like someone was talking from the bottom of an oil barrel, I called the operator.

"This is Dr. Love. Did you just page me?"

"Yes, Dr. Love. You're wanted in Dr. Ardsley's office."

My first thought was to be pleased. The chairman of the department of obstetrics and gynecology had never asked to see me before—I'd been granted hospital privileges without any direct meeting with him—so maybe he wanted to issue a personal welcome on my first day. Yeh, right. Heading toward the elevator, I laughed aloud. I was pleased with how I'd handled Mona's case, but thinking that Ardsley was calling to be pleasant was the first sign of an encroaching God complex.

Ardsley's secretary, Ginny, was in her usual place outside his door. Fortyish or so, she was Ardsley's polar opposite—a warm and encouraging den mother who nurtured overtired residents and interns. If a resident had a problem, she would quietly switch shifts and schedules without ever telling Ardsley, and she was the one who had put through the papers for me to get privileges. Everyone talked to Ginny, confided their problems, and her old-fashioned, flamboyant style didn't get in the way. Today, she was wearing a too-tight low-cut wool dress that showed off her generous cleavage, and when I came up she blinked her excessively mascaraed eyelashes at me and said, "So, how's the big jump from resident to staff doctor going?"

"You tell me," I said. "Is he furious about something?"

She giggled. "Always. But don't worry about it, honey. He's just an old teddy bear. Go on in."

Dr. Ardsley—or should I call him Gus?—was standing by his desk, holding a patient's chart. Teddy bear was not how I'd describe him. His long white coat was spotless and sharply ironed creases were evident in his black pants. Overbearingly tall, he had a pair of reading glasses perched at the end of his aquiline nose. If you're going to be an arrogant Wasp bastard, you might as well look the part. He could act the part, too. The moment I stepped onto his Oriental rug, he took off the glasses and gazed down at me as if he'd just noticed an odd-shaped bug on his carpet. "That was a very unusual case you handled this morning," he said. "What are your thoughts on the etiology of the tear?"

I swallowed. Okay, maybe "Welcome to the staff" was a bit much to expect, but whatever happened to "Hello, how are you?"

I cleared my throat. It was obvious that Dr. Ardsley wasn't making small talk—at least with me—so I plunged right in. Two can play the arrogant-bastard game. "It was a large baby and an extremely fast delivery. The combination led to a jagged tear that extended all the way up to the parametrium. I was able to suture it quickly enough that there was no significant loss of blood and no need for transfusion. The patient is resting comfortably now with a drip of penicillin, four million units every four hours, and gentamicin, eighty milligrams IV every eight."

"When did you put in the IV?"

"As soon as I realized there were unusual circumstances. There was no delay in proceeding. I had the line in place well before anesthesia even arrived." I knew my stuff and I hadn't done anything wrong. I could answer questions as fast as he could ask them.

"Nurse Dolton tells me you were quite disrespectful

to her and refused to have the patient properly prepped. That would have included putting in an IV well before your, quote—unusual circumstances—endquote."

He wasn't just rude, he was obnoxious. I tossed back my red hair—maybe he'd figure out I was Irish and had a temper. I felt like decking him. The kick-punch I'd learned in karate class would no doubt be justified in these circumstances. The sensei had said to wait for signs of "dangerous aggression" before attacking—and I sure didn't have to wait any longer. But somehow reason prevailed.

"The patient was upset before I got there, and Nurse Dolton wasn't helping the situation—in fact, she was aggravating it. Labor was progressing extremely fast, and I decided to stay there myself. I calmed the patient and her husband and used an external fetal monitor to determine that everything was normal. It was. I used my best medical judgment as to what other prepping was necessary."

"Your best medical judgment?"

"Yes." I sounded snappish, which probably wasn't smart, but the truth was I'd take my medical judgment over hospital policy any day.

Dr. Ardsley raised an eyebrow but decided to move on. "Why was there no anesthesia used?"

"The patient had requested no anesthesia or painkillers during delivery, and there was no medical reason to go against her wishes."

"Demerol can slow labor."

"That's not what we usually try to do, is it?"

"What about forceps?"

"Not used. There was virtually no intervention until

I discovered the tear. Nothing I did caused the tear, and nothing I can think of would have prevented it.''

Dr. Ardsley threw the chart on his desk. ''You have an answer for everything, don't you?''

I didn't have an answer for that.

''As far as I can tell, you made at least one mistake. Let's run through it without a lot of double talk, okay? When exactly did you start the IV? Before or after the actual delivery?''

''After.''

''Once you'd discovered the bleeding?''

''Yes.''

''You endangered a patient's life, Dr. Love. The blood vessels could easily have collapsed by then. That's why we start IVs before any delivery. Any. Hospital policy. I'll investigate this further, but you can expect to be cited for that.''

He gave me a nod of dismissal, and I was no doubt supposed to slink off, but I was too mad. ''The patient is doing fine and is very happy with how I handled the case.''

''Then you won't be sued for malpractice, and we can keep this as a matter only for professional review,'' he said acidly.

How do you say ''screw you'' to the chairman of the department?

While I mulled that over, Ardsley said, ''Being a resident is very different than being an attending, you know. So don't get cocky just because you did well as a student. I tried to tell that to John, but he insisted on hiring you and I gave you privileges as a favor to him.''

He didn't bother to say he'd tried to talk Franklin out of hiring me, but it was pretty obvious.

"As long as you're here," he continued, "you might as well accept the key term, which is that everybody practices at my forbearance. In case John didn't give you any advice, I will. Don't make waves and follow department policy. And I might add, don't spit in the faces of the nurses."

I had a few choice words for the recent behavior of the nurses, but I kept them to myself. Instead, I said, "Some of the nurses may have a little resentment toward the women doctors—however few there may be on this staff."

"That's your problem, Dr. Love. If you can't get along with the nurses, guess which one of you will have to go?"

"If that's a threat, Dr. Ardsley, I should mention that I'm not planning on leaving. And I don't think you really want me to. I know how to fill beds." I tossed my head again, realizing I should shut up, but burning to keep going. "This hospital needs me for the same reason Dr. Franklin does—I attract the patients your bureaucracy has been scaring off."

He looked slightly off balance, and for the first time in the conversation, I had the pleasure of being one up on Gus Ardsley. But he recovered. "Of course you're here to fill beds. But that doesn't have anything to do with the case we're discussing."

"Yes it does. I don't manage health care, I manage patients. I pay attention to their needs, not just the hospital's. Squelch that and you don't do any of us any good." I was speaking loudly, but it was hard to stop myself.

"We have policies here meant to meet the needs of the patients."

"No, you have policies to keep the hospital bureaucracy going smoothly. I was at Mona Simpkin's bedside, Dr. Ardsley. What I did had a positive medical outcome and also made the patient feel comfortable and happy. Shouldn't that mean something to your policies?"

Obviously it didn't, because he said, "I'm not continuing this discussion. I'll be reviewing this case. And following it closely. You made a mistake with the IV, and you'd better admit it."

"Is that another threat?"

"It's a fact."

I left the hospital, and still raging, went back to the Beacon Hill office where I saw half-a-dozen patients, but only ran into Dr. Franklin in the hall. It was just as well. What good would it do to let him know that his buddy, the chief of the department, hated my guts—and that I'd just made it worse? I finished with office hours at about 6 P.M. and saw that the snow was billowing down in giant flakes. But some combination of concern for Mona Simpkin and fear of Dr. Ardsley led me to trudge back to the hospital. The nursing shift was just changing, and a young nurse who'd recently come on duty smiled when I asked for Mona's chart.

"She sure is a popular patient," the nurse said, handing it to me.

"Why's that?"

"Dr. Ardsley was by just a few minutes ago."

"Oh. Did he say anything?"

"Not really. He spent a long time looking at the chart and just a couple of minutes with the patient, but he left the medication as you ordered it. I know because I specifically asked. Sometimes he writes notes changing orders—or just gives something to the patient—and forgets to tell us."

I looked in on Mona, wrote a note on the chart to show I'd been there, and noticed that Dr. Ardsley hadn't written anything. He'd just come by to check on me. Hoping for a mistake, no doubt. Well, he wouldn't find one.

I finally headed home, taking a subway this time and then traipsing through the snow. After a while, I stopped thinking of Ardsley and started picturing myself opening the door and being taken into Paco's arms. Me, the hard-working doctor with a passionate lover like Paco. I still wasn't sure how it had happened.

But when I opened the door, Paco didn't come rushing to greet me. The place was chilly, and I was welcomed by the dank smells of oil paint and turpentine. Paco had dragged a huge canvas from his upstairs studio down to the living room, and he was sitting on a stool, his long legs sprawled in front of him, staring at the painting and holding a tiny brush that was dripping with fiery red paint.

"How was the first day?" he asked, not quite looking at me.

"Fine. Actually, kind of traumatic. One tough delivery that ended up well. Then an unpleasant meeting with the head of the department, who's threatening to cite me for not following hospital rules and being rude to nurses.''

''Is that serious?''

''Just an annoyance.''

He didn't say anything more, and I wasn't surprised. Funny, this had sounded just like a conversation, but I knew Paco had at least half his attention on the canvas. I put down my tote bag and umbrella and slowly unbuttoned my coat. I was wet all over, my wool coat as sopping as my hair. I sighed and tried not to think about the hot shower I wanted to take. Paco was waving the paintbrush in front of the painting, and I wondered where it was going to land.

''What are you going to do with that red?'' I asked. ''It looks like blood.''

Now I had his full attention.

''You think so?'' he asked. He looked from the paintbrush to me, then over to the canvas again.

''Yup,'' I said. ''Blood.''

''Okay, if it's blood''—he waved toward the canvas—''then where does it go in what I'm trying to create here? Can you see it?''

I groaned. I wasn't indifferent to art—it was just that I'd spent more time studying organic chemistry than Picasso. Give me a picture from a sonogram and I could tell you what it meant, providing the subtlest of interpretations; but show me a canvas that didn't have an image of flowers, churches, or Jesus Christ and I was stymied.

I went over and kissed the back of his neck. ''I love you, darling, but you know I'm lousy at discussing art.''

''No, come on. This one's been inspired by you and

I think you see it. You just don't want to admit it.''
Paco was looking at me, his deep blue eyes gleaming
with anticipation. ''I'll give you a hint. It's called 'A
Day in the Hospital.' ''

''Then all the red in it is blood,'' I said, trying not to
sound helpless.

''Seventeen different shades of red,'' he said triumphantly. ''And the deepest red in the center hints at the
despair at the core of our hearts.''

I cocked my head to contemplate the vivid crimson
glistening in the center of the picture. It looked to me
like wet paint, but I tried to think of it as despair. Something in my expression made Paco burst out laughing.
''You don't know what the hell I'm talking about, do
you.''

I made a face. ''Not really. The colors are gorgeous
and I like looking at it. But it's so beautiful that I don't
see how it can be about the despair in our hearts.''

''What do you see in it?''

I always hated that question. I knew that ''Nothing''
would not be an acceptable answer, so furrowing my
brow, I stared at the picture and waited for it to speak
to me.

''I guess I see the mystery of birth,'' I said. ''At the
center is just what you suggested—blood, despair, terror.
The primal scream. That eruption of something new—
whether literally a new life or metaphorically anything
you choose to begin—is frightening. But then you
emerge from that and the terror turns into the sunlight
that's all around it. You have those beautiful swirls of
yellow and blue that promise clear skies and bright sunlight. So to me, the picture is about emerging from de-

spair into the promise of a brighter tomorrow.''

Paco looked at me, then back at the painting. He stood up slowly and I saw a small smile playing at the corners of his mouth.

''You really see all that?''

I shrugged. ''That's what it says to me.''

The smile was bigger now. ''You're full of crap.'' He kissed me, but seemed to keep one eye on the painting. ''You don't see anything like that in it.''

''I see 'A Day in the Hospital,' '' I insisted, laughing.

He ran his fingers up the back of my neck and lifted my hair, as if testing its heft. ''Well, you were damn close to what I was thinking. Blood and pain. Hope and promise. As I said, my ode to you. Fact is, I probably don't understand what you do any more than you understand what I do.''

''But you're trying to understand. And I'm trying. And I love you.''

''I love you too.'' He kissed me, swiveling his hips gently, and in a few minutes we were lying on the dhurrie rug, understanding each other perfectly. He massaged my thighs, and somehow my clothes came off as he pulled me on top of him. Paco was always intent on being a perfect lover, and I had to admit I didn't mind. When at last we were finished, we went into the kitchen and I made sandwiches while Paco uncorked a bottle of white wine. We took our winter picnic into the bedroom and tumbled into the huge iron bed Paco had made for us when we moved in together. After we ate, we made love again, then snuggled for a long time, stroking and talking, and when Paco fell asleep his rhythmic breathing was like a lullaby. When I finally fell asleep,

I dreamt that Archibald Ardsley was chasing me through the corridors of the hospital with a whip, and that Paco was fending him off with the dripping paint of his red heart.

I had two cesarean sections to perform at the hospital the next day, both managed-care patients I didn't know, prearranged by Franklin. It wasn't how I liked to practice medicine, but I just had to do them. After the first delivery, I checked on Mona, who was just getting off the phone when I came into her room.

"I've told at least a dozen of my friends about you," she announced cheerfully. "Expect a huge surge in your practice. All my friends plan to start coming to you, and trust me, once they see Rose, they're all going to get pregnant."

"That's nice," I said looking at her chart.

She laughed. "You don't believe me now, but you'll see. I'm not kidding. Anyway, how soon can I get out of here?"

I felt her belly and checked her stitches. Everything seemed in order. The chart showed her temperature was normal, with no signs of infection.

"Maybe tomorrow," I said.

"How about today?"

"Tomorrow." I laughed. "Most women beg me for longer stays after a tough delivery. They complain about getting thrown out of this lovely hospital."

She made a face. "This hospital gives me the creeps. That evil nurse from yesterday kept coming by this morning and asking me questions. When I wouldn't answer, some old doctor who looks like he belongs in a horror movie swept through.''

''Ardsley?'' I asked, a half-suggestion.

''Yup. You know him. He asked me twenty questions about you.'' Mona adjusted her pale blue nightgown and smiled at me. ''In case you're wondering, I told him you're God's gift to the medical profession. Period. I had nothing more to say.''

''Well, thank you.'' I wrote a note on the chart adjusting Mona's antibiotics and cooed over the baby, sleeping in a bassinet a foot from her mother's bed. ''Rooming-in working all right?'' I asked.

''Of course.'' She smiled at the little bundle. ''My baby. Rose. Why would I let her be in a big hospital nursery when she can be right here with her mom? I don't understand some women.''

I patted her on the shoulder. ''Rose is a lucky baby. You're going to be a great mom.''

''And Rick's a great dad. He just went out to get something to eat and he'll be right back. He'll be sorry he missed you.''

''Tell him he catches even better than I remembered,'' I said as I left the room.

Since I still had a little time before my next surgery, I went to the doctors' lounge. As I was washing my hands, someone tapped me on the back.

''Can you still talk to me now that you're a Beacon Hill doctor?''

I turned around. ''Eric!''

''Ah, she remembers. How's it going?''

I turned off the faucet and looked for someplace to dry my hands. The only towel by the sink looked grimy, so I decided my cotton skirt would be just fine. "I'm in Day Two. And it hasn't been that great, I can tell you."

"Then tell me."

"Really want to hear?"

"What kind of question is that? Of course I want to hear. Mind if I change while I listen?" He was still in surgical scrubs, so we went to the lockers at the back of the room. None of the doctors—including Eric—had abandoned the habit of peeling in full view just because there were now some women surgeons on the staff.

Eric was my best friend and had been since the first year of medical school. We had been lab partners in anatomy class, and he liked to tell people we had lost our virginity together—his way of describing how that first time of cutting into a cadaver changed you forever. Now, as he took off his scrubs, I told him about Mona and Ardsley and my first day on Beacon Hill, and I knew I was getting his full attention.

"Medicine's great sometimes, isn't it?" Eric said when I was done and he was back in street clothes. "If the malpractice bastards don't get you, your own colleagues will."

"I hate to think of Ardsley as a colleague. Why would he hate me already?"

Eric looked at me appraisingly. "Maybe because you have nice tits. He's probably so busy looking at them that he doesn't know what he's saying."

It was only Eric talking, but I blushed anyway. "I'm a doctor. You're not supposed to notice."

"You can bet Ardsley notices. He sees tits and he thinks he's supposed to have sex, not a professional conversation. Face it, babe, Ardsley doesn't love working with women, so he usually just pretends they're men. With you, that's hard to do.''

"I'll take that as a compliment."

"Good. How's your big dick of a lover, by the way?"

"Paco's fine," I said, ignoring Eric's obscenity. "And if you'd meet him sometime, you'd probably like him." I looked across the room at an older surgeon, fresh from the shower, sitting on the bench in front of his locker wearing nothing but a towel. "Where would you change if you were me?" I asked.

"Right here," Eric said. "You're an attending surgeon, right? You use the attending surgeon's side."

"I know, but I'm not into flashing. I generally sneak off to the bathroom—though there's no such thing as a ladies' room in here."

Eric grinned. "That's because we've moved beyond the need for gender distinctions. Wake up and smell the political correctness."

"Wake up and smell a hospital that doesn't know women exist," I retorted. "Come on, Eric. Seriously. What do the other women do?"

"Make themselves scarce. They're not quite as confrontational as you." He grinned, then added, "I mean that in the most loving way, of course. Stop being so worried about what everyone will think. If you need to change, do it the way the rest of us do. Screw them. Or better yet, screw me."

I rolled my eyes. It was a joke between us, our unconsummated affection. Eric and I had slept together once—really just slept—when we were both interns. Eric had just spent twelve hours in the operating room, trying to save a thirty-one-year-old man whose wife and baby daughter sat sobbing all night in the waiting room. The patient, not much older than we were, had come into the hospital by ambulance after a truck smashed into his Volkswagen on Route 128. He left by hearse. Overwhelmed by the tragedy, Eric had stumbled into the on-call room at 3 A.M. and sat on the edge of the cot where I was sleeping. When I woke up and saw him there, I asked, "What happened?" and he started to shake. I held him and hugged him—not like a lover, not like a mother, but like a best friend. We lay down together, our arms tightly wrapped around each other, and stayed like that—both of us fully clothed—until 6 A.M., when I was called for another delivery.

Now Eric pulled a medical bag from his locker and said, "Speaking of screwing, tell me more about Paco."

I shot him an exasperated look, but said sprightly, "He had a really successful show at the Massol Gallery and he's preparing for another one."

"And you told him it was the most brilliant show you'd ever seen, which made his dick even bigger and gave you yet another reason to stay with him."

"You're being obnoxious."

"No, I'm not. It just bugs me. You're the smartest doctor I know, and you fall for the poet."

"He's a painter."

"Oh, excuse me. What a difference."

"He's sensitive. Liberated. I met him at a women's rally, remember?" It was true: I'd met Paco at a gathering in Harvard Yard to fight for more tenured women on the faculty. I liked to think that Gloria Steinem had introduced us, because it was during her speech that Paco tapped me on the shoulder and asked, "Is this yours?'' He was holding a stethoscope, which must have fallen out of my pocket. I said, ''Thanks,'' and took it back. I noticed he was wearing a button that said ''Single Men for NOW.'' He wouldn't be single for long, I figured. He was ethereally handsome—tall and slim with a surprisingly broad chest and shoulders. His longish hair was clean and shiny, his beard neatly trimmed. I'd always been attracted to sexy, creative types, but they weren't usually looking for a woman who could understand the structure of DNA. I couldn't help glancing over at him when Steinem finished and Susan Faludi approached the podium. He winked, and edging closer to me, whispered, ''The pocket is ripped. You're going to lose that thing again.'' I put my hand to my pocket to rescue the wayward stethoscope, but his hand was there first, and when our fingers brushed he said, ''Oh, sorry,'' but didn't seem to mean it.

''A clever one.'' Eric sat down to tie his shoes. ''Didn't I ever tell you my theory on that? He was cruising for a liberated broad who'd put out easily. Somebody who figured an artist had to be sensitive. It pisses me off that you fell for it.''

I shook my head. ''I need to fix you up with someone. You must be working too hard. If you're still into bimbo types, there's a nurse in my office named Juliette. Big chest and a come-take-me look on her face. Only problem is, I think Dr. Franklin has her getting more than his coffee.''

Eric grinned. ''Now you're talking. A nurse who grovels at the doctor's feet. Or some part of his anatomy. It's what they teach you at nursing school, you know. Make a guy feel like he's a god and of course he wants to have sex with you. You should try it with Paco.''

"I do.''

Eric slammed his locker door shut and stared at me.

I turned my palms up to the ceiling in a gesture of giving in. What did he want from me? I'd decided when I was in high school that I wanted to be a doctor instead of a nurse. The nuns went crazy and told my mother there was something wrong with me. And it hadn't gotten much better. I was always fighting for everything I wanted. "I'm the one who doesn't have a goddamn bathroom to use in the doctors' lounge, remember? I have to sneak in at odd hours and lock the door if I want to pee. So, yes, when I'm at home, I get tired of fighting. I make Paco feel good and he makes me feel good. Is that so terrible?''

"No, it's not so terrible.'' Eric kissed me on the cheek. "You're right. If it's making you happy, I'll shut up.''

The alarm went off Monday morning at six o'clock and when I reached across Paco to turn it off, he sleepily kissed my neck and slid his hand into my nightgown, searching for my breasts.

I pulled away, whispering, "Not now. I have to get up.''

He opened one eye. "Let's make love first.''

"I can't. I have to get to work.''

He yawned and asked, "Is it Monday?'' When I nodded he said, "Never on a Monday. I should remember.''

He rolled over to go back to sleep but I asked, "What do you mean?'' and when he didn't answer I asked, "Why never on a Monday?''

"Monday is the day you despise men," he said, his voice slightly muffled by the pillow. "The day you save women from the wrongs we've committed."

"That's ridiculous."

He sat up and kissed me, and when I stiffened he said, "Don't worry, I understand. You can't want sex when you're angry."

"Could it be that I'm just in a rush this morning?"

"Maybe," he said, lying back down again. "But I happen to think I'm right."

I went off to the shower, annoyed by the twists of the male ego. Why did there have to be a deep, psychological reason if I didn't want to make love? Men couldn't stand the pinch of personal rejection—they had to make it cosmic. I felt myself getting angrier as the hot water drummed on my back, but when I stepped out of the bathroom and saw that Paco had fallen back to sleep, my heart suddenly melted. He was right about one thing: On Monday mornings sex wasn't about passion, it was about trouble.

I had a quick breakfast of a slightly stale bagel, then drove carefully through Cambridge, across the bridge, and zig-zagged through Boston to the run-down decaying streets of Roxbury. I maneuvered into a space directly in front of the small gray building where I was headed. At this hour, nobody was hanging out on street corners, and anyway, my Honda was sufficiently beat-up that I didn't mind parking it in full view. Paco always worried about my walking alone through the neighborhood, but the high crime rate didn't faze me. I was here to do good, and that had to be some kind of protection.

I took a deep breath, then went inside the building. It

was just a little after seven, but there were already four young women in the waiting room. One of them, who couldn't have been more than fourteen, was fair-skinned, wearing a heavy coat, open to reveal a tight stretch top that bulged over her belly. She sat quietly, while two of the others, Hispanic girlfriends of about sixteen, were chewing gum and talking. The final girl, black and studious-looking, was flipping through a magazine.

They all looked up expectantly when I came in. "Just give me a moment, please," I told them, and went into a small office where I put on a white coat and made sure my hair was tied back neatly. I checked my supplies and realized we were almost out of prenatal vitamins. Damn. We needed to do some private fund-raising. The new governor of Massachusetts had targeted clinics for the poor for major cutbacks, and it was hurting. I thought of the stacks of vitamin samples that pharmaceutical reps left in the office on Beacon Hill. The ironies of life. I could give free samples to the rich women who could afford to pay for them, but not to the poor.

I called the pregnant fourteen-year-old in first. She'd been coming in every month for prenatal care and was doing well. I gave her the last of the vitamins and cheered her report that she'd completely quit smoking. Her boyfriend, who was doing heroin, had disappeared, but her mother had stopped beating her and said she'd help take care of the baby, so all was well.

Next patient.

The morning went quickly. I treated herpes and chlamydia, vaginal warts and yeast infections, and tested several times for AIDS. I dispensed condoms and urged the girls to use them, but most of the time they just shrugged. Sometime in mid-morning it occurred to me that Paco was right: On Mondays, men were trouble. The girls came in, one after another, and not one of them had a boyfriend along to hold her hand or offer support. It was a sisterhood here, and a painful one.

But also, in my heart of hearts, it was why I was a doctor. To help people who needed help. The governor had tried to hint that women's clinics for the poor must be abortion mills, but I'd seen hundreds of patients and done exactly one abortion—for a thirteen-year-old girl from a housing project in Dorchester who had been brutally raped by her cousin. I didn't believe in abortion, but that's when I'd learned that every life isn't the same. The girl, raped, abandoned, and treated like garbage, looked at me beseechingly, and I told her we'd take care of it. Right then. In the face of the hard realities of life, ideology didn't seem to mean much. Besides, I'd already figured out that people only got worked up about abortions at clinics for the poor. Nobody thought twice about good Dr. Franklin, attended by Juliette, doing them quietly in the Beacon Hill office for Wellesley College girls who forgot to take their pills and wealthy young mothers who had gotten pregnant by their lovers instead of their husbands.

By eleven o'clock, I'd seen about twenty patients and I had to leave and get back to my real life. I locked the clinic and put up a sign saying another doctor would be in at two. We did what we could. I walked over to my Honda, where three teenage boys were hanging out, smoking cigarettes and drinking from a forty-ounce bottle of malt beer. When I went around to the driver's side and took out my keys, they made a few lewd comments, tossed an empty beer bottle, and sauntered away. One of them was holding a boom box that he turned up to earsplitting volume. I got in my car and drove back to Beacon Hill, the sounds of gangsta rap still ringing in my ears.

III

JUST TO MAKE sure that the day had enough contrasts, the first patient I saw when I got to the Beacon Hill office was Hollis Taft Brewster, who came in wearing a cashmere coat in charcoal-gray over a pale silk Donna Karan suit that I'd seen on the cover of a Saks Fifth Avenue catalogue. She looked slightly wan, but I had to glance at the chart to see that she was also about fourteen weeks pregnant. I pegged her as one of those reed-slim women who barely show until their last trimester and then regain their figures immediately after delivery.

I also noticed that she had been Dr. Franklin's patient, and that made me pause. As far as I could tell, the chance to treat a rich, old-money patient like Hollis Taft Brewster was exactly why he'd stayed in practice.

"It's good to finally meet you," Hollis said. "Dr. Franklin has been telling me about your joining the practice since the day I found out I was pregnant."

"Really?" That caught my attention. Unless she was exaggerating, there was a good chance Hollis had known I was joining the practice before I did.

"Not you exactly," she amended. "But he said somebody new was arriving who would be perfect for me. I wondered about it, since he was well aware that I wanted to leave his practice." I didn't say anything and she looked out the small window in my consulting room, her eyes growing distant. "I have pretty mixed feelings about this office," she said. "Some are personal. Some medical."

"Let's start with the medical. I can probably help on those."

She turned back to me, and I was struck by how stunningly pretty she was, her long swan neck and slim arms unaffected by the pregnancy. The Tafts—like the Kennedys—were Boston royalty, and I'd grown up observing Hollis the same way children in London must have followed everything connected with Prince Charles. I remembered Hollis's tenth birthday party better than my own because I'd spent hours poring over the newspaper pictures of Hollis and her friends at a special performance of the circus. Hollis got to ride on the back of an elephant, wearing a glittering tiara. At the time, it seemed to me like the most wonderful treat in the world.

Hollis's mother, Lily, was famous for running charity balls that raised millions of dollars for the cancer fund. Her grandmother, Dulcimer Taft, was the grande dame of Boston society. When we were little and my brothers and I had bad manners at the table, my mother would say, "We could never have Mrs. Taft to this house, could we?"

My mother had clipped Hollis's marriage announcement out of the paper and sent it to me at college, as if Hollis were a close friend. It was a classic match of old money and new. Sloane Brewster's family had made a fortune building an insurance empire in Boston, and the gleaming new Brewster Building, proof of the incredible family wealth, towered over the Boston skyline. They were also generous with their newly acquired funds. The Brewster Special Care Pavilion at P&S Hospital had been built with a five-million dollar donation from Hollis's father-in-law.

But right now Hollis looked troubled, and however much her history resounded with me, I looked at her with a professional eye.

"The first medical problem," she said, "is that I'd like to have a natural delivery this time. And my last two babies were by cesarean."

"Not necessarily a problem," I said.

"Not?"

She seemed sufficiently surprised that I checked the notes on her chart and saw the C-section in the first delivery was attributed to "failure to progress." That was standard lexicon for any number of problems, so I asked if she remembered any of the details.

"All of them," she said, "because I was in labor for exactly one hour. One hour in the hospital. And I'd come in right away, because that's what Dr. Ardsley told me to do. Do you know him? He was my doctor then."

"Of course. Archibald Ardsley. He's the chairman of the department."

"He'd been a friend of the family for years. He checked me when I came in and then an hour later told my husband we should do a cesarean. Not me, my husband. When they finally bothered to tell me, I started to cry and asked if we could wait, but Gus laughed and said women like me weren't meant to struggle through labor. He thought he was doing me a favor. Plus he told my husband that the sex would stay better if I didn't get all stretched out."

Since it wasn't right to trash the chairman of the department, I didn't say anything, and Hollis continued. "Gus's practice became more hospital-oriented after that, and he recommended Dr. Franklin. With my second baby, Dr. Franklin told me to pick a date and come into the hospital like a lady. I never even went into labor—I just had another C-section."

"That's standard practice, you know. Maybe not necessary, but not really unusual, either."

"Is it what you would do?"

"No." I sat back. "Hospital policy used to be once a cesarean, always a cesarean. Your uterus has been cut and stitched and there's always a fear of rupture. That could be life-threatening. But it's also very rare. I don't believe a second cesarean is always necessary—and there's good research to back mc up. Same for a third C-section, by the way. I strongly believe in what we call VBAC—vaginal birth after cesarean. But that's still a little threatening to the old guard around here, and I fight for every one."

"Dr. Franklin said you were the expert at it, and it shouldn't be a problem."

"He did?"

"Absolutely." She smiled for the first time this visit, and again I had the sense of something being just slightly off-kilter. Franklin singing my praises to Hollis Taft Brewster was curious. Most of the other patients he'd passed along to me so far were from health plans and managed care. Wouldn't Franklin do everything he could to keep Hollis happy, instead of turning her over to me?

I felt things tumbling out of my control, and trying to

get them back in hand, suggested we hold off further discussion until I'd done an exam. In the examining room, I went slower than usual, and suggested a sonogram. She sighed. "I know it's important, but I hate drinking eight glasses of water and feeling like I'll bust."

"That's the old days," I said. "Dr. Franklin agreed to buy new sonogram equipment before I even started." I held up the simple rod. "No fuss or muss."

I slathered the tube with jelly and slipped it gently inside her. We both turned our eyes to the screen. I jiggled it slightly—and saw the baby. "Do you see it?" I asked. She didn't answer, so I leaned toward the screen, to give meaning to the Rorschach-like shapes. "There's the head. And the heart. Watch and you can see it beating."

She looked at the screen another minute and then gasped. "My baby. I didn't expect to see this today."

"I can make a copy of the screen image. The first picture for your baby book. Or for your husband."

Bringing Sloane Brewster's name into the examining room with us seemed to change the atmosphere. Did I just imagine a cold chill sweeping through the room? "Sloane would only want to know how much the new sonogram machine cost, how much you charge for each use, and whether Brewster Managed Care is giving you excessive reimbursement," she said.

"I haven't a clue about any of that," I said, pushing a button to print the image and gently ending the procedure. "So I'll keep this in your records."

I finished the exam and decided that Hollis seemed completely normal and healthy. "I can't promise that there will be a natural delivery," I said, when she sat up and pulled a sheet up around her examining gown, "but that's what we'll aim for. I'll be with you the whole time and try to do what you want. It's your baby. Your life. Your health. Those are the only things that are going to matter when we're making the decisions."

She nodded, relief etched on her face. "You know, I'm not bitter about the other deliveries," she said. "James is six and Porter is three and a half and they're both perfect, so I can't be too upset about how they got here. But I'd just like it different this time."

"We'll try," I said, but I didn't know then that "different" could also be deadly.

Unlike the patients at the Roxbury clinic, the pregnant women coming to the Beacon Hill office usually brought their husbands along on at least one visit. My late office hours on Tuesday nights, which I had planned for the convenience of working women, quickly became Husband's Night. But Sloane Brewster was never one of the husbands. I mentioned it to Hollis during one visit, and she said she'd bring him the next time; when that didn't happen, she said she'd remind him on the one after that. Each time I brought it up, Hollis looked distraught. In fact, she often looked distraught when we spoke. I had the feeling that she wanted to confide something but could never quite bring herself to do it. She danced around the subject: We talked about her husband and his business, about Dr. Ardsley and hospital policy, and the crazed state of medical insurance in Massachusetts. Once, sitting in my consulting room, she admitted that

Sloane didn't mind that she'd left Franklin—but he was adamant about her delivering at P&S.

"Something to do with a big deal he's putting together," she said. "That's the kind of nonsense we argue about—which is more important, his deals or my delivery."

"What's the deal?" I asked innocently, not wanting to pry into the details of her arguments with Sloane.

"P&S is trying to get an exclusive contract with Brewster Managed Care. That means anybody insured by BMC who's being hospitalized has to come to P&S." She shrugged. "Bad news for pregnant women, don't you think? I mean, there aren't a lot of young, forward-thinking physicians on Ardsley's staff. But Sloane's going to make a fortune off it and so will the hospital. The governor is pushing for it to happen because of some Sloane-manueverings that I don't care to follow."

"I hadn't heard about it. But then, I'm not very well plugged into hospital politics."

Hollis suddenly looked concerned. "Actually, I can't believe I mentioned it to you. It's really top secret. Put it right out of your mind, okay?"

"Okay. It's gone."

"I mean, I couldn't care less who knows, but Sloane gets furious. He thinks I'm always on the wrong side when it comes to his managed care deals because they usually seem so slimy to me. So many games you have to play to get them through. He calls me an old-money snob because I don't think you should screw the poor to get rich." She sighed. "Notice that the last generation of Brewsters donated a wing to the hospital. Not the library, not the museum, the hospital. I used to figure that they'd made a fortune off people who needed medical care and wanted to give something back. Now I think it was just for good publicity.''

She blushed slightly after she said that—it wasn't like Hollis to make critical remarks about her husband's family. Or about charitable giving. I looked down and pretended to write a medical note in her chart, not knowing quite how to respond. No doubt some of the Taft giving had personal motives behind it, too. But there was an anger that I couldn't quite interpret when she discussed the Brewsters. It made me even more interested in meeting Sloane.

But he didn't come to the next visit either, and we were into the final trimester. During the exam, I listened to the baby's heartbeat, then turned up the volume so the Doppler amplified the sound enough to fill the room.

"Sounds great," Hollis said, smiling. "But isn't it a little fast?"

"Fast is normal," I reminded her. "Your heart goes about seventy beats per minute but a baby's in utero is about one hundred twenty."

We did another sonogram and watched the baby sucking its thumb, then counted its toes—all ten. All Hollis's vital signs were fine, but she hadn't gained very much weight, and I urged her to put on a bit more.

"You're kidding. Gus always said not to gain more than twenty pounds. He teased me about being pudgy."

"You're not pudgy, you're pregnant—and the new recommendations are to gain slightly more weight. A big baby is often healthier." I didn't add that a small baby was easier to deliver—which is why doctors used to put women on restrictive diets. But Gus Ardsley probably just hated to see women get big.

Hollis got dressed and came into the consultation room. "So it's all agreed, right? I'm not going to have another C-section."

"You'll be carefully monitored throughout," I said to her, as I had on nearly every one of our visits. "The goal is a healthy baby, not a heroic delivery, so if there's any sign of trouble, we'll do the section. But right now, I'm optimistic."

"You know, my mother still uses Gus as her gynecologist, and when she saw him a couple of weeks ago, she spoke to him about me. And you."

I could just imagine what he'd said. I felt my heart beating about as hard as that baby's in utero. As far as I could tell, Ardsley's attitude toward me hadn't softened a bit. He was proceeding with the investigation into Mona Simpkin's delivery, and he seemed to have spread the word that people should watch out for me. The times I'd run into him personally he'd been as cold and brusque as that first day. "So what did Gus say?" I asked, keeping my voice from shaking.

"He said you're the best doctor on staff for a procedure like this. He told Mom that you're young and smart and completely up-to-date and that you're the most patient and skilled doctor he's put on staff in years—the two traits vital for a VBAC." She sat back with a smile, waiting for my reaction.

It was slow in coming, because my first thought was to tell her that her mother must have gotten my name wrong. Or the message wrong. I waited a beat until a more professional demeanor could settle in. "I'm pleased to hear that,'' I said, ''because we've occasionally had our differences.''

Hollis sighed. ''Anyway, I'm in good hands—yours—and I'm hoping that it all works out so I'm home from the hospital quickly for Porter and James. Mostly Porter, I must say. She's been a little shaky about having a new baby in the family, and she's not going to understand if I can't pick her up to hug her.''

I nodded, wishing I could give her some guarantee.

''Is Sloane getting excited?'' I asked, wondering about the man I hadn't met.

''The truth, Sarabeth? Sloane didn't want this baby. In fact, he was pretty furious when I got pregnant. We had an awful argument.'' She stopped, and looked at me with wide eyes. ''I never told that to anybody, including my own mother. But Sloane and I can have terrible battles. Isn't that amazing? Calm, crafty Sloane Brewster, never ruffled in business, fights with his wife.''

She looked at me, as if waiting for me to ask a question, but I was taken aback, not quite ready to see this side of Hollis.

''I'm sure he'll be thrilled when the baby arrives,'' I said, sounding platitudinous even to myself.

''Of course,'' Hollis said. She must have sensed my discomfort, and too well-bred to let anyone feel ill at ease, quickly changed the subject.

Her next visit was scheduled for Monday afternoon at one o'clock, and I arrived twenty minutes late. The moment I came in, Hollis followed me into my consulting room, but I wasn't ready to talk to her. I straightened out the papers on my desk, took out some charts, and tried to calm down.

"You seem upset," she said.

"I am."

"I always tell you what's wrong. Now you tell me."

I wouldn't have, but there was a gentleness in her voice, a sense that she really cared. "I volunteer at a women's health clinic in Roxbury on Monday mornings," I blurted. "I thought I'd seen everything, but I was wrong. I did a D and C this morning on a woman who was thirteen weeks pregnant. Her husband beat her with his fists so badly last night that the baby was dead."

"My God." Hollis's hand fluttered to her own stomach. "How awful."

"The worst part is that after I finished, she told me she was going back home. She said she loves him, and anyway, she has no place to go. Of course, he promised not to touch her again. No chance. I think she'll be dead by the end of the week."

Hollis looked pale, and I quickly said, "I'm sorry. I didn't plan to discuss this with you. But I can't get the image of that poor woman out of my mind. Monday mornings are kind of draining. It tends to be one thing like that after another."

"I wish I could help somehow," Hollis said. "Maybe join you some morning when you're there." I didn't say anything and she added, "I'm quite serious. I can't offer medical help, but maybe I could talk to the women about getting control of their lives. I have the same X chromosome they do—the one that carries the gene for acting stupid around men. I could probably learn as much from them as they could from me."

I looked at her and saw she meant it.

"Okay. After the baby's born, I'll have you come."

"Why after? You're the one who said I can do anything I want. I'll meet you there next Monday."

I didn't really think she'd show up, but when I arrived at 7:30 the next Monday, I saw a limousine idling at the curb and found Hollis already inside the clinic, drinking coffee from a plastic foam cup and laughing with Ruby, the clinic administrator. Ruby had been hired full-time when the clinic was a government project, but now that it had been summarily dropped, she could only afford to come in once or twice a week. But she was dedicated and deeply caring, an older black woman who had found her way out of Roxbury but wouldn't forget her sisters still there.

"You made it," I said to Hollis, who must have been trying to dress correctly for a morning in the slums because she was wearing a plain black maternity dress. Still, her pale, creamy skin was glowing and she had a pearl choker at her neck.

"I can't stay too long today," Hollis said, "because I'm meeting my mother at a nine o'clock breakfast. But Ruby said there should be a couple of women for me to talk with this morning. Another lady who's being abused at home. And a pregnant teenager."

"Good luck," I said. "This might be tougher than you think."

I got busy and didn't see Hollis the rest of the morning, but she knocked on my door before she left. "This is a good place and I actually enjoyed those talks," she said to me. "I'm not going to forget it. I'll be back."

• • •

Foolishly, I started to think of Hollis as a friend. She wasn't, of course—she was a patient. If not for our professional connection, we would never even have met. I knew all that, but I just liked her. I always left extra time when she was coming in to the office because talk about her pregnancy invariably drifted to other, nonmedical subjects, and I found myself looking forward to our chats. Maybe I was waiting to hear the secret she seemed ready to tell about the Brewsters. And maybe I was still hoping to get invited to that ten-year-old's birthday party.

And finally I did. When she came to see me in her eighth month, a week after her visit to the Roxbury clinic, she suggested I come for dinner. "Sloane really wants to meet you, but he's never available during the day, and usually has meetings on Tuesday evenings. It would be much better if we make it social." She nodded to the picture of Paco. "Bring your artist, of course."

Paco agreed to come, and on the following Wednesday evening he changed from his usual jeans to neat khakis and we drove into downtown Boston. Hollis had told me about a private-parking entrance for the Brewster Building, and when we drove up to it, a uniformed guard asked "Are you Dr. Love? Mr. Callan?" When told that we were, he took the car keys and turned them over to another attendant, then ushered us from the garage into a private, back lobby. I felt like I was in Versailles. The ceiling soared at least ten stories, and on one side a waterfall tumbled fifty feet down a granite wall, landing in a series of softly lit pools at the bottom. I would have stayed to stare, but we were quickly turned over to a white-gloved elevator operator who introduced himself as Morgan.

"Been to the Tower before?" he asked closing the door and pushing the button for the penthouse—the only place this elevator stopped. I guess we looked like we hadn't, because he chatted for most of the sixty-seven-story ride. I answered mostly with "Mmm" and "Oh," but that was enough to keep him going while I stood on the red plush carpeting, held Paco's hand, and studied the vaulted ceiling superimposed with a three-part mural. It was a trompe d'oeil that created the illusion of ascending to heaven—and, I quickly discovered, we were.

Hollis greeted us in black jeans and a white silk over-shirt—and we immediately giggled since my long black skirt and tailored white shirt made us look like sisters. I introduced Paco, who had her charmed in moments as he exclaimed over the Picasso and Miró paintings in the foyer. Then he turned his attention to a small Chagall in the corner.

"That's my favorite, too," said Sloane Brewster, coming out of the shadows. He was of medium height with sandy-brown hair and a surprising air of calm. He looked as if he'd just come home from work, since he was still in a well-cut business suit and expensive Italian dress shoes, though he'd loosened his tie.

Introductions were made, and as Paco and Sloane fell into a discussion of the Chagall, Hollis offered to show me around. We walked across the marble foyer and through the huge living room which boasted so many exquisite antiques that I stopped to gasp every few steps. Hollis pointed out a Louis XIV armoire and writing desk, and when I admired a pair of extraordinary chairs, she said, "They're real tortoise shell, but they've been in the family for over a century, and I figured hiding the

chairs away wouldn't bring the tortoises back to life.
They're gorgeous, aren't they? Maybe they died a natural death.'' She laughed sweetly, then added, ''Everything else from an endangered species is in Sloane's
study. It bothers me to see them, and we never let the
magazine photographers in there.''

''You have a lot of those?''

She made a face. ''There was a big story on Sloane
in *Fortune*, so they came by, and of course *House Beautiful* and *Better Homes and Gardens* wanted family features. When this building opened—gosh, I guess it's two
years ago now—we were inundated with photographers
from all over the world. Sloane thought the publicity was
important, but I got tired of it quickly and my mother
thought it was horrible. Particularly when one of the
magazines photographed our bathroom.''

''You weren't using it, were you?''

She laughed. ''No, but Porter was sitting on the floor,
wearing nothing but a diaper. Mind you, she was eighteen months old.''

''If that's as close to scandal as your family gets,
you're doing okay.''

''And if it isn't?'' Her voice was suddenly brittle,
stopping me in my tracks. It was a moment to be serious,
but I missed it, too overwhelmed by the splendor around
me to be either friend or doctor or confidante. Instead,
sensing her anxiety, I rattled one of the door handles and
asked, ''A lot of skeletons in these closets?'' The small
joke worked, in its way: She laughed and the moment
passed. Later, much later, I would wish it hadn't.

We continued our tour. The sprawling space, really
too enormous to be called a living room, was divided

into at least six separate seating areas. Most were positioned to face toward the windows, which ran the entire length of the far wall and offered a panoramic view of downtown Boston and the suburbs beyond. The lights by the windows were low, making the view even better, and despite its size and opulence, the room felt almost cozy. The area had clearly been designed for entertaining, since the vast space swept toward a dining room, with a banquet table that could easily seat two dozen. An elaborate arrangement of antique brass candlesticks occupied the center of the table, and for a moment I thought of the single beeswax candle and hurricane lamp Paco and I used at home. A few steps down from the dining room was the closed door of Sloane's study and two libraries where guests could retreat after dessert. In one, a handsomely carved wooden table was set for our informal dinner.

"I'll show you the upstairs later," Hollis said and I realized that the four of them, soon to be five, lived in a space that elsewhere in the skyscraper held entire corporations with hundreds of secretaries and bosses and managers. Next to the winding staircase that led up to the family quarters, I noticed a glass-fronted cabinet filled with Steuben animals and a child-sized Porsche parked right next to it. "James's favorite toy." Hollis grinned, following my gaze. "And Porter had to have one if he did. Of course hers is pink and always filled with dolls. Sloane hates it when they ride down here, but I think there's plenty of room, don't you?"

"Even enough room for another one." I laughed, eying her stomach. "Besides, your children must be very well-trained. You don't usually see Steuben crystal and kids' toys side by side.''

She laughed too. ''Amazing, isn't it? They never try to touch them.'' Impulsively, she opened the cabinet and took one out. ''Here. An elephant. Put it on your desk for me. Elephants are good luck.''

''I couldn't.''

''Please. Take it. I owe you a lot.'' She held it out to me, and I couldn't refuse gracefully.

''Thank you. It will be on my desk until you deliver— as good luck for you.''

At dinner, I tried to talk seriously to Sloane about the baby and delivery, but he was all wit and surface charm that I couldn't penetrate. He didn't seem to care at all that the two previous deliveries had been less than perfect for Hollis. They had their children and she was well, so wasn't this all a lot of feminist posturing about how the babies arrived? I pointed out that if we did it differently this time, there was a good chance Hollis would be home in a day or two, instead of a week. I was sure James and Porter would appreciate that. Sloane made a joke about it, and I realized that I didn't quite trust him: He might be the impossibly rich and well-dressed president of Brewster Insurance, but at heart he was just another slick insurance salesman.

Hollis, ever the gracious hostess, moved us on to other topics. She had kept the menu simple—smoked salmon to start, then a cheese soufflé with fresh asparagus and a raspberry tart for dessert. Two waiters served everything from gleaming platters and Paco sent me a quick wink across the table as he sipped his cappuccino. Maybe he was thinking of the cheese sandwiches we sometimes had for dinner on the nights I was too tired to cook. But at least we ate them cuddled up together in bed, or in front of the fireplace while Paco massaged my toes. I tried to imagine Sloane being sweetly romantic with Hollis but the image just wouldn't come.

When we were finally leaving, Hollis hugged me and offered her cheek to Paco. Sloane, more distant, shook hands with Paco, then turned to me and said, "I have the feeling that Hollis has told you a great deal about our family. She confides in you."

I swallowed, realizing he might be worried that I knew about his early reluctance to have another baby.

"Let me just make one thing very clear," he went on. "I love my wife. I don't care how this baby gets delivered as long as my wife is safe."

"Always the first priority," I agreed.

"All I care about is my wife," he said, putting his arm around her. I waited for Hollis to look up at him adoringly, but she didn't. In fact, she turned slightly away so that his grip seemed dangerously viselike and she seemed unable to escape it.

Since Hollis was going to deliver soon, she was coming in for weekly checkups. She was still slim everywhere, except for her stomach which stuck out in front of her like a basketball. "My mother, my grandmother, and people I don't even know keep telling me I'm carrying like I have a boy," she said at one visit. "But the amniocentesis said it's a girl. Could it be wrong?"

"There's always a chance the amnio got your cells instead of the baby's, but it's highly unlikely. The test is about ninety-nine percent accurate. I'd put folk wisdom at about fifty-fifty.''

Hollis laughed. "It's sort of strange knowing it's a girl. I was about to paint her room pink, but I stopped myself. I feel like amniocentesis means we can start stereotyping in the womb.''

"If not there, in the delivery room, about two seconds after the baby is born,'' I told her. "Trust me, I hear it every day. I pull out a boy, no matter what size, and everyone says how big he is and how strong. When it's a girl, they begin cooing about how beautiful she is. I know we've heard the lectures about stereotypes so often that they sound trite, but when you stand in a delivery room day after day, it all becomes very clear.''

"I'm guilty,'' Hollis admitted. "I put Porter in pretty dresses and then tell everyone that she insists on wearing nice clothes. And she does. But I guess babies aren't born wanting pink lace.''

I shrugged. "I was delivering a first-time mom a couple of weeks ago. It was a long labor with a big baby and one of the first things she said after it was over was, 'Typical girl. She's already giving her mother a hard time.' Just jokes, I know, but these are babies. I sometimes think what it would be like to deliver a baby and wrap it up without telling the parents the gender. They'd freak out, don't you think? They wouldn't know how to talk to it.''

"I wish you could try it on me, but it's too late,'' Hollis said. "We all think we're doing such a good job at raising our kids equally, but I don't know.''

"The pink Porsche,'' I said, remembering what she'd told me about Porter's toy car.

She smiled ruefully. "It's always a struggle. When I was in college, I thought ours would be the break-through generation. We wouldn't fall for all the non-sense about men's and women's roles. But then we all got a little older, and nothing changed."

"So why do we do it?"

"Because it's what's expected. I don't know, Sara-beth, maybe you don't always do what people want you to, but the rest of us get pretty well snared in that trap." She looked at me with pained eyes, and I realized she wasn't just talking about babies and gender anymore. "Going through this pregnancy with you has given me a whole new sense of control. When I was talking to the women at your Roxbury clinic, I realized that I never tried to direct anything about my own life before. But now I'm going to. I've told that to Sloane, too. Things between us have to change. He's trying, and that makes me happy. Once I get through this delivery, I'm going to take what I know about myself and the world and—well, make a difference with it. Wherever that gets me."

"Sounds like a good goal, Hollis."

"Wherever it gets me," she repeated.

IV

IT WAS EXACTLY on her due date, Sunday July 4, that Hollis called me at six in the morning to say she was in labor. She slipped quietly into the hospital at 10 A.M., and I had her up to the labor room almost before anyone knew she had arrived. We'd made our deal weeks be-fore: I insisted on an IV, and an external fetal monitor. No drugs, because I needed her alert to any unusual symptoms. At the first sign of a problem, we would do an emergency C-section.

By early evening, Hollis was in transition, and she stayed calmer than anyone I'd seen. No signs of rupture. Two weeks earlier, I'd sent Dr. Ardsley a memo telling him what we were planning and including an inch-thick stack of articles from medical journals supporting the decision. I knew he already knew about it and—if Hollis was right—supported the decision. But I was trying to avoid any repercussions. I asked him to let me know within the week if he had any problems with the plan, and I never heard from him.

At 6 P.M., we took Hollis into the delivery room, and at 6:30, I saw the head crowning. Moments later, the slithering bundle of life emerged and I cried, "You've done it!" I'd wanted Sloane to cut the umbilical cord, but he shook his head at the suggestion, so I did it myself—and placed the brand-new baby girl on Hollis's stomach. She touched it and I saw tears streaming down her cheeks. Sloane kissed his wife and put his hand on the baby, overcome by the moment.

"This is Kristin, right?" he asked.

Hollis nodded and lifted the baby to her. "Kristin Taft Brewster," I heard her whisper, "you can be anything you want to be. First lesson. And never forget it."

Hollis and baby Kristin were sent to the largest private room on the floor, and somehow, it was already filled with flowers. Hollis nursed the baby and then Sloane sat rocking her for a long time, until she fell asleep in his arms. He carried her to the tiny bassinet, looking as if he'd like to curl up inside it himself.

"You should go home," Hollis told him. "Get James and Porter from their grandparents and tell them all about their baby sister."

"I will." He lingered for a moment and then we heard firecrackers popping outside the window.

"The whole city's celebrating her birth," I said, smiling.

We all went to the window and watched the colors exploding in the sky over the Charles River. It was well after ten o'clock when the huge display was over, and Hollis got back into her bed. I was in no rush to leave, but finally Sloane kissed her good night, and we walked out of the hospital together. Outside, I saw Sloane's limousine waiting on the corner. "Can I drop you someplace?" he asked.

"No, thanks. It's such a wonderful night, I think I'll walk for a while." For a summer night in Boston, it was surprisingly cool; with the fireworks over, I saw a full moon and a sky full of stars. I imagined Hollis holding Kristin to the window and letting her witness the majesty of her first night on earth.

"You did a fine job tonight," Sloane said, but there was a certain edge in his voice as he added, "Let's just hope that all stays well."

"Of course it will," I said. "You have a beautiful, healthy daughter to join the rest of that lovely family. I wish you all boundless love and joy."

Sloane nodded tiredly, as if he didn't believe that the future was boundless love and joy. As if he had a premonition. As if.

V

THE NIGHT THAT Kristin was born, I thought I could do no wrong. I have thought about that night often. The full moon and the stars, the blissful walk home. The sense that the whole city had gathered to cleebrate this special birth. I had become a doctor to change people's lives, and that's what I was doing. I was full of myself, full of pride and pleasure at the life I had chosen. I was fighting a network of old boys who were sometimes wrong in their ideas and I was helping women like Hollis Taft Brewster stand up for themselves and define the course of their lives. Somehow I sensed that Hollis hadn't just given birth to Kristen—but to a new future for herself. And how could I know that night, when I thought that changing the world was so easy, that the world had decided, that very night, to change me?

two

THE EYE OF THE STORM

I

THE NEXT DAY, Monday, I got to the hospital at a little after noon. The elevator was taking forever to come, so I sprinted up to the fifth floor, eager to see Hollis. I knew her well enough by now to expect that she'd already be eager to be discharged. Instead of lying around in a sunny hospital room full of summer flowers, she'd want to be in her own home in the Brewster Tower with her children and new baby, back in control of her life. She was definitely the least-spoiled rich girl I'd ever met. I smiled to myself, looking forward to seeing her with her baby.

Preoccupied, I didn't notice the silence on the floor or the strange looks I was getting until Nurse Dolton marched up to me, blocking my path.

"Where are you going?" she asked.

It wasn't a question I would normally bother answering, but instead of getting hostile, I said, "Room five-oh-one. To see Hollis Brewster."

"I'm afraid that's not possible." She was as offi-

ciously overbearing as I'd ever seen her. I noticed small
sweat stains under the arms of her too-tight uniform.

"Why not?"

"She died this morning."

"*What?*"

"She's gone."

What she was saying didn't compute. My mind
wouldn't accept it. "Gone? You mean she went home?"

"Doctor, she died five hours ago. At about seven-
fifteen this morning."

"That can't be." I stared at her blankly, too stunned
to say anything more. Then suddenly I was babbling.
"I'm her doctor. I was never called. What are you talking about? Where's Hollis? What happened to her?"

"Dr. Ardsley happened to be on the floor, so he handled the arrest. We spent close to an hour trying to re-
vive her, but there was nothing we could do."

Handling the arrest. That meant doctors and nurses
pounding on the chest, inserting an endotracheal tube,
administering epinephrine and magnesium, trying to get
a heart that had stopped to start beating again. But why
on earth had Hollis Brewster gone into cardiac arrest?

"I saw her late last night and she was fine." My voice
sounded as if it were coming from across the room, ech-
oing in disbelief. "This can't be. It can't." I felt myself
starting to fall apart, reached for the wall to get steady
on my feet, and took a deep breath. Across from me,
Nurse Dolton stood implacably, her face unreadable.
Healthy women didn't die twelve hours after giving
birth.

"What caused the arrest?"

"I certainly don't know." Nurse Dolton clamped her

jaw firmly shut and I had the feeling I could faint at her feet and she wouldn't reach out to help me. Almost without realizing it, I began cataloguing all the rare complications of childbirth. The ones that could lead to death. "Embolism?" I ventured.

Her lips were pinched tight. "I couldn't guess."

"It doesn't make sense," I whispered. Too dazed to think about what I was doing, I continued toward Room 510, but Nurse Dolton blocked my way again. I looked up at her and felt my hands beginning to shake. "Where's her chart? I need to see her chart."

"Dr. Ardsley took it. He asked that you have no further contact with this case while he"—she paused for a moment, then said with emphasis—"investigates."

I looked at her blankly. "Where's Hollis's husband?"

"I don't know."

"Has he been here?"

"He got here during the arrest. Dr. Ardsley spent some time with him afterwards. I don't know any more than that."

There were a million things I wanted to find out, but Nurse Dolton wasn't going to help me with any of them. She didn't know. Or she wouldn't tell. I stared at her briefly, then stumbled away, blindly making my way to the elevator. I leaned heavily on the Down button, trying to choke back the fear and nausea that were rising in me. Two nurses passing by glanced at me and began whispering. The wait for the elevator was interminable, and when it finally did arrive, I took a step in, then hesitated, not sure where I was going. An orderly was holding onto a wheelchair, and the patient, a young woman attached to an IV, looked up at me. For a moment, I thought it was Hollis, and I began to shake so violently that I backed out of the elevator. The door closed. I needed desperately to get a grip on myself, decide my next step. Two deep breaths. My brain had to unfreeze. I moved back to the call buttons and pressed Up. Another wait. Somewhere on this floor, I had five other patients, but I couldn't see them now. I'd be useless.

This time, when the elevator door opened, I stepped in. Two doctors I recognized from the ob-gyn department were talking in soft, urgent voices. They never looked up at me. My hands were shaking hard as I hit the button for the seventh floor. They got out at six, and suddenly alone, I wondered if I would faint or cry or scream. I felt my fingers forming into fists: Stay in control, I would stay in control.

The seventh floor had a slightly different atmosphere than the floors I normally frequented, and I felt it immediately when I got off. A knot of men in business suits were standing at one end of the hallway, and they disappeared into a conference room. I went in the other direction, to Dr. Ardsley's office. Ginny, the den-mother secretary with the generous cleavage was there, but when I came in this time, she didn't smile.

"I have to see Dr. Ardsley urgently," I said. "Tell him I'm here waiting."

"He's not available."

"I'll wait. Or I'll find him. Where is he?"

She looked at a paper that had nothing written on it, then said, "He's in conference. But not here. And I don't think he'll be available for the rest of the day."

"I have to talk to him about Hollis Brewster."

"Oh. Well . . ." She hesitated. "Tomorrow, maybe. I think he'll be available about four o'clock."

"Ginny, she's my patient. Or was. She died this morning, and I don't know why. I don't know what happened. Nobody will tell me. Dr. Ardsley was there and took the chart. I have to know what's going on."

I could see her struggling to keep her face blank. "He's just not available and I can't disturb him. His direct orders."

I leaned over the desk, my face inches from hers. "What the hell is going on, Ginny?"

She pulled back, looking scared. From her secretary's perch, Ginny had been running the department for years, and she was everybody's friend, everybody's comforter and protector. But today she had obviously been given her orders—and being helpful to me wasn't included. "Just go away," she hissed. "I mean it, go away." There was a look of fright in her green eyes.

"Ginny, what's going on?" I asked again.

Two men drifted by in the hall, and Ginny got up abruptly. "I'm going to the ladies' room," she announced. She pulled a huge key chain with a big wooden W from her desk and marched out with it. I waited for a minute, then followed her. When I got there, the ladies' room door had been left unlocked, so I pushed it open and went in. Ginny was leaning against a sink with her arms folded, as if waiting for her turn in the bathroom, but there were only two stalls in the room, and the doors to both were ajar. The room was empty. She was expecting me.

"Listen to me," she said softly, without any preface. "There are a lot of people buzzing around Gus's office this morning. Tafts. Brewsters. Lawyers. Cops. I frankly

don't even know who they all are. A lot of people to be in
town for the Monday of a holiday weekend. The governor's office called, and Gus is meeting with the governor
later today. I don't know how you're involved or what
you did, because that's not my business. But I like you.
You've always been a nice girl. You just have to understand that the politics on this are a lot bigger than you.''

"She was my patient," I said. "She shouldn't be
dead. I need to know what happened.''

"I can't tell you anything because I don't know anything. But I think you should keep your mouth shut until
you see how this plays out. Let Gus handle it. He's the
chairman. He knows what he's doing.'' Ginny straightened up and the gold cross she always wore on a thin
chain danced at her cleavage. "That's my advice. I don't
know how much longer I'll be around to give it to you.''
She disappeared into one of the stalls, and after I heard
the lock click shut, I left. This time, I didn't wait for an
elevator—I raced to the staircase. Down seven flights
even though I didn't know where I was going. I ran
down the staircase, into the doctors' lounge, thinking I
had to find Eric. But of course he wasn't sitting around
the lounge waiting for me. I picked up the house phone
and asked the operator to page Dr. Linden and put him
through to me immediately. A minute later, I heard his
name being bellowed over the intercom, and I counted
out the minutes until he would call the operator and she
would transfer him to the doctors' lounge. But the phone
didn't ring. I paced around the room, poured a cup of
coffee from a pot that had been brewing too long, and
tried to figure out what to do. Finally the house phone
rang and I pounced on it as if it were my last chance on

earth. The operator put Eric through, and the minute I heard his voice, I began to cry.

"Hollis died."

"What?"

"This morning. Before I got here. Have you heard anything about it?"

"What would I hear?"

"Anything. I don't know. There's a wall of silence and nobody will tell me what happened."

Eric didn't say anything for a minute. Then he asked, "Where are you?"

"The doctors' lounge."

"Give me half an hour and I'll be there."

I paced. I picked up the phone three times to call Sloane Brewster, then put it down. What was I going to say? Hi, this is the doctor—do you know why your wife died? Twice I went to the door, thinking I'd check on the patients I had in the hospital, but the thought of going back to the fifth floor right now was too distressing. I sat on the sofa in the lounge and pretended to read a medical journal, but my eyes didn't focus on a single word.

A couple of doctors drifted in and out of the lounge, but I didn't know them and they didn't pay any attention to me. Out of the corner of my eye, I noticed Dr. Oliver Pierce walking in briskly. It took a moment to place him—we shared an office, but I almost never saw him since he spent most of his time in consultations and surgery. He noticed me, too, hesitated, then came over. He wasn't as dramatically handsome as Dr. Franklin, but he looked like a doctor should—solid, competent, and respectable. He was one of the world's experts in uterine cancer, which meant he was a genius but not exactly a fun guy.

"I heard about Hollis Brewster," he said. "I'm sorry."

"Thanks. It's hard for me to believe."

"I know. The advantage of your side of the specialty over mine is you don't deal with death very often."

"It's pretty devastating."

"Things go wrong. It happens." He reached over and touched me on the shoulder. "I'm sure it wasn't your fault."

"I'm having trouble getting the details of what went wrong," I ventured.

Dr. Pierce shrugged. "All I hear around the halls is that it was a uterine rupture. She bled out. I don't know more than that, either."

It was more than I knew, a lot more, but I wasn't going to tell him that. Pierce offered a few more kind words and moved on.

I sat there, pretending to look back into the journal, but feeling more shocked than I had all day. Uterine rupture? What the hell was that about? By the time Eric came in to the lounge and gave me a quick hug, I'd worked myself into such a lather that I needed one of those paper bags I'd given Mona Simpkin. I was either going to hyperventilate or vomit.

"Want to go somewhere for a cup of coffee?" Eric asked, after taking one look at me.

"There's coffee here. Made yesterday and burning ever since, which is the way I like it."

"You have to calm down."

"No I don't." I paced up and down in front of him.

"I have to know what happened and why nobody will tell me anything."

"Uterine rupture," Eric said abruptly. "She bled out. That's all I could find out."

I stared at him. "Who told you that?"

"Jay Tucker, who's the resident on the floor. He was called in during the arrest. Actually, he didn't tell me—he told one of the other residents, who passed it along." Eric paused, then said, "People are buzzing about it around the hospital. I didn't have to ask a lot of questions to hear."

"I know about this rumor already," I said tremulously. "Oliver Pierce was in here and told me. Of course, he didn't know he was giving me the news. I'm the doctor, remember?"

"You had no idea about the rupture?" he asked.

"It didn't happen," I said.

"This stuff can be tough to believe," Eric said piously.

"It didn't *happen*," I said furiously.

Eric pulled on his chin, stroking the beard he didn't have anymore. "Did you do the VBAC as planned?" he asked.

I nodded. "VBAC, uterine rupture. It goes together, right? But think for a second. If a uterus is going to rupture because of a previous cesarean, it'll happen under stress and strain. During labor or delivery. I was with Hollis for hours after the baby was born, and there wasn't any sign of a problem. If there was, I never would have left."

"So what do you think happened?"

"I don't know."

"That's not much of a defense."

"I didn't know I needed one."

Eric shook his head. "Look, don't fight with me, okay? I'd like to help, but I don't know what I can do. You've obviously got to get the details. Ardsley has to talk to you. Or the nurse on the floor. Or Tucker. You can't be making guesses from rumors."

"I don't have a choice at the moment," I said. "Nobody's talking to me. Usually residents call me in the middle of the night to report a patient's temp has gone from ninety-nine point six to ninety-nine point eight. They call me before they prescribe a Tylenol. Now it's July, when there are new interns, and they usually call before they get a cup of coffee. But my patient dies— actually dies for God's sake—and I don't hear a murmur until I get to her room. Something's strange here."

"I agree. Have you spoken to your office? Maybe Franklin has something intelligent to say."

It was a good point. I picked up the phone and called. The receptionist who answered passed it along to Juliette, who almost immediately put me on hold.

"Waiting," I said, looking up at Eric. I tapped my foot against the leg of the chair, anticipating what I would hear. There was nothing for a while but the music that went on at our office with the hold button. Finally Juliette came back. "Dr. Franklin can't get to the phone at the moment, but he said to tell you that he's heard about Hollis. You can go home if you want and he'll round later in the day."

"Thanks, Juliette, but I need to talk to him."

"He can't right now."

I took a breath, trying to control my temper. "Okay

then, if you want to play middleman, go back and ask him how he heard about Hollis. And what he heard.''

"I can't do that right now. Why don't I see if he can call you later.''

I didn't answer. Juliette only followed the party line. Whatever Franklin told her, she repeated. But she'd know one thing.

"Did anyone at the hospital call our office this morning looking for me?''

"Uh, what do you mean?''

The question was pretty straightforward, but I rephrased it for her. ''Nobody ever beeped me when Hollis arrested. I wondered if any calls came into the office for me this morning.''

"No,'' she said. Then, worried that she had uttered a single word undirected, she quickly amended it. "I mean, not that I know about. Maybe. You could ask Dr. Franklin. But not that I know.''

I thanked her—for nothing—and hung up. Eric had picked up the substance of the conversation from hearing my side, and now he had just one question. "If you weren't at the hospital this morning and you weren't at the office, where were you?''

I looked him straight in the eye. "It was a Monday morning, Eric. You know exactly where I was.''

Eric was quiet for a moment, then said, "Damn, I forgot. You still volunteer at that clinic in Roxbury.''

"I had my beeper on. If anyone tried to reach me, I'd know.''

"Well, if anyone asks, maybe you should just say you were at home.''

"I saw fourteen women this morning, Eric. I wasn't

at home. Fourteen poor women. And anyway, what difference does it make? Where I was has nothing to do
with what happened.''

Eric shrugged. ''I know that. Rationally, I know that.
And I can't explain why it seems like it would matter.''

He was pissing me off. The whole world was pissing
me off. I shouldn't be helping the poor if I was supposed
to be tending the rich? Is that what people were going
to say? ''Look,'' I said abruptly, ''you have to get back
to work. Thanks for coming to talk to me. I needed it
and I appreciate it.''

Eric knew he was being dismissed, and he didn't try
to fight it. Maybe he was grateful. ''What are you going
to do?''

''Round,'' I said. ''I have five more patients on the
floor, and I'm going to see them.''

Early in the evening, I got home to a perfectly quiet
house. Paco was in New York, talking to a big-deal gallery owner in SoHo who was thinking of representing
him. I wanted to call him, but I knew Paco wasn't going
to be relaxing in his hotel room at this hour and I didn't
know where else to try. Besides, I'd already played out
our conversation in my head, and I knew where it would
lead. What I was making into a big conspiracy, Paco
would see as paranoia. And maybe he was right. All the
little things that had happened today didn't add up to
much. Ardsley was investigating the circumstances of
the death and didn't have time to talk to me just yet.
Franklin was busy with a patient when I called. Ginny
may have liked the mystery of a ladies' room meeting,
but all she was doing was telling me to back off and let
the hospital bosses handle things. Nurse Dolton, who

had every reason to hate me, wasn't rushing to my assistance. Big surprise. I needed to curl up in bed with a cup of tea and try to stop making mountains out of molehills. By tomorrow, things would start straightening out.

I changed out of my work clothes, pulled on old jeans and a baggy T-shirt, and went over to the CD player. My favorite disk of Beethoven piano concertos was lying on top of the player, which meant that Paço had taken it out to put in his music while he was painting. I turned it on, and the raucous strains of Pearl Jam filled the room. Not my style, but it made me feel as if Paco were nearby. When the doorbell rang a few minutes later, I didn't bother switching off the music. I peeked through the side window and saw a heavyset man standing there, dressed in wrinkled bluejeans and a shabby green cotton sweater. He looked vaguely respectable, so I cracked the door open.

"Yes?"

"You're Dr. Love?"

I nodded and he pulled a notepad from his back pocket and flashed it at me. Taped to the front of it was a business card that I could hardly make out in the dim light. "I'm Marty Stenopolus from the *Boston Tribune*," he said. "I need to talk to you about Hollis Brewster."

I should have just shut the door then. Maybe things wouldn't have gotten out of hand as quickly as they did. But instead I asked, "What about her?"

"She's dead, you know."

"Well, yes, of course I know."

He scratched his head, peering at me through the crack in the door. "I'm trying to find out why a healthy woman would have died in childbirth."

I stared at my bare feet for a moment, since I'd been trying to find out exactly the same thing. Hollis Brewster was perfectly healthy when I left her on Sunday night. When I got to the hospital today she was dead, the body had already been taken from the floor, and Archibald Ardsley was in charge of the case.

But I wasn't going to tell Marty Stenopolus all that.

"The hospital will have to help you. I'm sure they've issued a full statement."

"I'll rush right down and get it," he said sarcastically. Then switching tone almost immediately, he became conspiratorial and said, "Look, I don't need press releases, I need real information. I'm part of the paper's investigative team."

"This story's not exactly Watergate. Or even Whitewater." I didn't mean to sound snappish, but it was either that or break down sobbing at his feet. "People die in hospitals every day."

"But not like this. And not someone as important to the city as Hollis." He was sweating profusely even though the night was cool, and I could see big wet stains under the armpits of his cotton sweater. He wiped his brow with the back of a grubby hand. "Think I could come in and we could talk a little more about it?"

"No." Paco wasn't there, and I certainly wasn't letting a strange man in my house.

"How about tomorrow morning in your office?"

"Uh, sure." I didn't know if I'd go to the office the next day, but all I wanted was to get rid of him.

"Let me just make sure I'm right on one thing. You're her doctor. You delivered the baby."

"Yes."

He looked me over carefully, taking in my bare feet, my cut-off jeans, and my T-shirt. I didn't have on any makeup, and my hair was wilder than usual. In the brief silence, the cacophonous sound of Pearl Jam roared at us from the living room.

"Will you be at the funeral? I think it's Wednesday. Maybe Thursday."

"Probably. I guess so."

He handed me one of his business cards, pulled from his pocket. "I'll call your office in the morning and find a time we can talk, okay?"

He walked back to his beat-up car, and as I watched him go, I felt my heart beating too hard.

II

MY BEEPER WENT off at five o'clock the next morning. All I'd thought about for the last eighteen hours was Hollis, but apparently the world was still in motion. A patient named Katie O'Rourke, pregnant with twins, was in labor. Her water had just broken, and since it was twins I wanted her at the hospital right away.

"You'll meet me there?" she asked, her voice tremulous.

"Of course."

I dressed and drove over to the hospital, crossing over the Eliot Bridge and onto Storrow Drive. There was no traffic at this hour, but still I drove carefully, watching as the rising sun cast a pinkish glow on the Charles River. I couldn't help wondering if Hollis had seen the sun rise the day before or if she had been struggling for her life by then. Did she know she was going to die?

Was she scared? Or was it sudden—looking out her window at the summer sunrise, relaxing in the warm glow of her new baby cuddled against her breast and then suddenly . . .

Suddenly what? I slammed my fist against the steering wheel. These were questions I should know the answers to. Her husband, her parents, her in-laws—all the people who loved Hollis—were asking themselves the same kinds of questions right now. It was my job to call them with answers. But I didn't have any.

I parked and went into the hospital, which for a moment felt like a foreign country. It was getting close to the time that Hollis had died. Most of the staff worked the same hours each day, and I couldn't help feeling that some of the people who were here right now had the answers I needed.

I made my way to the fifth floor, taking the stairs slowly. Katie had arrived before me, and her name was already on the board. The floor seemed quieter than usual. I signed my initials next to my patient's name and went into the labor room. Her husband was there, holding her hand. An external fetal monitor was attached, and a notation on the chart said she was three centimeters dilated when she came in. But there was no labor nurse in the room. Another time, I would have tried to find out why, but now I just turned my complete attention to Katie.

She'd had a fairly easy pregnancy, but the labor wasn't going to be simple at all. She was in back labor when I came in—fairly common in delivering twins—and the pain of that was registering in her face. There were beads of perspiration on her forehead and she had bitten her lower lip so hard, it was cracked and bleeding. I pulled up a chair to her bedside. It was going to be a long haul.

I didn't want to leave her, but the day turned out to be a full one. A patient who'd very recently come to me from Brewster Managed Care arrived an hour later in an advanced stage of labor. I immediately spotted an active herpes infection and whisked her off to the operating room for an emergency cesarean. If her water broke or the labor went much farther, the baby could be infected—and that was dangerous. The surgery wasn't. The anesthesiologist gave an epidural, I made the incision, opened the uterus, and removed the healthy baby.

"That was so fast," she whispered.

But it wasn't quite over. Closing the incision took about thirty-five minutes. I focused intently on the surgery, and the operating room was quiet. I know some doctors tell jokes in the operating room or chat with patients who are awake, but I never could. I don't want to be relaxed when I'm cutting and sewing through skin, tissue, and muscle; I want to be thinking about the person in my care, the heart beating because I'm there to make sure all goes well. And especially today, focusing on the surgery was a relief. Thinking about that, I couldn't be thinking about anything else.

But then it was over, and as I pulled off gloves and scrubs, Hollis immediately came back into my mind. This delivery had been so easy. Would Hollis be alive now if I'd followed the old rules, done a cesarean, and not let her worry about a few extra days in the hospital? No, it didn't make sense.

I checked on Katie, then got paged again. Another

pregnant woman had just come into the hospital. She was a patient of Franklin's, but he wasn't on call today. I went to the labor room just in time. She was having her third baby and delivered fast. No problem there. She didn't want to stay in the hospital, and in other circumstances I would have made a joke about McDelivery and sent her home a few hours later. But I was nervous today, on edge. I urged her to stay overnight and promised a cot in the room for her husband. The woman with the cesarean would have to go home in three days under the BMC plan. That's all they'd pay for. Well, if she needed more, I'd let her stay. I had a degree in medicine, not business.

Feeling a bit like I was on a treadmill, I checked on Katie again, who hadn't progressed any further. But she was well within the range of normal, and we weren't going to rush anything. An epidural had relieved the pain and she was lying in bed, watching television and joking with her husband. I went to the hospital cafeteria to grab a salad and some iced tea.

Very late in the evening, I brought Katie to the delivery room. The epidural had worn off, which meant she could push, but the pain had returned, too. For an hour, she pushed and screamed and sweated while her husband held her hand and I kept murmuring, "You're almost there. Good job. Deep breath and push." And then it all paid off as the first twin was born and Katie held her baby and began crying for joy; but the second baby flipped around into a breech position, and I couldn't turn it. For three hours we waited and tried. The baby wasn't budging and Katie was at the end of her coping powers.

"Don't twins come out minutes apart?" she asked in

a hoarse whisper as we went into the third hour.

"Usually. But this isn't that rare. The first baby was very low down. Baby number two is actually still quite high in the uterus."

"How long could it be?"

I'd once heard of twin babies who were born ninety-four days apart, but I wasn't going to tell Katie that. "Anything can happen when twins are premature, but you're full term. Don't worry. We can't go much longer."

After another hour the only choice was an emergency cesarean, which meant poor Katie had the worst of everything—a long labor, an episiotomy, and a C-section. But both babies were lusty and pink, and the moment Katie heard the cries of the second baby she grabbed her husband's hand and said, "We did it! Let me hold him!" Her husband, a fireman, finally relaxed enough to swagger at the realization that he'd sired two eight-pound boys.

Katie didn't leave the recovery room until after 2 A.M. By then, I was too bone-numbingly exhausted to go home, so I stumbled into the doctors' lounge and curled up on a sofa by the window. Just a quick nap, I told myself. Then I'd be okay to drive home. But it was six in the morning before I opened my eyes again, awakened by a heart surgeon I knew vaguely, who came in to make some phone calls before his early-morning operation. I sat up, realizing I had a crick in my neck from the couch and that I also had a hospitalful of patients to round on and office hours that began at nine. Propriety be damned. I went to the bathroom in the back of the lounge, peeled off my clothes, and stepped into the large stall shower.

The hot water felt good and I didn't care who walked in. If the men didn't like me in their bathroom, let them give me one of my own.

I stood under the shower for a long time, only gradually aware that someone was pounding at the bathroom door. I ignored it and let the hot water drum against my back and flow over my hair. Hard to believe that I'd regularly worked thirty-six-hour shifts when I was an intern.

"Sarabeth, are you in there?"

The pounding at the door finally penetrated my groggy senses.

"I'll be out in a minute." I turned off the shower and stepped out, wrapping a towel around me.

"Sarabeth, let me in." Only now did I realize it was Eric, with a trace of hysteria in his voice.

"I have the morning paper. Did you see it?"

"I haven't seen anything," I said, calling back through the door. "I've been delivering twins since seven o'clock yesterday morning. Can't it wait?"

"No." He pounded on the door again. "Goddamn it, Sarabeth, let me in. I'd better show you this before anyone else does."

Still in a towel, I opened the door and Eric charged in, waving a copy of the *Boston Tribune*. Even before he came to a stop, I could see Hollis's picture fluttering across the front page of the tabloid. I tried to grab the paper, but I was suddenly shaking from head to toe. Eric held it out to me and I saw the six-inch headline: SHOCKING DEATH OF SOCIETY GIRL *Complete story, page 6*. Eric flipped the pages, and there was another headline, screaming across two full pages, reporting the death of Boston's beautiful Hollis Taft Brewster. Below it was a half-page picture of Hollis, smiling sweetly and looking like a princess. A box announced that this was a special investigative report by Marty Stenopolus.

I pointed shakily to the name. "He stopped by my house Monday night. But I didn't talk. He never called to meet again."

"He talked to someone. He has more details about what happened than I've heard anywhere."

I tried to look at the text of the story but the words blurred. I focused on the small pictures running along the side: Hollis and her mother in evening gowns at a charity ball; Hollis with Sloane at a ground-breaking ceremony; Hollis and James romping on the grounds of what the caption described as their mansion in the Berkshires. I shoved the paper back at Eric.

"I can't read this," I said. "Just tell me what it says."

He took a deep breath. "The gist is that Hollis had an unsafe medical procedure—that is, a vaginal delivery after two cesareans. A simple cesarean, and she'd still be alive. Instead, her feminist physician—that's a direct quote—encouraged a natural delivery, and her uterus ruptured. Chairman of the Department Ardsley did everything he could to save her, but it was too late."

"No." My mind refused to take in what he was saying. All I was aware of were the hairs around Eric's forehead, beginning to curl in the steamy room.

"They also mention that while she was bleeding to death, you were neither at home nor at the hospital, and couldn't be reached. An anonymous source is quoted as saying that you secretly work at a clinic on Monday mornings. The implication is that you're some wild-eyed liberal feminist, taking her revenge on rich, conservative Hollis.''

My heart was slamming against my chest. I was as stiff with fear as if a rapist were holding a knife to my throat. I couldn't begin to speak.

''You really never talked to this guy?'' Eric asked.

''Maybe for three minutes.'' My voice was hoarse.

Eric turned a page in the paper. The article apparently went on and on. ''Right here. He makes it sound like he interviewed you for hours. He describes you as, quote—the barefoot doctor with long hair tumbling down her back and full breasts unhampered by anything as conventional as a bra—endquote.''

''It was at night,'' I whispered, then added more forcefully, ''This is all lies.''

''Lies in print. He says you're more interested in winning feminist points than in being a doctor.''

I took the paper and threw it at Eric. ''Get the hell out of here, will you? That paper is garbage. It's a tabloid. Why are you quoting it to me?''

Eric deflected the paper and was suddenly as angry as I was. ''I quoted what everyone else in the hospital is going to be reading and believing. Only I'm trying to make some sense out of it.''

''It doesn't make sense. I'm not the demon doctor and Ardsley's not a hero! I didn't kill Hollis so I could make a point! I did what was medically right and there's no explanation for why this happened.''

I was shaking uncontrollably and Eric put his hands on my shoulders to calm me down, but I shook them off and began swinging wildly at him, missing every blow but trying to connect. He grabbed at my hands and I lunged at him, slipping on the wet tile floor and landing with a thud on my side. I gasped in pain and shock, and didn't even try to get up from the floor as I shouted, "Get out of here and leave me alone!"

"I won't, goddamn it! You can't pretend this isn't here!"

"I can pretend whatever I want! I can pretend I'm a real doctor who doesn't kill people! I can pretend Hollis isn't dead and the world hasn't turned upside down! I can pretend some of this makes sense."

Suddenly, our fight was over. Eric was lying on the floor next to me, and I buried my head in his shoulder and began to sob. I felt him stroke my hair and murmur words of comfort, but I was shaking and sobbing with such violence that nothing could make me stop.

I don't know how long I lay there clinging to him and pretending that he could protect me, but after a while he stirred and tugged at my bunched-up towel, and I sat up, pulling the towel over my breasts and holding it in place with crisscrossed arms. I rocked back and forth like a frightened animal and then heard a knock at the door. I looked in alarm at Eric, but he didn't seem startled at all, and I wondered if he had been alerted by a previous knock, unheard by me through the sobs that resounded in my head. He looked at me with an even gaze, and then turning toward the door, called out, "I'm sorry, but it'll just be a couple more minutes." The footsteps outside the door retreated.

"You'd better get dressed." Eric stood up and looked around the small room. My clothes were hanging from a hook, and he handed them to me and moved away, pointedly turning his back. I rose shakily and began to dress, aware of Eric picking up the scattered newspaper pages and putting them back together. I pulled on my panties and the sleeveless flowered dress I had put on the previous morning. It was slim on top and belted at the waist with a long, pleated skirt. I slipped my bare feet into flat shoes and reached to the zipper in the back. I had pulled it only a couple of inches when it got caught in a thread. I tugged at it in frustration, trying to rip through the thread, but the zipper would go neither up nor down. After a minute, Eric came over and word-lessly brushed my hands away. I felt his surgeon's fin-gers extricate the thread and slowly close the zipper over my bare back.

"I'm your best friend, so I can make rude sugges-tions," he said. "Start wearing a bra. And pantyhose wouldn't hurt."

I turned around to face him. "It's hot in the hospital. You want me to wear a hair shirt, too?"

"If you're going to prove this article is a pack of lies, you better start with the basics. Everybody's going to be staring at you the moment you step out of here. Are you ready for that?" I grabbed for the edge of the sink know-ing I wasn't ready for that at all. My eyes felt swollen and sore from the crying, and I didn't know what I was going to say to anybody who had seen the article.

"Can you take a walk with me?" I didn't want to be alone.

Eric glanced at his watch. "I have surgery scheduled at eight. Gives me about half an hour."

We left the doctors' lounge, which was empty; we didn't have time to go to Boston Common or the Charles

River, so we settled for the park outside the hospital. The weather wasn't cooperating with my mood. There should have been gray thunderclouds and flashes of lightning against a graphite sky, the ominous rumbles of a storm moving in. But the sun was bright and the humidity rising only enough to fill the air with the pungent sweetness of nasturtiums. Walking slowly Eric said, "If Marty Stenopolus didn't get his information from you, it came from somewhere. The medical examiner?"

"There was no postmortem. That much I've heard."

"Who signed the death certificate?"

I shrugged miserably. "Ardsley, I assume, but I haven't investigated. I'm a doctor, not a detective."

"Maybe you should get one."

The sharpness in his voice cut through my fog.

"Look," he said. "Yesterday you were trying to explain to me why this death didn't make sense. Okay, I heard you, but nobody else did. So now you're taking the fall for something that wasn't your fault. You can't change what's in the paper, but you'd better be ready to fight it with facts, and that means chapter and verse to present to a jury."

"A jury?"

"Obvious setup for a malpractice suit, wouldn't you say? Maybe Sloane Brewster leaked all the information to Stenopolus to make his case stronger. Somebody had to give him those pictures. Brewster gets the whole world believing you're guilty before he even files a suit. By the time it goes to trial, the jury thinks he's generous asking for only ten million."

I blinked hard. Eric had to be off base. Sloane Brewster wouldn't try to profit from his wife's death. He didn't need the money, and besides, he had to know that the newspaper's interpretation of events was all wrong. I said as much and Eric snorted.

"Wanna know how the rich are different from you and me? They have fewer morals. People only become as rich as Sloane Brewster by not caring how they make their money. I've heard the Brewster Building is a black hole, devouring money. It wouldn't be that hard for Brewster to turn on you and rake in a few million from your malpractice insurance."

Suddenly I laughed. "He'd just be getting it from himself," I said. "Remember? He's Mr. Insurance. He built the Brewster Building with our malpractice premiums."

Eric stopped walking and glanced at his watch. The sunlight bounced off the dial and reflected like two magic beams on his forehead.

"I've got to get back to the hospital. Maybe I'm wrong about the insurance, but I just want to make sure you keep your eyes open here. You're the one who thought something was wrong yesterday. Now I'm agreeing. Just CYA."

Cover your ass. Great. The rule of thumb in the hospital, that I'd always refused to follow. I wanted to cover my patients first, not my ass. But now it felt brutally exposed.

Eric kissed me on the cheek, then put his arms around me and held me for a moment. "Hey," he said softly, "I'd like to burn every copy of that newspaper. You don't deserve this garbage."

"Thanks." I didn't want to start crying again, but his kindness brought an unexpected lump to my throat.

I hadn't had much sleep, but it didn't matter. Doctors weren't supposed to need sleep. I knew that was ridiculous, but it was one of those things ingrained in your head after four tired years at medical school, a year of internship, four years of surgical residency, two years of ob-gyn residency . . . I hadn't slept through all that, so why should I now?

I walked around the park for a few minutes after Eric had left, plotting my day. See my patients. Morning office hours. But there was something I wanted to do first. I returned to the hospital, waited for the snail-like elevator and went back to the seventh floor. Outside Dr. Ardsley's office, a heavyset, middle-aged black woman stared up at me from the place where Ginny usually sat.

"Is Ginny around?" I asked.

"No," said the woman. "Can I help you?"

"Well, I actually need Ginny. Do you know when she'll be in?"

"She won't be. She's gone."

It was the phrase Nurse Dolton had used in telling me about Hollis, and suddenly my heart was pounding again.

"Gone . . . where?"

"I don't know, but she doesn't work here anymore. I'm just a temp. I was called in this morning. Sure I can't do anything for you?"

"Perhaps I could see Dr. Ardsley."

"Are you Dr. Love by any chance?"

"Yes."

"Oh. He said you might be by." She consulted a note on her desk. "He said he'd talk to you at four o'clock this afternoon, in his office."

"He's not in now?"

"He's in now. But he said he wanted to talk to you at four o'clock." The woman was like a brick wall.

I checked on the three women who had delivered the day before, plus two other patients of Dr. Pierce, then left the hospital, walked over to Beacon Street to get on the subway and noticed a man on the corner selling the *Boston Tribune*. At the next corner, a kiosk had a pile of the papers displayed, and as I slowed my step to look at the headline again, see Hollis's smiling face, the vendor asked, "Paper, lady?" I just stared, transfixed by her image. "A quarter and you can read the whole thing," he said. Smartass. I wanted the paper, but I couldn't bear to buy it. Ignore this nightmare, I told myself. Ignore it. Maybe Ardsley would clear some things up this afternoon.

Juliette barely glanced at me when I came into the office, except to toss her blond hair and flounce away when I asked her to talk with me for a minute. "Sorry, I'm busy," she said. Fortunately, my patient schedule was light. Nobody wanted to be in downtown Boston in the heat of July, and certainly nobody wanted to be in a doctor's office. The first two patients were routine gynecological exams, the third a newly married woman who beamed when I confirmed the positive result of her home pregnancy test. The next patient was a strikingly pretty forty-four-year-old named Pia Davis, a vice-president at one of the big banks in the city, and one of those rare women who managed to look powerful even in a paper examining gown. It was her first visit and she crisply explained that she'd left her last gynecologist only because her bank had switched health insurance carriers and she might as well go to someone where the visit would be covered.

Great. I was free.

She'd come in after several months of erratic periods, and I gave her the news—I'm never sure if it's good or bad—that she was hitting menopause. She seemed momentarily surprised, but quickly recovered.

"Then I'd like to begin estrogen treatment immediately," she said briskly. "I've read a lot about it, so you don't have to tell me. Estrogen's the miracle hormone that relieves menopause symptoms, preserves your skin tone, your bones, and a good sex life."

"You've done your homework," I said. "I don't recommend hormone replacement for everyone, but forty-four is the early side of normal, so there are a lot of years to protect. There's not much downside. Taken at very low doses and combined with progesterone, estrogen does exactly what you say. The new research also suggests that at the right dosage level, it doesn't promote uterine cancer and in fact may be protective against some cancers and heart disease."

She nodded impatiently. "Good. We agree."

"But you should understand that we can't start it just yet."

She stared at me coldly. "Why not, Doctor? Another of those feminist positions of yours that I read about this morning?"

I felt my cheeks getting hot. I should have told her that if she doubted my medical judgment, she should get out immediately, but the nerve was so raw, I could do nothing but protect it. I ignored the comment and stayed professional.

"You're in what's known as perimenopause," I told her. "That means you've stopped ovulating and therefore stopped making progesterone. But you're still producing enough estrogen to build up the uterine lining. Without the balancing progesterone, the lining sloughs off unevenly and irregularly. Hence, your erratic bleeding. For most women, this interim stage lasts anywhere from a few months to a couple of years."

She wasn't paying attention—just waiting to talk. "I was told to start estrogen quickly—to avoid the symptoms of menopause, like hot flashes. I don't need those, thank you."

"No, you don't. And if they begin during perimenopause, we can put you on some carefully monitored hormone therapy. But let me say again that you're still producing estrogen. In fact, estrogen levels typically soar at this time. If we add more on top of that, there's a good chance of developing endometrial hyperplasia—which is an excessive buildup of cells along the uterine lining. That can incite a malignant growth."

She looked at me dubiously, then said scornfully, "So I should do nothing? Follow that stay-natural philosophy that's already gotten you in trouble once this week?"

I looked down briefly, bit my lip, and silently vowed to stay calm. "We can begin progesterone if the irregular bleeding is unnerving you. Ten milligrams a day for one week a month. That will put you back on a predictable schedule and make sure the endometrial tissue is cleanly shed."

"So I get to continue my periods for the rest of my life. Not what I had in mind."

Her voice was dripping contempt, but I wasn't going

to be riled. I wouldn't get off track. I couldn't. Like a robot, an advice spouting medical robot, I continued:

"When your body stops producing enough estrogen to build up the uterine lining, the progesterone has nothing to act on. Your periods stop. At that point, we do some blood tests to determine hormone levels, and assuming all is normal, we can begin the estrogen replacement."

"I want to begin it now," she said arrogantly. "I guess I'll have to find a doctor who sees things my way." She jumped off the table, pulling her gown close around her. "As I told you, I only came here because my bank just switched to Brewster Managed Care for health insurance. Your name was on the list and I picked you because you were nearby. After that article this morning, I probably never should have come in."

I walked to the door of the examining room. "I'm sure you'll find a doctor somewhere on that list who does what you tell him. And after you develop cancer, come back and ask for Dr. Pierce. He's the best in the field. I'll try to find out how he feels about treating an arrogant know-it-all." I walked out, slamming the door behind me as hard as I could.

Down the hall, I saw Juliette exchanging looks with one of the other young nurses, who then hurried over to me.

"Everything okay, Dr. Love?"

"No," I said. "It's not." I went into my consultation room and shut the door. Stupid bitch. She could run a bank or approve loans or whatever it was she did, but that didn't make her a doctor. So she'd picked my name from a health-insurance list. That did a lot for the doctor–patient relationship. Doctor as God? When it went this way, it was more like doctor as cat, purring at the feet of the patient and trying to make her happy. Let somebody else collect her fees. I had better things to do.

I'd never really stopped thinking about Hollis, but now my mind snapped back to her, full attention. For a moment, I stared at the shelves that Dr. Franklin had filled with textbooks, then took down the thickest obstetrical treatise there. I held the book, but didn't open it. I'd worked harder than anyone to make sure I was the smartest doctor in Boston. Nine years of studying. Chief resident. But somewhere I'd missed something. Somehow Hollis had died. I could proclaim as much as I wanted that I had done everything right, that none of this made sense, but the end result was the same. Like the old joke: The surgery was a success but the patient died. My patient, my friend, had died.

There was a knock on my door, and when I said "Yes?" Dr. Franklin walked in. He worked here, too, but I was still surprised to see him. I wasn't sitting, and he didn't sit down, either. Nor did he bother with small talk. He must have been taking lessons from Ardsley.

"I heard there was a little fracas with your last patient," he said abruptly.

I nodded. "She's insisting on estrogen replacement, but she's still in early perimenopause. It would be irresponsible."

"You slammed the door and told her you hope she dies of cancer."

"I did not," I said defensively. "Tell her that, I mean. Yes, I slammed the door. I told her to get her estrogen and come back and consult Dr. Pierce."

Franklin leaned against my desk. "Understandable that you're a little overwrought, Sarabeth. But you can't talk to a patient that way. No matter what she says."

"Sorry," I said. "I was delivering Katie O'Rourke's twins all night and had two other deliveries. And then this morning . . ." I trailed off. Dr. Franklin of the good manners probably wouldn't mention the article if I didn't. I suddenly wondered if his name had been in it. Damn, I should have bought a copy after all.

Franklin paced across the room and stopped at the picture of Paco and Betsy.

"Everything okay with you at home?" he asked.

"Fine," I said.

"Good. Then maybe you should take off the next couple of weeks to study for your boards."

I looked at him, astonished. "I don't really need to do that."

"It'd be a good idea."

"You want me out for a while?" I asked bluntly.

"I want to make sure you pass your boards, and this would be a little insurance. They're at the end of July, right? Work out the dates with Juliette. I'll go talk to her about it." He strode over to the door and was out of the room before either of us could say anything important or let down our guard for the briefest moment.

I collapsed in the chair behind my desk and picked up the phone. I had to talk to Paco. I called every telephone number that I knew in New York, finally reaching his agent, Deke Passer, who told me to try Paco at a gallery on Fifty-seventh Street.

"Everything okay?" Paco asked, finally coming to the phone. "Because everything's hunky here. The

SoHo gallery didn't work out, but this incredibly classy uptown gallery agreed to show three of my pieces at the end of the summer.''

"That's great."

"You don't sound excited."

"I'm thrilled, darling. I'm just having kind of a bad time here."

"Oh." The sudden change in his voice—was that concern?—was vaguely satisfying. "I tried you last night, but there was no answer. I would have beeped you, but it wasn't important enough to drag you out of an operating room."

"Are you in a place you can listen to a long story?"

"Hang on." I heard muffled voices, the phone was put on hold, and a couple of minutes later he was back on the line. "There. I'm in an office now. Shoot."

So I did. I told him about Hollis's delivery and what happened afterwards. I told him about going to the hospital the next morning and Marty Stenopolus at the door that night and Katie O'Rourke having twins. I didn't mention Eric's coming in while I was showering and just told him about the newspaper article and Dr. Franklin's wanting me to disappear for a couple of weeks. I wasn't crying as I talked, only because I was too numb.

Paco listened, and except for a few exclamations along the way, said nothing. At the end he just sighed.

"Hey, baby, I'm sorry. I can't believe I'm not there to hold you."

I smiled to myself. My Paco. Love conquers all. Well, what had I wanted, advice? An insightful medical diagnosis as to the probable cause of death?

"Listen, I'll come right home," he said. "I should be there."

"It's okay," I said weakly.

"Well, then why don't you come here? Get out of there for a few days. Deke took me to dinner last night at Odeon and introduced me to Julian Schnabel and Brice Marden. We can go there again tonight."

I hesitated. Sometimes it seemed that our worlds were too separate to ever merge. Who the heck was Julian Schnabel and why should I care? But I knew Paco was trying to be sweet.

"Let me figure it out," I said. "I'm seeing Ardsley at four and Hollis's funeral is tomorrow. Maybe after that."

"I can come home."

"No. I'm okay." As I hung up, I wondered why I'd said that.

At five minutes before four o'clock I was standing outside Dr. Ardsley's office, and at the stroke of the hour, he opened the door and told me to come in.

I was armed with a list of questions and ready to spew forth my anger and outrage at how I'd been treated. But the moment I walked into the office I realized that I wasn't the one setting the tone for this meeting. A uniformed policeman was sitting in a chair, and two other men I didn't recognize were standing by the window. With his usual lack of preliminaries, Dr. Ardsley pointed me to the chair beside the cop, sat down behind his desk, and said, "We're here to discuss the death of Hollis Taft Brewster. Let's begin with the details of the delivery. At what point on Sunday did you first hear from Mrs. Brewster?"

The good girl in me started to answer—after all, I'd been asked a question—but then I stopped myself. Eric's advice: *CYA*. "Dr. Ardsley, I've been trying to talk to you about this since it occurred. In private. Could you tell me who these people are?"

He nodded. "Officer Greg Curry next to you. The other gentlemen are John Doheny and Peter Vicente."

"And why are they joining us?"

"Because a death has occurred. Hollis Brewster was a well-known figure in this city and people are asking a lot of questions—as you know from the paper this morning. The governor asked my cooperation Monday in investigating the circumstances, and I was happy to comply. I assumed you would be, too."

Monday. Today was Wednesday. A lot had gone on without me. I turned to the men at the window. "So you represent . . ." I let the sentence hang, assuming they would finish it, but neither did. They just looked over to Ardsley.

"Mr. Doheny is from the governor's office and Mr. Vicente is from the district attorney's office. Okay? So let's start again. When did you first hear from Mrs. Brewster on Sunday?"

If I had a choice about answering, it didn't feel that way. Maybe I should have asked for a lawyer or demanded to be read my rights, but it never occurred to me. This was a hospital. I figured that even with our guests in the room, we were still just exchanging information. Ardsley would ask his questions and then I'd ask mine.

I went through the details of Sunday, which weren't very dramatic: Hollis's arrival at the hospital early in labor, the carefully monitored delivery, the by-the-book VBAC, the immediate postpartum recovery which seemed completely normal. Ardsley scribbled a note or two. The other men just listened. When I was finished, Ardsley led me through the delivery again, asking about signs of danger that had never been there. I shook my head, rejecting each point he raised, but just voicing the possibilities made them real. I saw where he was headed—that there was a small rupture in the uterus during delivery that wasn't immediately catastrophic and so went undetected.

"Not only do I reject that possibility," I said, "but it's one that I've never seen described in the medical literature." From the corner of my eye, I caught the two men by the window exchanging looks. Was this what Ardsley had been suggesting to them since Monday?

Ardsely closed his notebook. "Very well, Dr. Love. Thank you for your cooperation. I'm sure we'll need to talk to you again."

He stood up, but I kept my seat and said, "Dr. Ardsley, I have a few questions that I'd like to ask you at this point. Nobody's filled me in on what happened Monday morning. The chart was gone when I arrived and nobody's been forthcoming. Can I know what you found?"

It was a mistake to have remained sitting after he stood up, because now he peered down at me as if from Mount Olympus. "This isn't the proper time for it," he said. "Once the investigation is finished, I'll issue a complete report." He opened the door to let me out, and with everyone sitting there, I somehow didn't plead my case. A lot more had been left unsaid than said, but I kept my head as high as I could as I left the room.

• • •

The notice in the paper said the funeral would start at ten o'clock in the morning, and when I arrived at ten minutes before the hour, there were so many cars lining the streets near the church that I had to park blocks away. I rushed toward the church, not wanting to be late. The last thing I needed was to draw attention to myself.

The temperature must have already hit the nineties and the humidity was nearly unbearable. The sun glared in my eyes and my long black skirt clung uncomfortably to my legs. I'd searched my closet for a plain black top, but the only one I could find had small white flowers in it. I convinced myself it was appropriate—from death springs life; flowers were symbols of renewal and hope.

Nobody looked at me as I entered the church and I had the fleeting impression that some even looked away. Despite the July heat, people were dressed in dark clothes, a few specks of white, some dark green and navy, but otherwise it was a sea of black. In the church, I saw a few empty seats near the front but realized that I couldn't bear to walk down the long center aisle like the bride I'd never been, walking to death. There was a single seat in the center of the very last pew, and excusing myself, I made my way to it. At least there was only one row of people disturbed by my entrance.

The music began almost the moment I was seated, the organ resounding through the huge church and seeming to bounce off the glistening stained-glass windows. From a side room, where he had allowed no visitors, Sloane Brewster slipped in, clutching the hands of his two small children. A nurse followed, holding the new baby. At the sight of them, there were a few gasped sobs in the packed church. Beautiful little Porter dressed in white, an angel like her mother had been. Her big brother, six-year-old James, dressed in crisp chino pants and a blue blazer, looking stunned beyond words. They went to the casket and bowed in front of it, Sloane whispering a prayer. The baby, who had been resting sweetly until then, began to wail, a cry that might have been hunger or fatigue, but pierced every heart in the church like an arrow of grief. The minister ascended the pulpit and the nurse took the baby away, but it seemed the most eloquent prayer had already been said—a child's cry for her mother.

I found myself shaking and feared that I would break down and begin sobbing relentlessly here in the last row. I concentrated on the mechanics of the service: time to stand up, time to sing a psalm, time to bow my head. Toward the front of the church I noticed a row of men in gray suits, unrelieved by any female presence: Dr. Ardsley, Dr. Franklin, Dr. Pierce, the president of P&S Hospital, the governor, the mayor. I thought I recognized the two men from Dr. Ardsley's office, Doheny and Vicente. I felt a chill that I couldn't explain, as if they were all bonding together against me. I turned my eyes away, gazed around the church, and saw various well-known faces—local newscasters, the publisher of the *Boston Tribune*, a famous actress. Two rows in front of me but across the aisle, Juliette was sitting straight up, attentive, and I wondered briefly why she had come. Hollis didn't like to deal with the nurses in the office, so they'd scarcely known each other. I remembered only one time they'd met and had an angry, whispered conversation in the hall. Juliette no doubt had wanted to draw blood; Hollis liked me to do it, so I had. Without much personal connection, Juliette was probably here for stargazing today; she'd go back and tell her girlfriends what all the rich people had been wearing.

After the service, people stood in tight little clumps on the sidewalk, clutching moist handkerchiefs as the casket passed by. But even when the casket reached the hearse, nobody seemed able to leave. A long row of black limousines stood waiting at the curb, but only Sloane and the children ducked into one. The thick perfume of flowers hung heavily in the humid air, and the quiet conversations on the sidewalk were punctuated by an occasional gasping sob. A thin, older woman in a black suit came up to me and said in a quiet voice, "You were her doctor?"

"Yes."

"You are Dr. Love, then?"

"Yes, I am."

"You evil woman. You evil, evil woman." There was a crazed look in her eye, but her voice was flat and soft, with little intonation. A white-haired man hurried in our direction, calling, "Sylvia! What are you doing?" She turned abruptly toward him. "I've found the murderer, Manville! She's right here!" Now her voice rang out and people stopped to look at her and to glance nervously at me. "The murderer! The evil woman who killed our Hollis!" The man reached us in two more strides and put an arm around her, trying to lead her away. But she looked back at me over her shoulder. "How can you stand there? May you be damned to hell!"

I stood frozen to the spot, aware of the quiet that had fallen around me. I looked up and unexpectedly caught the eye of Dr. Ardsley, who turned away quickly and murmured something to the governor. A few of the pall-bearers seemed to be conferring, and one came over to me and said quietly, "I'm sorry about Sylvia. She was Hollis's great-aunt."

"It's all right."

"Thank you for coming to the service. The interment is of course just for the family."

"Of course."

He was lying and we both knew it. They didn't want me at the cemetery. I hadn't really planned on going, but knowing that they wanted to keep me away was painful. I hurried toward my car and noticed that Ardsley was stepping into a limousine that was in the cemetery procession. Through the tinted glass, I caught a glimpse of the governor already inside, in deep conversation with Doheny.

III

I GOT IN my car and began to drive, turning away from the church and the long line of cars headed to the cemetery. In my rear window, I saw two police cars, lights flashing, and realized that the funeral procession was getting a police escort. Was that because the governor was in the procession? Was the mayor going too? Or were there just so many cars that they'd block traffic?

Whatever, it was definitely not just the family.

I turned onto the Mass Pike heading west and after nearly an hour picked up Route 84 into Connecticut. The road was straight and boring and I turned on the radio to a classical music station that was playing Wagner. Great music, but there was only so much I could take of it. I flipped to all news and listened to the weather and sports, then found an oldies station and drove for a few miles to the Beatles. But nothing was giving me comfort today. I went back to Wagner.

An hour later, the signs pointed me to Route 91, and then before too long to the turn-off to Route 95 south. I passed the exit for Yale and then the Yale Bowl. I'd been there only once for a football game, Harvard versus Yale, and all I remembered was that nobody paid much attention to the game, but everybody had silver flasks and tailgated from the back of their BMWs. The other exits in Connecticut didn't mean much to me—I drove past one after another, the names of the suburban towns falling into a rhythm.

I'd been driving for more than three hours and was suddenly aware that I was hungry. But I didn't want to stop. I found a stick of gum in the glove compartment and wondered how long it had been there; in my mouth, it was strangely stale but the taste of fake peppermint was enough to keep me going as the miles went by. Route 95 was packed with trucks trying to get into New York. I sat in traffic, waiting to get over the Triborough Bridge, which would take me into the city. Inching my way past the toll booth and at last into Manhattan, I finally realized where I was going—and it wasn't to see Paco.

Driving slowly on the FDR Drive, I rifled through my pocketbook until I found an address book—and there, fortunately, was the name I needed. I exited at Fifty-first Street, went crosstown to Park Avenue, and pulled into the first parking garage I saw. Emerging onto the street, I was happy enough to be on foot that I bought a pretzel from a vendor and munched it as I crossed Park Avenue, looking for the right building. The glass-and-steel structures all looked the same, but finally I found the one I wanted, went up to the thirty-third floor, and walked through the heavy wooden doors of Bender, Golson, Gray and Wiley, one of the more formidable law firms in the city. Their name was inscribed on the door in gold script. A thick Oriental carpet in the reception area muffled my steps, but the well-dressed woman at the front desk looked up and asked pleasantly how she could help me.

"I'd like to see Alicia Rice, if she's in. My name is Dr. Sarabeth Love. I don't have an appointment, but she knows me and it's—well, a business matter."

"Certainly, Doctor." The receptionist smiled. "I think Ms. Rice is in. Let me check." She motioned to a leather sofa and I sank into it, realizing that for the first time all week, I didn't feel as if people were avoiding me. But it was only a receptionist. What would Alicia think of my showing up unannounced at her office door? The receptionist hung up the phone and said, "She'll be here in a minute," and it wasn't an exaggeration. Before I had time to pick up one of the magazines on the glass-and-marble coffee table, Alicia came through a set of double doors. She stopped briefly when she saw me, as if trying to place me in a context outside the office, to conjure the person she once knew. That done, she said, "Sarabeth, it's nice to see you," and we shook hands. Her grip was cool and strong. However surprised she was by my presence in her wood-paneled haven, she made no comment and her expression was pleasant. Neutral. A perfect lawyer.

Which was why I was there.

I followed her back through the double doors and down a maze of hallways into her office, which was large and sunny. Alicia Rice was doing well. Her properly tailored blue suit was expensively cut, accessorized with elegant gold jewelry and a silk scarf knotted at her neck. She was tall, slightly heavier than she should be, with a commanding style. I'd met her when we were both undergraduates at Radcliffe—she was a couple of years ahead of me—and bumped into her a few times in Cambridge when she was at Harvard Law School and I was at the med school. We'd been on a panel together about Women at Harvard, part of the same group that organized the rally where I met Paco, and stayed casual friends after that. Instead of joining a big firm after law school, she went to the district attorney's office and got shunted into the organized crime task force. In Boston, it was kind of a joke, since nobody went after organized crime. But Alicia acted as if she didn't know that, and at age twenty-seven brought a case against Tom DiSalvo, one of the city's best-known crime lords. Newspapers called her tough and fearless, but they didn't see her as I did one night in the middle of it all—weeping miserably in the P&S emergency room after a DiSalvo crony had wooed her to his apartment with promises of information, then tried to rape her. She'd fought him off and was worried that if word got out, it could cost her credibility. I disagreed, but it was her decision, so I quietly sewed up the gash in her thigh and gave her antibiotics and a small can of Mace. A few weeks later her picture was on the front page of the paper when DiSalvo was convicted, and not much later, I heard that she'd

decided to cash in and move to Bender, Golson. She
sent me a printed announcement with her new office
address in the Big Apple and the formal notification that
she had been named a partner. On the bottom, she'd
scrawled, "I owe you a big one. Come visit me sometime in New York."

So here I was.

We made small talk for a very few minutes, and
though Alicia was too polite to ask immediately what
the hell I was doing there, I could see the question in
her face. She finally asked where I was staying in New
York, and deciding to take her out of her misery, I said,
"I really just arrived. Paco is here negotiating with a
gallery on Fifty-seventh Street, but the fact is that I came
to see you. I need some advice."

Her body stiffened slightly, her professional antennae
coming out, and she moved from behind her desk to
close the door. When she sat down again I asked, "Did
you hear about Hollis Taft Brewster?"

Her eyebrows shot up. "God, yes. Was she your patient?"

"Bull's-eye."

"Oh, Sarabeth, I'm so sorry. Fill me in on the details."

I started doing that, but I caught myself slanting the
story. I wanted to present it straight on and see what
Alicia thought. So I told her about Hollis's desire for a
VBAC and how smoothly the delivery had gone. I described my staying there until late at night and then leaving with Sloane, coming back the next day to find Hollis
dead, Ardsley in charge, and nobody telling me anything. I skipped some of the details—like my conver-

sation with Ginny and the men in business suits all
gathered on the seventh floor—because in this expensive
office, with its view all the way over to the East River,
they seemed mostly irrelevant. But Alicia was nodding
and jotting down the occasional note. When I got to the
Boston Tribune article, she interrupted to ask, "Do you
have a copy of it?" I shook my head and she pushed an
intercom button on her desk.

"I need a Nexus search, please," she said to the assistant on the other end. "Input the names Hollis Taft
Brewster and Sarabeth Love into the computer. I need
any article where both names appear. Go back a week—
or better yet, a month. Bring it to me as soon as you
find it—and drop whatever else you're doing. I want it
immediately."

She let go of the intercom button and turned to me
again expectantly, so I went on, describing the meeting
in Ardsley's office and then the funeral and the men
sitting there like a row of jurors—the governor and
Ardsley, the president of the hospital and Dr. Franklin.

"So you started to think conspiracy," Alicia said, and
when I nodded slowly she asked, "But what's the conspiracy about? Getting you named in a malpractice suit
instead of the hospital?"

"Maybe. But that doesn't totally explain the article."

As if on cue, the assistant, a frizzy-haired redhead
wearing a blue suit that looked like a cheaper version of
Alicia's, knocked on the door and came in holding a
sheaf of computer pages. Alicia introduced her to me as
Dana Bracco.

"Here's what I found in Nexus," Dana said, turning
over the pages. "I had the computer check for any article

that appeared during the entire month and included the names you said, but the only articles that matched were in the last two days. There was a long article in the *Boston Tribune*, then fairly short pieces in six other newspapers.''

"*Six*?" I echoed, shocked.

"There could be more, but the Nexus program we have only searches the major newspapers.''

"Thanks,'' Alicia said. "I appreciate the quick work.'' She managed to be dismissive without being curt, and Dana smiled at both of us as she went out.

I turned back to Alicia, who was reading quickly and circling some facts as she flipped through the pages. "*Six*?" I repeated.

"Our Nexus program searches fifty or sixty city newspapers—so don't be shocked. It looks to me like the wire service picked up the *Boston Trib* article, which is how it showed up elsewhere. I don't see any fresh reporting. Just this Marty Stenopolus.'' She sat back and fiddled with her pencil. "We need to know where he got his information. As I recall, the *Trib* is a classic tabloid—they print pretty much anything as long as there's a source. But they do need a source—however disreputable he or she may be. Somebody talked to Stenopolus, and it wouldn't hurt to find out who it is.''

"How much trouble am I in, Alicia?''

Someone else would have tried to placate me and say all would be fine, but she didn't. "It's hard to tell, frankly. The man you met in Ardsley's office—Doheny—is a powerful guy. He does special investigations for the governor, but I've been away from Boston for over a year, Sarabeth. I don't know what he's investi-

gating anymore. I also don't know at the moment why
someone from the D.A.'s office was at that meeting,
though I can think of a number of possibilities. Vicente
is new there—he was coming in just as I was leaving,
so I can't really call him directly, but I'll make some
inquiries and see what I turn up. I believe he's the D.A.'s
link to the governor." She was scribbling on a legal pad
as she talked, all business. "The other thing we need to
do is find out Stenopolus's source." She tapped her pencil against the back of her hand, thinking about it. "If
anything dramatic develops, we'll subpoena source material—or try to—but right now, I'd like to do something a little less official. Do you know anybody at the
Trib?"

When I shook my head, she snapped open her pocket-
computer organizer and began pushing buttons, which I
quickly realized was the high-tech way of flipping
through an address book.

"Juan Garcia!" she exclaimed triumphantly a moment later, scanning the *g*'s in her organizer. "He wrote
most of the stories when I was doing the DiSalvo case.
I talked to him off-the-record enough that . . ." She
didn't finish the sentence, but added his name and number to the notes on her pad. "Even if he's not a buddy
of Stenopolus, it's a good place to start. I won't get to
it this afternoon, I'm afraid, but I'll try him tomorrow."

"Alicia, do you have time for all this?" I asked anxiously. What I really meant was that I'd come here on
a whim, and now didn't think I could afford the high-
priced guns of Bender, Golson.

"At the moment, this is in the friend-in-need cate-
gory," she said, with a small smile. "If it goes beyond

that, we'll figure out what to do. You might need a lawyer in Boston at some point—right now I can't tell. By the way, you need to do some work on this, too. I have some connections, but you have a lot better ones. Talk around at the hospital as much as you can. Make some inquiries. Sometimes what your gut tells you is more important than any other evidence we can gather.'' She looked over her pad. "So have we missed anything?"

"Just one thing." Hesitatingly, I told her about Dr. Franklin wanting me out of the office for a couple of weeks and his feeble excuse about my studying for the boards.

She shrugged. "I can guess how that's making you feel, but trust me, this one's not worth fighting. Think of it as his having given you two weeks to play detective. That's what you're going to do. But we'll compare notes before then, believe me."

Her intercom rang and Alicia said, "Yes, Dana."

"Are you taking calls, Ms. Rice? I've told everyone you're in a meeting, but I have three people hanging on, anyway."

I stood up to go. "I can't thank you enough, Alicia. I know you have a lot of work to do, and you're wonderful to take this time for me."

"My pleasure." She waved me off. "We'll figure out what's going on. I promise."

Outside the office, I asked Dana if I could use her phone, and she directed me to one of the lines that wasn't lit up. I called Deke, Paco's agent, who told me that Paco had left the city about noontime, heading back to Boston.

"He was eager to get back to you, and I'm surprised

he's not home already," Deke said unctuously. "He should be there any minute."

"Actually I'm not home either," I admitted, but I was too embarrassed to tell him that I was in New York, about six blocks away from his office. Missed connection with Paco—and it had been my fault.

Saying goodbye to Dana, I noticed that Alicia was still on the phone. I wrote down my address and phone number for her, added my office phone, then crossed it out, explaining I wouldn't be there for a while, then wrote it down again when Dana asked to have it anyway for the records. I headed back out to Park Avenue, and once outside, I glanced at my watch, trying to decide what to do. It was nearly dinner time, and I hadn't even eaten lunch, so I was starved. But I was also eager to get back. Paco would be wondering where I was, and even more compelling, I suddenly felt as if I had a mission. Two weeks of detective work, Alicia had said. Or whatever it took to unscramble this confusing mess.

I turned right on Fifty-second Street and walked over to Lexington Avenue. People were starting to leave their offices for the evening, which meant that if I got in my car now, I'd just sit in traffic for an hour or two with all the commuters heading toward Connecticut. Instead, I walked up Lexington, which was jammed with vendors selling jewelry and scarves and watches from briefcases and folding tables. Shoppers crowded around them, spilling into the street, where cars and taxis honked as they tried to make illegal turns. I heard one man assuring a woman with a French accent that the two-dollar earrings she was looking at were 14-karat gold. And the watches for ten dollars were genuine Rolexes. "They be eight hundred dollars in there," he said, nodding toward the Bloomingdale's on the next block. "Here only ten." I couldn't resist peering over, and even to my untrained eye at ten paces, the gold looked cheap and shiny. But the woman handed him a ten-dollar bill and turned away happily.

I continued up the street, past Bloomingdale's and a Gap, past Banana Republic and Express and dozens of small shoe stores. I looked in windows but didn't go inside because the street scene seemed so lively. Just a few more blocks and the frantic market-atmosphere gave way to a quieter neighborhood, so even though it was getting dark and I wasn't all that familiar with the city streets, I felt comfortable. A few more blocks, and I spotted a bedraggled sign that said Le Bistro. Peering in the window, I saw a cramped room with red-checked tablecloths and waiters with white aprons tied around their waists. The menu, stuck in the window, promised old-fashioned French bistro food, and without further thought, I went inside. Just a few tables were taken, and the maitre d' was happy to seat me. I ordered a glass of red wine, and a basket of hot, crusty French bread appeared with it. Then came an omelet, light and fluffy, with cheese and mushrooms, accompanied by a mountain of crispy *pommes frites* that I ate with my fingers. Feeling much better, I was ready to leave, but the waiter persuaded me to try the chocolate mousse. It was so rich and creamy that I felt sinful after one spoonful but managed to eat down to the very bottom of the bowl.

"It was good, mademoiselle?" the waiter asked, appearing with my check. By now the restaurant was almost full, the tables taken by an assortment of couples and singles and a few business pairings.

"Excellent. All I could use now is a phone. Would that be back by the ladies' room?"

"No, let me bring it to you." He reappeared with a cellular phone, and sipping my *cafe au lait*, I punched in various codes, then the number of our home in Boston. Paco answered on the second ring.

"Where are you?" he asked the moment he heard my voice.

"In New York. It's a long story, but I guess I went a little crazy after Hollis's funeral and had to escape. I'm just finishing dinner and trying to decide if I should stay over—but I don't know where I'd go. I didn't realize you were coming back today."

"I did." There was a brief silence and then he asked, "Was everything okay with the house when you left?"

My heart pounded too hard for a moment and then I said, "I think so. Is anything wrong?"

"I can't really tell. The lock was broken when I got home and the door was open, but nothing seems to be missing. I checked the obvious things—CD player, TV, VCR—and they're all here. My paintings and drawings don't seem to have been touched, and as far as I can tell, all my sketches are still here. I never would have worried about that before, but I can tell you the dealers in the New York art market are nasty. Now that I've met them all, I figured God knows what could happen."

"And my things?" I asked, a little too breathlessly.

"I wasn't sure what to check for, honey. Everything looked neat in the drawer where you keep your jewelry. I couldn't find the ring and bracelet I made for you, but

I thought maybe you were wearing them."

I looked down at my left hand and said, "I am. Both of them. I always do."

"Good." He paused, and I pictured him on the phone in our bedroom, sitting on the large bed with the sculpted steel headboard, looking around, trying to make sense of the puzzle. "Your desk looks a little messy, but I don't know your papers, so I can't imagine what someone might take. Any ideas?"

"No," I said. "I was probably distracted when I left this morning because I was going to the funeral, but locking the door when I go out is automatic. I would have noticed if I couldn't do it. Somebody broke the lock after that."

"Could be vandalism," Paco said. "That's what I was just starting to settle on. Plain old teenage vandalism."

"Maybe," I said. "But that's usually more on the lines of smashed windows and spray-painted graffiti. If someone gets a door open, you'd think it would be for a reason."

"I'll report it to the police," Paco said. "But don't worry. I'm here and I have a locksmith on the way, so we'll be secure tonight."

"Maybe you shouldn't report it to the police," I said.

I could hear Paco's surprise across the phone line. "Why not?" he asked.

"I can't explain it, really. It's just—I don't know. There's nothing they can do about it now, and until we know what's missing, it seems kind of silly. Anyway," I added, "I'm coming right home. I guess I'll see you around midnight."

I gave the waiter back the phone and took a final sip of coffee. I added a large tip to the bill and realized that I didn't really want to leave the restaurant. Wild, exuberant New York seemed like a haven from the storms I felt brewing over Boston.

The drive home flew by. I've never had a great sense of direction, and in the dark, going in the opposite direction, it didn't really matter that I'd driven the same route earlier in the day. It took all my concentration to keep on the right roads and not miss any turn-offs. Trucks rumbled along the highways with me, and after I passed one eighteen-wheeler on an uphill, he shot past me at demon speed on the downhill side. For several miles after that, it seemed we were playing cat-and-mouse: He would inch up and then fall back, pass me where he could, and then slow down so that I had no choice but to pass him. It wasn't a game I liked very much. I wonder who else was playing cat-and-mouse with me.

When I finally got home, I realized how exhausted I was, and I stumbled up our front steps, anxious about what I'd find. A brand-new lock was on the door and my key, of course, didn't fit. I knocked softly, concerned about waking Paco, but there wasn't any alternative. I knocked again, a little louder, and he came to the door, opened it wide, and hugged me. He was bare-chested, dressed only in a pair of the silk boxer shorts he liked to sleep in, and clutching him, I felt the ripple of his back muscles and the stirring of his pleasure at holding me again.

"I missed you, honey. Come in. You must be knocked out." Solicitous, he took my hand and led me inside. "You're okay?"

"I guess so. Exhausted. And pretty shaken." There was a long stairway leading to the upper floor and I sank down on the bottom step. "Now that I'm here, I should try to figure out what's behind this broken lock, but I'm too tired. I've been thinking about it the whole ride home, and I'm convinced it has something to do with Hollis and the article, but I don't know how."

Paco leaned over and rubbed my neck. "It could be something completely different, honey. We live in Cambridge—it's a crazy neighborhood. All sorts of strange things go on."

He was trying to make me feel better and I appreciated that, but I needed some facts, too. "You got a new lock. What did the locksmith think? Did you ask him?"

Paco hesitated for a moment, then said, "He pointed out that it was a surgical break. Somebody knew what they were doing."

"Which speaks against vandalism."

"I suppose so, but that doesn't mean it has anything to do with you or Hollis."

"Not a regular robbery. Not your art. What's left?"

I got up and staggered up the stairs, feeling drunk on fatigue and worry. I had a tiny office on the second floor and I stood at the doorway, wondering if it would yield any clues. The papers on my desk were so scattered that anybody trying to search through them would be on a needle-in-a-haystack mission. The laptop computer that I generally used to organize my life was in a corner of the desk, closed. I went over and turned it on. Various opening screens came up and then the program went automatically into Microsoft Word. I moved the cursor to File and held it there. Almost paralyzed, I kept holding it. Paco, hovering in the doorway, asked, "Everything okay?"

"No," I said. "Come here and look." When he was leaning over my shoulder I said, "Look what I have highlighted here—under File."

"New, Open, Close, Save, Save As, Restore . . ." he read out.

"Not there. Underneath the line."

"Print Preview. Print . . ."

"Under the *second* line." I tried not to sound exasperated, knowing that Paco believed in pen, pencil, and paintbrush—not computers.

"Current Finances. Loans. Insurance. Clinic Patients." He paused. "I don't get it. What is that?"

"A feature on the computer. It lists the last four files that have been opened—to make it easier to get back to the last things you've been working on."

"Okay."

"And those weren't the last things I was working on."

"You think someone's been in your computer?"

"I know it."

We both heard the tension in my voice, and Paco was rubbing my neck again. "Honey, I don't doubt you, but can you really be sure about the last four files you had open? You didn't have the computer with you today. You could have forgotten."

The stay-calm-and-life-will-be-okay routine was starting to get to me. "For God's sake, Paco, I may be upset, but I'm not a raving lunatic. I was home myself last night, remember? I stayed up until midnight writing down everything I remembered about my dealings with

Hollis. Cover your ass material, as a few people have called it. I named that file Hollis Report. Then I wrote down everything that happened right after I heard about her death—the stony silences and everyone ignoring me. I called that Hollis Folo-Up. Just before I finished, I drafted a letter to Ardsley, posing all the questions I wanted answered. I haven't sent it—or even printed it.''

I moved the cursor to Show Existing Files and quickly found one labeled ''Ardsley/lett.'' ''There it is,'' I said to Paco. ''I didn't dream any of this. I don't know what the fourth one would have been, but those were the three I worked on last night. And unless the computer's broken, those three should have shown up.''

''And the computer's definitely not broken.'' It was part question, part statement—Paco learned quickly and he wasn't going to doubt me again. For an answer, I opened the Ardsley/lett. file and then closed it again. I moved the cursor over to where the express files were listed. ''Ardsley/lett. Current Finances. Loans. Insurance,'' I said, reading the new list. Most recently opened file listed first, last one dropped off.

''No, not broken.'' Paco folded his arms across his bare chest, then inched his thigh onto the edge of my desk and perched himself on the corner. ''Okay, then, here's a question. If someone came in to find out what you know about Hollis, why wouldn't they have gone into those files you did last night? They were the last ones you worked on, so they would have been easy to find. Just listed right there in the easy access.''

I shrugged. ''Let's assume they came in and turned on the computer. They took a disk from there—'' I glanced at my box of unused disks, and then looking inside, saw there were only two left. Had there been more? I couldn't possibly remember that detail. "Anyway, they put the disk in the computer to copy from my hard drive. It takes about five seconds to copy a file. The first four were a snap. Once they had those, they kept looking for other things that might be of interest."

Paco rubbed his fingers through his beard. "All conjecture, as I guess lawyers would say. No evidence for any of it, but I have to admit that it makes sense. The problem is that you've figured out the 'how' but you still don't have the 'who' or 'why'."

His confidence in my theory warmed me, and I looked up with a sigh. "That will have to wait until tomorrow," I said. "Or at least until later this morning."

"Thank God."

We crawled into bed and it felt good to be in Paco's arms again. His silk boxers rustled against my skin, and when he finally climbed on top of me, my fatigue seemed to melt away. Sex was a sweet distraction tonight, and Paco, sensing this wasn't the night for bells and whistles made love so compassionately that I was able to escape into the warmth of our tenderness and feel a flicker of hope that the whole cruel world hadn't turned against me. I fell asleep curled up next to him and didn't think I dreamt. But I half-awoke, startled, at 6 A.M., and grabbed Paco in fright. "Ginny," I said aloud. Then again, "Ginny!" and sat bolt upright in bed.

Paco, foggy with sleep, reached for me, and I shook him away like a bug, then flung off the covers. My mind was a complete blank—whatever had awakened me, or whatever dream had ended in this panic, was gone from my mind.

"Ginny?" Paco asked gently.

"She's not working for Ardsley anymore," I said hoarsely, as if a blinding revelation had just struck. "And when I spoke to her that first day, she seemed to know that she might be gone."

Paco dropped his head into the pillow. "You think she broke in last night?"

"No, of course not." But as the first light of morning crept in from under the blinds, I couldn't imagine what I had been thinking or dreaming that made Ginny so important. Even as Paco settled back beneath the covers, I roused myself and went to the study, wondering if my laptop might hold some answers. I turned it on and stared at the opening menu for a while. Then I clicked on Program Manager and played around with various options, finally finding the one I wanted. I entered some data and clicked on the mouse, and the screen filled with the names of all my files, and next to each one, the date on which it had last been opened. The pattern was clear the moment the screen lit up, but I couldn't afford to be careless, so I checked the calendar on my desk carefully before looking back at the screen. Seventeen files had been opened yesterday. Seventeen. Yesterday, when I hadn't been home all day. That was all the confirmation I needed.

IV

ALICIA CALLED ME midafternoon with bad news and even worse vibes. She had reached Juan Garcia, who was now the news editor of the *Trib* and knew the story about Hollis because it had passed his desk for approval. Juan and Stenopolus didn't seem to get along very well, Alicia said. Now, there was a surprise. A young Hispanic kid from Harvard rises to news editor where he oversees an older, crotchety reporter. It had the makings of either a TV sitcom or a lot of newsroom tension. The hint of distaste must have made Juan more willing to talk, though he told Alicia that he'd help us because he remembered me from Harvard and didn't mind playing Deep Throat for a classmate. I didn't remember him at all, so I figured he'd either been afraid of Radcliffe women—a not uncommon condition among Harvard men—or had other reasons for wanting to cooperate with Alicia.

"According to Juan, the reporter had good sources," Alicia said, "and they came from very high up in the hospital. The really interesting part is that the sources apparently came to Stenopolus with the story, rather than the other way around. Juan usually assigns the pieces to the investigative unit, and he'd never heard of this story until Stenopolus came to him with it. Juan wouldn't give me names for the sources just now, but he seemed to suggest the chairman of the department."

"Ardsley," I said. "But where would he have gotten those pictures?"

"I don't know, and I'm not sure it matters right now. The fact is that somebody influential is talking, and pointing a finger. Which makes my other news all the more disturbing." She took a deep breath, like a doctor would before telling a patient she had cancer. And that was about how I felt, anyway: as if I had something alien and inexplicable growing inside me, taking over my otherwise normal life. "I've poked around the governor's office and got a line on Vicente and Doheny. It's all very strange, Sarabeth. I'm starting to hear talk about a possible indictment. There are rumors, but no facts, that a secret grand jury is meeting—maybe even right now. If what I hear has any validity, they could be considering a murder charge.''

I was about to ask, ''Against whom?'' and then it sank in. There was silence, and for some reason, all I could think of were smart-aleck comments.

''Think you can get me a cell next to DiSalvo?'' I cracked.

''Stop it, Sarabeth.''

''Or maybe you can get me locked up in L.A. near Lyle Menendez. Or that Night Stalker guy in San Francisco. Is he still in jail?''

''Sarabeth!'' Alicia's voice was louder now, as if trying to penetrate my shock. And that's what it must have been—that moment when all rationality finally leaves your mind. I was glad to discover, though, that shock turned me into Don Rickles rather than Camille. Trying to control myself, I asked flippantly, ''Do I at least get to testify?''

Alicia missed the forced flippancy, or at least took the question seriously. ''From what I hear, not at the grand jury. Rules for a secret grand jury are pretty obscure, and how this case fits under them is even more obscure. Due process seems to have been totally thrown out the window, and I can't get a handle yet on why.''

''Would this have anything to do with why my house was broken into yesterday?''

''*What*? When did this happen?''

''About the time I was with you in New York, I guess.

Somebody broke the lock and came in, but didn't steal anything. The only thing I've found disturbed is my computer. It looks like somebody was riffling through the files.''

"Which ones?"

"Seventeen of them. Do you want the whole list? Everything I'd written about Hollis. Then all sorts of personal files I have on finances and loans and things like that. And my personal files on clinic patients.''

There was a brief pause, and then Alicia asked, "Isn't that the clinic the governor is trying to close down?"

"Yup. Nothing's computerized there and we didn't want records stolen, so I keep my patient information in my laptop. I thought it would be safe. By the way does this make any sense to you?"

"I'm thinking, Sarabeth, and unfortunately, I'm starting to see some connections I don't like. Dangerous ones, in fact. I want you to be careful these next few days.''

"Hey, I haven't been looking for trouble, it just seems to be finding me. Any guesses who might have broken in?"

"I have some ideas, and I don't like any of them. Did you call the police?"

"No. Paco came home and he couldn't find anything missing, so he just called the locksmith. I figured out about the computer when I arrived, and by then it was late and it all seemed so confusing that we just went to bed. But I used the computer to figure it all out, and I didn't think about fingerprints or anything. Do you think they could still raise any prints?"

"Probably, but that's not the point. I can't explain

this, but don't call the police. And don't mention your theory about the computer to anybody else.''

After we hung up, I had a vague sense of looming danger, but whether it was the break-in, the reporters, or the secret grand jury, I couldn't tell. Alicia left me to brood about it until she called the next morning at eight sharp. She'd confirmed the report on the secret grand jury, and she had a theory on the break-in, but she couldn't share it yet.

''I'm thinking of coming up to Boston, Sarabeth, to act as your lawyer. If you'd like that.''

''Of course I'd like it. But how can you manage it? With your firm and all. How long can you be here?'' I was rambling like a bad talk-show host.

''As long as it takes. Look, I won't lie to you. My excuse is that Bender, Golson is thinking about a Boston office and I'm the obvious person to look into it. So that gets me to Boston for a while. But the truth is that becoming involved in this case started to get my blood boiling, and I realized that I haven't felt this way since the DiSalvo trial ended. I know it doesn't make you feel any better that I'm getting an adrenalin rush out of your case, but I am. It just reeks of corruption and we've got to root it out. That's what I do best, I guess. Much better than I do the big–New York–lawyer routine.''

I had the feeling that Alicia was having a career crisis right in front of my eyes, but if that made her decide to take my case *pro bono*, I wasn't going to argue. Rooting out corruption seemed like an excellent idea—as did keeping me out of jail.

For the next few days, Alicia called at least twice a day with updates, and none of them were encouraging.

In one conversation she told me she was now in Boston, settled in at the Ritz-Carlton in a room on the sixteenth floor, and that things were at the point where I should come over and talk with her. For the first time in ages I was glad my father wasn't around. I'd been weak with grief after he died suddenly of a heart attack seven years before, and I spent my whole medical training regretting that he hadn't lived to see me become a doctor. But now I was grateful that Dad, the ex-cop, didn't have to hear my name said in the same sentence as "possible murder indictment."

I happened to mention my dad to Alicia, and she discreetly asked if there was anybody left on the force with allegiance to him. The fact was that when I was little, I hung around the station house so much I considered it my second home, and I called half the guys-in-blue in Boston, "Uncle." But now all those uncles were either playing pinochle with my dad in heaven or poker at retirement communities in Arizona. Only one or two of them were still on the force, and it had been so long that even if I wanted to turn to them, I couldn't remember their names.

So Alicia was keeping me up to date, but ever the lawyer, most of what she said was qualified by *coulds*, *woulds*, and *mights*, keeping me in a week-long state of denial. Even when I came face-to-face with her again over tea at the Ritz-Carlton, it didn't totally sink in. She told me about the indictment and what I should expect and where we'd meet the next day. I went home thinking I understood, but when the clerk from the court came to my door that night with the murder indictment in hand, I tried to turn him away. My hands were shaking, and for some odd reason, when I looked at the papers, I thought it had to do with Paco. Then I stared at the paper, and Hollis's name jumped out at me, and instead of horror, I felt confusion and pain. The clerk escaped back into his beat-up Chevy and left, and I kept staring at the document he had given me, trying to decide if there was any way I really could be a murderer. Funny, how those thoughts overtake you. When you grow up believing in law and order and even old-fashioned morality, it's hard to question the truth of a legal document—even when it's about you and your heart knows it's all calumny and deceit. I think that up until that very moment, I assumed this would all go away, and I could continue to live my life believing, as my dad did, that you could never get treated wrong for doing right. Now the indictment in my hands meant that either my dad was mistaken or I had taken a grave misstep that even now I didn't understand.

I stared at the indictment and tried to remember what Alicia had told me. All I knew was that my life was falling apart. And I was due in court the next day.

V

THE DOORBELL RANG at seven the next morning, and Paco, already out of bed, went to answer it. I peeked out the window and saw a wispy woman with blond hair and an ingratiating smile, and heard Paco telling her that Sarabeth Love didn't live there. The woman looked him over, taking in his tight bluejeans and paint-splattered T-shirt, his long brown hair and Fabio-esque chest and seemed to decide that there was a good chance he wasn't lying. He didn't look like a man who would be living with a woman doctor. Especially one indicted for murder. But the wispy blond was being paid to find Dr. Love and this was the address she had, so she tried to engage him in conversation. He closed the door. She rang the bell again, and Paco opened it up a crack. His voice was soft, seductive, as he told her that if she didn't get off his property, he would call the police and file a trespassing complaint.

He came back into the bedroom, where I was standing by the window.

"Who was that?" I whispered, as if the person might not have gone away and was standing in the foyer, waiting to pounce. "I couldn't hear the whole conversation."

"A producer from one of those tabloid shows. *Hard Copy*, I think she said. No, maybe *Hot Type*. Sorry, they all sound alike to me."

"And she wanted..." I hesitated, and Paco kept himself from saying the obvious. *She wanted you, honey. You're a hot story this morning.*

I walked toward the bathroom, aware that Paco was staring at me. Tense about the day to come, I turned on him.

"What are you looking at?" I asked angrily.

"Your arches."

"Pardon?"

He looked down at my bare feet on the polished wood floor, and I followed his gaze. Okay, I had high arches. He himself was flatfooted in scruffy sandals. His eyes dreamy, he said, "We have a million things to think about today and worry about, but somehow your feet caught my eye, and I realized you're going to be all right. There's a perfection about those arches that touches me. Someday I'll paint them because they speak volumes.''

I looked at Paco dubiously. His poetic imagery wasn't doing much for me this morning. Somewhere in his mind, perfect arches were a metaphor for goodness, but I wasn't buying it. Maybe he'd like me to show my feet to the judge and see if she let me off. Now that was likely.

I closed the bathroom door behind me as I ran the water to scrub my face, used the toilet, turned on the shower. Daily ablutions wouldn't wash away the stain that was covering me today. From the bathroom window I looked out and saw that the wispy blond producer was still there, standing on the sidewalk—public property, so there was nothing Paco could do—and she wasn't alone. A van had pulled up, and a man, probably from another show, was leaning against it. A dark, unremarkable car was parked across the street, double parked, actually, on the narrow Cambridge street, and the man in the driver's seat was scribbling on a notepad. Newspaperman, no doubt, but I couldn't tell from this distance if it was Marty Stenopolus. I let the shade drop down again.

I finally emerged from the bathroom, wrapped in a towel. Paco usually liked to watch me dress, but this morning he must have felt it would be an intrusion. Everyone wanted a glimpse of me and he knew I was going to feel the pain of that. I dressed quickly and went into the kitchen, where Paco was fiddling with the coffeemaker. ''Coffee?'' he asked.

''Sure.'' I reached for a mug and held it with a steady

hand as he poured. A waffle popped up from the toaster, and trying to sound pleasant, I said, "You're taking care of me." But it came out snappish and accusatory. He put down the carafe and took a breath before answering.

"Somebody has to. I wanted to make bacon and eggs, but I knew you'd never eat that. So a frozen waffle will have to do." He offered a small smile, and when I didn't return it he asked, "What time are you supposed to be in court?"

"Alicia said nine." I took a sip of coffee and turned away.

Still unfazed, Paco said, "You look different this morning."

"You noticed."

I had on a double-breasted blue suit, buttoned carefully over a plain white blouse, an outfit that probably made me look like a flight attendant, or maybe a teacher in a Catholic school. A pair of pumps with little heels pinched at my toes. Pain was going to be part of the day. Alicia had made it clear that my usual flowing skirts and flat shoes were not to be worn to court. My hair, normally tied back loosely or flowing around my shoulders, was today knotted severely in what could only be called a bun.

Paco sighed, trying to be sympathetic, but my frostiness was taking its toll. "Look, this is a tough day. I know that. But how about if we attack it together instead of your attacking me?"

"I'm not attacking, I'm just thinking about court." Even as I said it, I realized there was an edge in my voice that I couldn't make go away.

Paco hesitated, possibly feeling more fed-up than he

was letting on. "I'm going to change and come with you," he said finally, as if just deciding.

"You don't have to, you know."

"I'd like to."

"Maybe I should go ahead and you can meet me. I mean, you have to paint today, don't you?" I wasn't sure why I was turning Paco away, but I was afraid to have him along.

"I can take a day off from painting. Wait for me. I won't be long." He started toward the bathroom, then paused. "There are a bunch of what look like reporters outside."

"I saw them."

"If you don't want to deal with them, there's a back way out of here. You just go through the basement and there's a tunnel that connects over to that little street where the deli is. Happens I'm parked there, so it's probably the way we should go out anyway."

I looked at him, feeling surprised mixed with other, ambiguous emotions. Interest that I had lived here with him for nearly a year and didn't know about the underground exit. Shock, perhaps, that our roles were changing. I, the doctor, always took care of everyone. Paco. My patients. The details of our lives. Now he was trying to do that, and I couldn't bear the idea.

But I had to get used to it. I didn't want to be whisked through an underground passage to Paco's car like a criminal who had to be hidden from the press. But I didn't have the courage to go out and face those reporters this morning. I was, in any case, stunned by their presence. How did they know about this latest development, anyway? To see Marty Stenopolus wasn't a surprise. But a TV producer? I waited until Paco was ready, then let him lead me underground.

Once in the car, I smoothed my skirt and tried to prepare for what was about to happen. What had already started to happen. Paco drove carefully through the narrow streets of Cambridge, crossed the Eliot Bridge, and turned onto Storrow Drive. The day was clear, and a sailboat or two already dotted the Charles River. It would be a day for sailing and bicycling and strolling along holding hands. Or else it would be a day for having your life turned upside down in court.

Paco exited to downtown Boston, went past the Boston Commons, curved through Boston's notorious one-way streets, and pulled up in front of the courthouse. I couldn't imagine how he had found it so easily. He cut the motor.

"You can't park here," I said, looking around for a legal spot.

"I know, but I am. I'll get you inside, then come out and move it."

"That's okay. I'll just run in."

"No you won't." He was adamant, and I wondered if he had spotted more reporters. Had we been followed from Cambridge?

"You'll get a ticket," I said, and as Paco snorted, I realized how ironic that sounded. Indicted murderer worried about a parking ticket.

I let him come around to my side of the car, open the door, and slip his arm firmly around me as I got out. My steps were shaky, but his were firm, and he practically pulled me up the long flight of steps to the court, pushing open the heavy front door, and delivering me to the halls of justice. It took a moment for my eyes to adjust from the bright sunshine to the dim interior of the courthouse. When they did, I saw Alicia Rice, my lawyer, walking briskly toward me from down the hall. Dressed in a perfectly cut, bright green Dior suit with pearl earrings and a matching necklace, she was an immediately comforting presence.

"I guess you'll be okay now," Paco whispered. "But I'll be right back." He squeezed my hand, exchanged greetings with Alicia, and went back outside to move the car.

Now Alicia held on to my arm, leading me down the long hallway. "You doing all right?" she asked.

"I suppose. But this is just so unreal. I don't know how it could be happening. I'm having a hard time understanding that it's me everyone's talking about."

"That's fine, because what I'm going to suggest is that you don't take this whole thing too personally. I know that sounds odd, but the paths of justice can be strangely crooked, and what goes on sometimes is more an impersonal game than anything else. Today's details are just by-the-book stuff. They're not about you or the truth or even guilt and innocence. It's just what we have to do to move on from here." She stopped in front of a wooden door with a frosted glass inset and said, "For the rest of the day, just answer the questions you're asked, and nothing more. If anything confuses you, ask me and nobody else. Ready?"

"I guess so."

Inside, two uniformed cops were sitting at a table, drinking coffee and laughing at some shared joke. When we walked in, they composed themselves immediately and shuffled to their feet.

"This is Sarabeth Love," Alicia said formally. "She's here to surrender under the terms of the indictment issued yesterday."

One of the cops nodded. He was middle-aged and beefy-faced; the name on his shield was Murphy. I wanted to tell them about my dad, the Boston Irish cop, and that our surname had been changed to Love two generations earlier by my great-grandfather, who wanted to make himself more interesting to the New York showgirl he was courting. He had never married her, but the family name stuck, a symbol of Irish hopes in America. But the cop gestured to a hard chair by the table, and I sat down, saying nothing. Answer only the questions you're asked, Alicia had said. That meant suppressing my natural urge to make friends, too.

"We'll start with some vital statistics, ma'am," Murphy said. The other cop, slightly younger and dark-skinned, took out a long sheet of paper and the two of them huddled over it. They painstakingly went through name and address, height and weight, hair color, eye color, prior arrests.

"None," I said vehemently to the last question, eyes flashing.

"I guess we know that," said Murphy, filling in the box. "That's why we have our kid gloves on for you today."

I couldn't decide if the comment reeked of resentment or a desire to appease me. I looked over at Alicia; her face was blank. They continued with the questions until Murphy nodded that he was done and they moved me over to another room where a camera had been set up. "Picture and fingerprints and then we're done here," Murphy said.

Looking into the camera, I couldn't decide how to arrange my face. A smile seemed wrong, but I wanted to avoid the blank stare that made everyone look guilty in a mug shot. Defiance? Arrogance? Anger? I remembered the reporters waiting outside the house that morning and was suddenly terrified that the mug shot might appear in the newspaper the next day. Front view. Side view. The flash went off twice and I found myself shaking.

Murphy snapped on a pair of latex gloves—not very different from what I used in delivering a baby—and took my hand for fingerprinting. I'd expected the process to be high-tech by now—a light-box and computer chip taking the reading—but instead it was stunningly old-fashioned—dip the fingers in an inky mixture, then touch them to paper. Murphy put pressure on each finger, rolling it from side to side to get the clearest possible markings. He did it slowly, one finger at a leisurely time, seeming to enjoy this routine procedure required for every criminal, from petty thief to drug-dealing kingpin, who was caught in the system. I felt myself flushing, the heat extending from my cheeks down my neck and across to my ears. Again I looked over at Alicia, who stood by dispassionately and did not change her expression when I caught her eye. Finally it was over, and Murphy handed me a wet towel in a small packet to clean my fingers.

"We'll get those into the computer for cross-checking," Murphy said, snapping off his gloves. "National matching. Should take a couple of hours. You're scheduled to appear before the judge at two o'clock. If there's a delay with the fingerprints, we'll have to change that, but I don't see a problem.''

Now Alicia was at my side again. ''Thank you, Officer. Do you have any problem with my taking Dr. Love back to my office until then?''

''Better you stay in the courthouse.''

He gave no reason and Alicia didn't argue. Picking her battles, I assumed. ''Fine. We'll be on the premises if you need us.''

We left the room. ''Not so bad?'' asked Alicia.

I shook my head, numbed beyond speaking. There was nothing to compare it to, no way of knowing if it was ''not so bad'' or truly awful. Maybe what I had just experienced was like the early stages of labor, in which case I had to expect that the pain would keep getting worse. And result in what? ''Just a little longer and you'll be holding that baby in your arms,'' I would typically whisper to my patients when they cried out at seven or eight centimeters that they couldn't stand it any longer. But where was all this pain leading me now?

To jail, possibly.

Or to a verdict of innocence, which would be a relief but not a gift. Not a baby to treasure and hold, just a long fight to get back to where I started.

With my reputation forever besmirched unless the real truth emerged.

We went to the cafeteria and had coffee. Paco found us, and Alicia sat with both of us for a while, discussing plans and strategy. She radiated confidence; it gleamed like the gold circle pin on her lapel. Alicia was in her

element, back in the courthouse which was the scene of
her greatest triumph

At a few minutes before two, she led us up a back
stairway to the floor where the courtroom was located.
Paco peered into the hallway first, and immediately saw
the blond producer who had been at our front door that
morning. He whispered the news to Alicia, who closed
her eyes briefly.

"I wasn't expecting it this soon," she said, then
added to me, "I'll speak for us, if it's necessary. There's
no need for you to make any comments to the reporters."

But the reporters were surprisingly well-mannered,
not calling out, just following curiously behind us. I
spotted one video camera whirling and noticed the TV
producer pointing to me. I turned my head away, and
Paco and Alicia moved discreetly closer to me, providing whatever shield they could.

"No cameras allowed inside," Alicia whispered, as if
to suggest that the courtroom we were about to enter
was a haven.

But it wasn't. The moment we stepped inside, a wave
of nausea hit me. The room was much smaller than I'd
expected, but two men were already sitting at the table
up front on the right-hand side, hunched over portable
files and shuffling piles of papers that were spread out
in front of them. "Prosecutors," Alicia whispered to me.
She led me to a table on the other side of the room, and
when I sat down, she sauntered over to them. One was
tall, bearded and brown-haired, wearing an olive-green
suit that made him look sallow. He jumped up to pump
Alicia's hand, talking animatedly. I couldn't hear what

he was saying, but he looked like a kid at a school dance, trying to impress the most popular girl in class. After a moment, the other prosecutor rose—he was young, shorter and sandy-haired, wearing gold-rimmed glasses and a dark suit. His partner introduced him to Alicia, and after she shook his hand, she walked away.

"The tall fellow is Justin Bryant," Alicia said, sitting down next to me. "He's the assistant D.A. I worked with in arranging your surrender. I've known him for years. He was part of the DiSalvo team. The other fellow is new—Douglas Stineman. I don't know much about him. The judge will be here in a minute. Her name is Rosalie Snow—she's a distinguished, older woman, and I think you'll find . . ." But she didn't get to finish the sentence, because at that moment the judge herself walked into the courtroom, and everyone stood up. The blood seemed to drain into my feet, and I thought I'd faint. I sat down again quickly, but after a few preliminaries, I had to struggle to my feet once more.

The indictment was being read.

It seemed to take a long time, and Alicia kept her arm firmly wrapped around mine. Finally the judge asked, "How do you plead?" and when Alicia squeezed my arm, I said, "Not Guilty." It seemed like an anticlimax. I wanted to shout at the top of my lungs, "Can't you see I've been framed!" or "I'm the most innocent person in this room!" but instead my voice was shaky and barely audible. We sat down.

Justin Bryant approached the bench then to raise the question of bail. He asked that it be set at $500,000, and I looked at Alicia in panic. Her eyes told me to stay calm.

"Let's not be deceived by the appearance of this defendant," Bryant was saying, when I turned my attention back to him. "Yes, she's a physician with a previously clean record, but the charges against her are very serious. She has committed a crime that is an outrage to this society. One need only look at the newspapers to realize how horrified this city is by the crime. We must prove that we take this case seriously, that the state will not allow professional status or social position to interfere with the proper course of justice. The defendant is unmarried. She has no family in Boston. There is nothing to keep her from fleeing before the trial. That is why we must ask for bail, Your Honor, and demand that it be set high enough to assure that we will see this defendant again."

Bryant sat down, and Alicia, who hadn't taken a single note while he spoke, stood but didn't approach the bench. Bryant had been loud and forceful, she was soft and conciliatory. "Your Honor, you will see this defendant again. She has only one goal at this time, and that is to fight these charges and prove to you, to the prosecution, and to the world at large why they are complete flimflam. This is an innocent woman, and innocent women do not flee. The assistant district attorney raises the question of professional status and social position and requests that it not interfere with the proper course of justice. I ardently agree with that request. However, the social position we must ignore is that of the deceased. The case has aroused unusual interest in the press because of the name Hollis Taft Brewster. But this is a court of law, Your Honor, and it is shocking that the prosecution would attempt to put pressure on the court through the press. I find it hard to believe that I heard correctly, and that Mr. Bryant said we can understand the seriousness of the case by looking at the newspaper. I believe this court will reasonably turn to a newspaper to find out the weather and last night's box score for the Boston Red Sox, but not to determine bail.

"Let me also make something else very clear. Dr. Sarabeth Love is a physician and a good one. But she is also only just out of her residency program. Unlike the stereotype of a doctor, she is not rich. In fact, her accounts at the moment show major debts—for college, medical school, and living expenses during her residency. Perhaps you are already aware of that. The bail the prosecution asks is unconscionable—and virtually impossible for her to make.

"So the court has a decision to make—whether to let the press determine the course this case will take, or whether to send a message right now that it is seeking truth and will not be swayed by public opinion.

"Bail is not necessary, Your Honor, and to set any bail in this case is wrong. I ask that you so find."

Alicia sat down, and I expected we would have a long wait, but in a moment I realized the speeches had all been part of a show. Judge Snow flipped some pages in a notebook, seemed to consult a calendar, and then said, "The defendant, Dr. Sarabeth Love, is released without bail, pending the continuance of this case. I will hear any pretrial motions on August ninth and am setting a trial date of August twenty-sixth. Dr. Love, until that time, you are not to leave this state unless you have permission from the court, and you are to notify me immediately if you have any change of address. If there are no further questions, this case is temporarily adjourned.''

So that was it. My first day in court. Alicia didn't bother talking to her friend Justin Bryant as we left, and Paco grabbed my hand and fairly flew with me outside, to fresh air.

three

HOW THE WIND BLOWS

I

I WANTED TO stay in bed the next day. I couldn't think of a single reason to get up. Paco, trying to be kind, brought me a tray with cereal and coffee, and what he got for his trouble was my unmitigated wrath.

"I'm not sick," I said, sitting up abruptly when he walked in.

"I know," he said mildly. "But it's almost eleven. I thought you might be hungry."

"If I were, I could get up and get something," I snapped. "Or do you think I should just hide myself away? Is that it? Yesterday changed everything, is that right?"

At my barrage, Paco put the tray down on the floor. "Look, this wasn't meant to upset you. It's breakfast, that's all. Nothing more significant than that."

I immediately felt like a heel.

"Sorry," I said. "I'm not mad at you. Just the rest of the world."

"I know that. Though it doesn't make it a whole lot

pleasanter here.'' Paco looked down at the tray but
didn't pick it up again.

I'd been on the eleven o'clock news the previous
night and God knows what tabloid shows. I thought I'd
been so clever in avoiding the wispy blond producer,
but it didn't do any good. There I was, walking into the
courtroom, and since they had captured only about ten
seconds on tape, it was played over and over in slow
motion. Show Mother Teresa walking into a courtroom
in slow motion and she'd look guilty, too. The producer
also threw in some pictures of Hollis as a deb and a
society lady; along with shots of doctors walking outside
P&S, there were about two minutes of tape, which altogether was long enough for the reporter to offer all the
gory details and speculate on the truth. The only thing
missing was comments from the victim's family—those
well-bred, chin-up-in-adversity Tafts had refused to dig-
nify the tabloid frenzy by providing tear-filled sound-
bites.

''Look,'' said Paco, ''if you're worried that people
will recognize you from TV—''

''I'm not worried about that,'' I said, furious again.
''I'm worrying about finding some explanations and getting out of this mess.''

''Anything we can talk through?'' he asked.

''No,'' I snapped, flinging back the covers and stomp-
ing into the bathroom. ''I don't see how you can help
with this at all. It's not an ethics question or a touchy-
feely one or an artsy-fartsy one. At this point it's all
medical.''

I guess I'd gone too far, because when I got out of
the shower a few minutes later, sweet, loving, and sup-
portive Paco had left.

• • •

I met Eric at a coffee shop a half-block from the hospital. He was sitting at a table in the back when I got there, already sipping a cappuccino. If it had been Paco I was meeting, I would have made a snide comment about sitting in the back so nobody could see us, but you're never as nasty to friends as to the people who love you.

"Chapter and verse to present to a jury," I said, sitting down.

"What?" asked Eric.

"That's what you said the day the first article came out, remember? It's what you told me I'd need."

"I was figuring on a malpractice suit then, not this."

"I wasn't figuring on anything."

A waitress came over, glared at me for a moment, and stomped away after I ordered herbal tea. I looked at Eric, stricken. "Do you think she recognized me as the killer doctor?"

He laughed. "Don't worry. She did the same thing to me. Her feet probably hurt and you're sitting down."

The tea came, and I filled Eric in on what had been happening, skipping most of the details of yesterday's visit to the police and courthouse.

"The good thing," said Eric, "is that Ardsley can't keep the records from you anymore. I assume your lawyer has seen them."

I shrugged. "Yup, but they're mostly meaningless. It's my notes until the morning-of, then a lengthy note from Ardsley about the bleed-out. He describes it as an obviously ruptured uterus, and the hospital review concurred, saying the patient had a small uterus after the two C-sections and it ruptured post-delivery. The family refused to permit an autopsy, but the blood was tested extensively. Only unusual finding was trace morphine and a slightly low level of fibrinogen in the blood.''

"Morphine as a painkiller, okay. But what accounts for the fibrinogen?"

"I don't know. I never ordered morphine for her, by the way. And the review panel ignored the fibrinogen. No explanation that seemed relevant."

"Well, maybe we shouldn't ignore it. Let's play first-year med school. Ruptured uterus is one explanation for this death. But let's look beyond that. What could possibly cause the two conditions we know: a bleed-out, and a drop in fibrinogen?"

"DIC?" I ventured. Disseminated intravascular coagulation—a weird condition where you're clotting and bleeding at the same time. Ultimately there are no coagulation factors to stop the bleeding, and you bleed out.

Eric's eyes opened wide. "Good one. DIC could cause the same kind of bleeding and would look just like—" He paused. "Just like what you're being blamed for."

"O.K." I nodded. "Good medical possibility. Give me an A in the course. But this isn't grand rounds, it's real. What would be the etiology for DIC? After a normal delivery with no obvious infection? Come on."

"Make the list. What could cause DIC."

"You do it." I felt my spirits sinking. I knew it wasn't right.

He began ticking items off on his fingers. "Trauma. Infection. Pulmonary embolism. Blood incompatibility. Any others?"

"Not that I can think of. Good list, but none of them make sense. There was no trauma. Cultures were negative, so forget infection. No pulmonary symptoms. And the blood types weren't a problem."

"So you want to dismiss DIC?"

"Yup."

"Then we need a DIC look-alike. A different etiology that causes an unexplained bleed-out and a drop in fibrinogen."

"I'm listening."

Eric strummed his fingers on the table. "Actually, I was thinking about this last night, when I was in the ER. A forty-six-year-old guy came in with chest pains and the resident started heparin and IV nitro. We did a cardiogram and it was a massive infarct, so I called for TPA. The nurse brought it, I hung the bag, and an hour later, he was bleeding at the venipuncture site."

"Overdose?"

"Accidental. And it couldn't have been much. But enough to cause spurting."

"So you're thinking—"

He shrugged. "It wasn't a big deal last night, because we caught it fast. But I heard about a case a couple of months ago over at Mass General where a sixty-year-old came in with an infarct and was started on TPA. Next day, he had a gastrointestinal hemorrhage and died. At first the hospital claimed he died from the heart attack, but after reviewing the records, they admitted he'd been given four times the right dosage of TPA. The insurance company is offering the family a huge settlement."

My brain wasn't working too well, but I tried to follow his thinking. A patient who came in with an acute infarct—or heart attack—was often treated with TPA, or tissue plasminogen activating factor. It was a potent anticoagulant that had revolutionized cardiology. Given in carefully measured doses, it broke up clots in the coronary arteries, and given early enough after a heart attack, it saved heart tissue. But Eric was thinking about the other side of it. Too much TPA and all recent clots dissolve. The body can't stop bleeding at vulnerable sites. That, apparently, was what had happened to the poor patient at Mass General.

"Think about it," Eric went on. "Too much TPA would cause hemorrhage from any fresh wound. At Mass General it was the gut, and last night it was the venipuncture site. So why not a postpartum uterus? There'd be heavy bleeding—probably causing death— and no evidence of it, either."

I sighed. "Medically, I can't argue. But who would give Hollis TPA?"

"She didn't have a cardiac emergency during the night, I take it."

"Nothing. There's no record of her having called for anyone or asked for anything like pain medicine. Nurses, residents, and interns have all said that they didn't see her or hear from her at any time during the night."

Eric shrugged. "Then maybe it was an accident. Maybe the TPA was ordered for someone else and ended up being administered to her by mistake. Those things can happen in the middle of the night, you know."

"It would still have been noted on the chart. The error would turn up."

"Charts can be altered."

We were both silent, pondering it. "Administered by mistake would suggest a nurse or intern," I said. "Unlikely they'd have access later to alter the chart."

"But Ardsley would. Say he realized what happened and altered the chart to preserve his relationship with Brewster Insurance. The possibilities would be clear to him pretty fast: Sloane Brewster's wife dies from a mistake at P&S and suddenly Brewster Insurance doesn't cover deliveries at the hospital anymore. It could happen, you know. And it could also bankrupt the hospital. He'd rather sacrifice you than his whole department. So records get altered and the nurse on call is told to shut up."

"It was Nurse Dolton."

"Who would do whatever Ardsley told her, and you know that. It could explain Ardsley's iron grip on this case."

"Possible," I said. "But TPA isn't usually quietly administered in a patient's room. It's an emergency. There's a code and fanfare. If the wrong patient got it, somebody would remember. And talk. Ardsley wouldn't take the chance."

Eric sipped his coffee, thinking. "Then, another scenario. Somebody came in—quietly—with an ulterior motive that they didn't bother noting on the chart."

"Purposely killed her?"

"Pretty good crime, isn't it? TPA isn't a bad killer for a postpartum woman. It's readily accessible to anyone who has reason to be in the emergency room. And the symptoms that caused the death would exactly mimic a postpartum complication. Whoever it was knew the finger would be pointed at you. They probably didn't figure it would go this far. Just a good malpractice suit.''

"Who could possibly want to do that?''

"Hey, I'm a doctor, right? I told you that first day you needed a detective. Why don't you ask that Radcliffe-pal lawyer of yours to hire one?''

I'd been sitting on the edge of my seat, but now I sat back. "A detective to check out the dirty linen of Hollis Taft Brewster. Now there's a waste of money. There is none. The most radical activity that woman was involved in was helping raise funds for Reading Is Fundamental.''

"Maybe somebody hated the books she bought.''

I blinked my eyes a few times. "You're not funny, and I'm not in the mood.''

"Sorry. But you're being naive. Who would want Hollis dead? There's got to be a long list, Sarabeth. The Tafts and Brewsters didn't make as much money as they did without pissing off a few people along the way. Insurance is still a dirty business. Maybe Hollis knew too much about something at the hospital. Maybe she knew too much about some*one* at the hospital. Easy to get her while she's there. You know how many cases an insurance company handles and how many people get upset?''

I let it sink in, and Eric sat back. "I vote that TPA was the killer,'' he said. "But whether it was murder or mistake—well, take your pick.''

The possibilities swam in my head. A lot of fingers seemed to be pointing in the direction of Ardsley's office. "Ginny,'' I said.

"What?''

"Ginny. Ardsley's assistant. I've had the feeling that

she might know something. From the time I started at P&S, she'd been running the department, and then suddenly, the day after all this happens, she's fired. It seemed so strange to me.''

"Go visit her. Want me to come?''

"No,'' I said. "First time I'll try it alone.''

The hallway in Ginny's apartment building reminded me of a cheap hotel—orange carpet, slightly grimy walls, and a long row of identical doors, with solid locks. I came to 3H and knocked. The walls must have been thin, because I could hear a chair scraping back in what was probably the kitchen and footsteps approaching the front door.

"Who is it?'' Ginny's voice was close to the door.

"Sarabeth. May I come in? I just need to talk.'' I sensed her looking at me through the peephole, but a moment later, I heard the chain slide across its holder, two locks turn, and the door opened. Ginny was wearing cut-off shorts, house slippers, and an orange tank top that stretched more than any material should across her chest. Her hair was tangled and some ragged mascara and eyeliner clung to her eyes. It was early afternoon, but it looked like she hadn't been awake for very long, and that the makeup was detritus from the night before. In the office, with her push-up bras and cleavage and too much makeup, Ginny looked like a 1950s good-time girl. But oddly, without all that, she seemed harsher, cruder.

"I don't usually chat with convicted murderers, but come on in,'' she said, stepping back from the door so I could enter.

"Indicted, not convicted," I said, trying to sound as flip as she did. But it didn't work. My heart was pounding too hard. I followed her into the kitchen and she plopped down on the chair where she'd been sitting before my knock disturbed her. A half-drunk cup of coffee was on the table, along with a copy of *Cosmopolitan* and an ashtray filled with butts. She lit another cigarette as I pulled up a chair.

"I didn't know you smoked."

"I quit five years ago. But since Gus fired me, I've started again. Nothing else to do. And I want to lose weight."

"You look fine now."

"I want to lose weight," she repeated. I resisted the lecture about how losing weight wasn't worth the risks of smoking. Ginny wasn't fighting obesity with her cigarettes, she was fighting loneliness and anger.

"I'm sorry you're not at the hospital anymore," I said. Maybe she could say she'd been fired, but my instinct was to be more discreet.

"Yeh. Well, I'm sorry you're not, too."

"Kind of different circumstances."

"I hope so."

We weren't going to be friends—two girls just chatting about their off-track careers in a dirty kitchen, so I said, "Look, maybe I can help you somehow. And maybe you can help me. Would you mind?"

"Nope. What do you need?"

"Well, tell me your story first. I don't know why you were fired."

"You don't?" She looked at me as if I'd just landed from another planet. "I figured everyone did."

"I'm always the last to hear gossip. In fact, I was kind of worried when I stopped seeing you. I couldn't imagine why you wouldn't be there."

She gave a small snort. "You knew about Gus and me, didn't you?"

"It occurred to me that he liked you a lot."

"We'd been screwing for years."

There was no answer to that. How was he? sprang to mind, but I squelched it.

"It's not like I expected him to leave his wife and marry me," she continued bitterly. "I'm not that dumb. I was married once, to a man who was a drunk. I left that fast. I never understand these women who stay and get beaten and say they can't get out. I got out. I believe in my own independence. I don't need a man to live."

It sounded like she'd spent too much time watching Oprah. "Why'd you stay with Gus so long?"

"Good sex. Some nice trips to Florida and Bermuda and the Caribbean, for the conferences his wife was too busy to attend."

"Did Dr. Franklin and Juliette join you on those trips?" I asked, suddenly making some connections.

She laughed. "You picked that up? Juliette and Franklin were with us in January at a conference in the Caribbean, but that was it. She's been his on-again, off-again for years, but now it's over. Juliette plays a lot of angles." She shrugged. "Anyway, nobody lasts as long as I did."

"Why else did you last?"

"My daughter was little when I left my husband, moved here, and started working for Gus. She's sixteen now. Gus was good to me and good to her and that was enough. Being a mistress isn't such a bad thing. And . . .'' She sighed. "Maybe I really did love him. Who knows."

If that's all Ginny had wanted, Gus had been luckier than he deserved. An undemanding lover who was also a competent administrator and ran your whole damn department. A good deal. Which led me to the obvious.

"So why did he fire you?"

"As an administrator or a lover?" she asked, with a twisted smile.

"The first. I know you were good at that. I have no idea how you were as a lover."

She gave a faint smile. "At least you see a distinction between the two. Gus didn't."

"You mean you wanted to stop screwing, so he figured you couldn't answer the phone anymore?"

"No, *he* wanted to stop screwing. His wife had found out about us."

"Took her long enough."

"Yeh, right. What kind of woman wouldn't know? Trust me, she'd had it figured out a long time ago, but she wasn't working back then and she needed Gus around. Once her kids got bigger, she went back to law school and joined a ritzy entertainment law firm. All of a sudden she knew everything and our affair became a *cause célèbre*.''

"Had a fit and threatened to leave him?" I asked.

"I wish. That he could have handled. But she didn't say a word—just went out and had an affair herself with some twenty-five-year-old soap opera stud she was representing. She made sure Gus found out, and he went nuts. God forbid his family picture should be messed up.

He was terrified that his perfect—and now successful—wife would leave him, and he wanted me out of his life. And that meant *out of his life*. Completely. The wife demanded it. I like to think he argued the point.''

I didn't say anything while I tried to make sense of the story, figure out whether it could have anything to do with me or Hollis. It didn't sound that way, but something about the timing nagged at me. It was too coincidental. ''When did all this happen?'' I asked.

''Over the last couple of weeks.'' She looked at me squarely. ''You and I talked in the ladies' room on the day I realized it was all coming to an end.''

''So what did you hear about my case before you left?'' I asked.

The change of subject might have been too abrupt. Ginny was still busy feeling sorry for herself, not me, and she just looked down sullenly. ''Nothing. I didn't hear anything.''

''Nothing? Then what were you warning me about in the ladies' room?''

She was silent.

''Nice of you to try to protect Ardsley at this point,'' I said acidly. ''He's been so helpful to you, after all.''

''Yeh, well, I do have loyalty to him,'' she said sourly. ''And whatever he's done to me, he still knows how to handle the politics of a department. That's all I was telling you. To let him handle the details.''

''You could have told me that at your desk. We didn't need a private meeting in the ladies' room.''

She was silent again, so I decided to take a stab at it. ''You know something about Ardsley and Sloane Brewster," I said. "Some connection they have. And it was making you nervous."

Without looking up, she said, "They've had meetings. A lot of them. And we were always getting calls from Brewster Insurance. More than once Gus was over here when Sloane Brewster beeped him. It didn't matter what we were doing—he'd be gone within ten minutes."

"Did he ever talk to you about it?"

"No, and I never asked. I had other things on my mind. But somehow after Hollis died . . ." She shook her head, then started again. "Hollis died and I knew you'd be coming by the office, and my instructions were to keep you away. I didn't know what was going on, but it all felt strange. Dangerous. I wanted to warn you there could be trouble."

"Instead you were the one who ended up in trouble," I said.

Now she looked up. "My trouble had nothing to do with this."

"Are you sure?" When she didn't answer, I plowed on. "You said yourself that Mrs. Ardsley had known about you and Gus for a long time. So why was it suddenly urgent that you leave? The way you see it, the love affair ended, so you had to lose your job. Well, maybe it worked the other way around. Maybe you had to lose your job, and the only way he could think to do it was to end the relationship."

She looked at me as if I were crazy, and maybe I was. "You're as paranoid as the rest of the department. Give me one reason why I would have to lose my job."

"Because you knew too much." I was reaching, but

I had to go on. "You knew too much about Ardsley and Brewster."

I had her attention now. She was looking at me curiously. "If Gus wanted to keep me quiet, he wouldn't get rid of me. He'd keep me around."

"Not if he knew that you hadn't made the connections yet. You'd been sitting on this powder keg for ages, not knowing it was there. He had to get rid of you before you accidentally ignited the whole thing."

She played with her matches for a minute or two, then slowly struck one against the outside cover of the matchbook; when it caught, she held the small flame to a cigarette. Inhaling deeply a couple of times, she didn't remove the cigarette from her mouth as she asked, "So what's the powder keg."

I sat back. I had no idea. Wild guesses and carefully honed instinct had taken me this far. But if I was going to continue, Ginny needed to start filling in some of the holes. Silence filled the room. I had nothing to say, but Ginny clearly thought something deeper than that was going on. She looked at me uncomfortably, then stubbed out her just-lit cigarette.

"Are you referring to the cabinet?"

When you're talking, all the other person has to do is listen. But once you stop, they have to contribute something. Filling the vacuum, as it were. It's the oldest trick around, but I felt myself wanting to cheer, because it had worked.

"The cabinet." I repeated it, noncommittally.

"Look, I never really knew what was in there," she said defensively. "The files I needed were in my area. He kept that cabinet locked, in his office. I knew where he kept the key, but I didn't have any reason to open it." She puffed on the cigarette and added, "I suppose he has some stuff on Sloane Brewster in there. Only because I saw him open it once when Brewster was on the phone. But I don't know what it is. I swear."

I had no choice. "Look, I don't know how your Gus was tied up with the Brewsters, but I need to find out. I hate to be dramatic, but my life is on the line."

"You want to get into the cabinet."

"Right."

"Breaking in?" Her eyes were suddenly shining, the possibility of adventure bringing her to life.

"You have the key," I said. "I thought maybe you could give it to me." Five minutes ago, I'd never heard of this cabinet. Now I had a plan to break into it.

"I didn't say I have it. I said I know where Gus kept it. But it's too complicated to explain. You don't know the office and you'd never find it. You need someone to show you."

I waited a beat.

"You mean you'll come with me?"

"Why not?"

"It could be dangerous."

"My life is so terrific now I'd hate to put anything in jeopardy," she said sarcastically. And then she added, "Wasn't that your whole point in coming here? To point out that Gus has treated me like garbage and I should get my sweet revenge?"

"I think you're the one who figured that out, not me. I didn't even know you'd been fired, remember?" She shrugged and looked away, and before she could change her mind, I said, "Well, it's fine with me for you to come. I mean, it would help. But I don't want to wait. How about tonight?''

''Maybe tomorrow night.''

I didn't say anything, just looked down at my feet and fiddled with Paco's ring on my finger. Maybe she figured out that a murder indictment was a good call to action, because she said, ''Okay, tonight. I can manage it.''

Next we had to decide on a time. Ginny suggested nine o'clock but I'd worked enough nights at the hospital to know that half the doctors on staff could still be floating around then. Attending physicians would still come in from the suburbs at that hour to see private patients admitted with heart attacks and strokes; interns and residents who'd been distracted by emergencies earlier would be back on the floor, finishing the rounds that they'd abandoned for a bleeder on a stretcher, or a code four elsewhere in the hospital. Quiet set in only after midnight, when most of the residents on call tried to get some shut-eye and the private attendings needed a major crisis to drag them in. But we might be *too* obvious then. We settled on eleven-thirty.

I went home, puttered for the rest of the day, and at a little after eleven, pulled up in front of Ginny's apartment for the second time. Her street was narrow and poorly lit, with open garbage cans that seemed to have been permanently abandoned in front of several of the buildings. The meager street lamps cast odd shadows, like strangers lurking in the garbage. But I didn't have too much time for imagining, because Ginny came out promptly and got into the car. She didn't say much, and we drove away quickly, weaving through the crooked streets of her neighborhood, finally emerging onto Boylston Street and cutting over to Storrow Drive. We exited at Kenmore Square, where the lights were bright and crowds of young singles thronged the streets. Ginny, staring out the car window, said "Must be Thursday night." When I didn't respond, she added, "Bar night. Hang out and pick up your date for the weekend." Apparently, her affair with Gus Ardsley hadn't kept her too far from the singles scene.

Away from Kenmore Square, we got to what could only be described as the Hospital District: Beth Israel, Children's Hospital, Dana Farber Cancer Institute . . . they were lined up like dominoes. I took a right off the main street over to P&S Hospital, the next in the chain. A couple of ambulances were pulled up in front of the emergency room, but only one had its red lights flashing. I didn't see any activity around the ambulance, so either the patient had just been taken inside or the driver had gone in for coffee. We swung past the ER entrance and pulled into the underground parking lot. I slipped my magnetic card into the slot, and I was almost surprised when the barrier lifted. I'd somehow figured that all ways into the hospital would be barred to me. But the magnetic strip didn't know about indictments or murder or hospital privileges. All it knew was that I'd paid my parking bill for the month.

I eased my gray Honda to the spot I usually took. Then, thinking better of it, left the area marked DOCTORS PARKING and went across the lot to VISITORS. I pulled in, cut the motor, and looked over at Ginny, who wasn't making any effort to leave the car. "There aren't supposed to be visitors at the hospital after nine o'clock," she said. "Plus you have M.D. plates. The car will stick out like a sore thumb."

I hadn't seen Ginny as the brains behind this operation, but figuring she was right, I turned on the ignition again and moved the car back where I'd started. But I drove past my regular spot and parked it close to the wall.

This time Ginny got out.

We walked toward the Emergency entrance, where hospital bustle was the greatest. Another ambulance had pulled up, but I still didn't see much action. A security guard in the front lobby looked mildly at us, taking in the stethoscope hanging out of my jacket pocket and the ID clipped to my bag. I had put them both on carefully, feeling like a fraud, but now he just nodded us on through, without saying a word. Doctor's privileges.

We took the elevator, trying not to look self-conscious, and after a whispered conference got off on the sixth floor. Orthopedics. I didn't know any of the nurses there, so we wouldn't draw any stares. The elevator opened and we quickly walked the twenty feet or so to the staircase. Nobody saw us. Up one flight, and we reentered on the seventh floor. The halls were dark, and in hushed voices we debated turning on the lights. Ginny wanted to proceed in the dark so as not to attract anyone's attention. I insisted that if a guard happened by, finding us in the dark would make any activity seem suspicious. If the lights were on, we could talk our way out of it.

"You talk," Ginny insisted grumpily.

Fortunately, there was nobody to talk to as we walked down the corridor and made our way to Ginny's old desk. I looked expectantly at the file cabinet behind it, but she whispered, "The cabinet you want is in Gus's office." The door to that inner sanctum was as tightly shut as it had been that first day or two after Hollis's death, when I so badly needed to get inside. Ardsley had kept me out then, but he couldn't now. Ginny reached for her key chain, and as she fumbled with it, I wondered if Ardsley had thought to change his lock. But he couldn't have anticipated any need to do so, and the door gave way. We were inside the office.

Acting as efficiently as if she were still working there, Ginny sauntered over to Ardsley's big oak desk. It was littered with samples from drug companies, with sealed tablets of birth control pills like Levulin and Ortho-Novum tossed into a bowl as if they were M&Ms. A pile of vitamins was in one corner of the desk with a packet of Trojan-Enz next to them—whether for personal or professional use, I couldn't tell. Ginny flipped out another key from her chain, and opened the top desk drawer. Pens and pencils were neatly lined up, along with the usual office supplies like paper clips and rubber bands, and several small boxes. From one of them, she removed a key and held it out to me.

"Over there," she said, nodding toward a low, matching oak file cabinet.

My hands were shaking. Maybe I'd been accused of murder, but I wasn't much good at being a thief. *You're saving your neck*, I told myself, releasing the cabinet lock. It opened easily, and I flipped through the top drawer, which seemed to contain a lot of personal files—hospital contracts, personnel reports, tax returns. Interesting, but not what I wanted. The second drawer was more promising, but the variously colored file folders seemed to be labeled in code. I looked over at Ginny, who was still standing on the other side of the desk.

"Check the red folders," she said.

Green folders. Purple. Orange. Red. The first one was a gold mine. Letters from Sloane Brewster marked CON-FIDENTIAL. Financial statements. Private memos from Brewster Insurance to the personal attention of Gus Ardsley. Copies of three checks made out to Ardsley, including one for $250,000.

"Just take them," Ginny urged.

"I need a Xerox machine."

"Are you nuts? Take them. We can't stand here Xeroxing."

"I can't. It might be evidence. And if it's taken illegally, it's not admissible." I had no idea what I was talking about, but I was completely convinced I was right—probably from something maybe I'd once seen on *Law & Order*. In whispered voices, we argued about the Xerox machine which, she said, wouldn't even be turned on and would take five minutes just to warm up.

"Just show me where it is," I finally hissed. "You don't have to stay. I'll pick you up in half an hour at the coffee shop."

Released from responsibility for our escapade, she was now intent on keeping it. "You'll never figure out the machine," she whispered. "It's very temperamental." She flounced off, and I followed.

Without Ginny around, nobody had remembered to turn off the machine earlier in the evening, so it was already humming when we walked into the alcove where it was located, twenty paces from Ardsley's office. Once

or twice we thought we heard people walking nearby,
but nobody came in, and I decided it was just the natural
noises of the building. Still, I didn't want to take too
long. It took all my self-control not to stop and read the
pages we were copying. But even as they passed through
my fingers, I got the gist. The chairman of the department and the president of the insurance company were
in cahoots about something, but I wasn't sure what. The
more we Xeroxed, the more my heart pounded. Detailed
letters. Sample contracts. Several brief memos from
Doheny in the governor's office that were so cryptic I
couldn't begin to follow them. A handwritten note from
the governor himself. I couldn't figure out what was going on while I was copying, but I had no doubt that a
closer reading would reveal something.

We finished, undisturbed. Ginny put the folders back,
returned the key to its place in the desk drawer, and
locked up. The copies went into my big tote bag and we
took the elevator back down. The guard barely looked
at us as we left, and the car was where I'd left it in the
parking lot.

Ginny gave a big sigh as we settled into the car and
drove out into the street. "I hope you get something out
of all this," she said.

"Me, too. I'll read it as soon as I get home and let
you know."

I dropped her off in front of her building and waited
a few minutes until I saw the light go on in her apartment and knew she was back inside. Worrying about
someone else's safety takes your mind off your own.

Cross-town then, to my house. It was almost two in
the morning. Luck was on my side, because I found a

parking space barely a block from my front door. Getting out of the car, I checked the street. It was empty. I walked quickly toward the house, eager to get inside, wondering if Paco would still be awake. I was trying to decide if I had enough energy to read through the pages tonight or if I should put it off until morning. I still hadn't decided, when the knife went into my back.

II

)FOR THE FIRST instant, I didn't know what had happened or why I was on the ground. There was a horrible burning in my chest and lungs; "heart attack" flashed through my mind, but I knew that was wishful thinking. I had a sense of huge noise—blood pounding in my ears, gutteral cries of terror escaping my lips, feet scuffing by my head, which was flat against the cold cement of the sidewalk. My eyes wouldn't focus for a few moments, and when they did, I saw blood, my own blood, pooling at my shoulder in a mounting heap. *Sometimes it looks like bloody murder and it's an inconsequential amount of blood.* The words of my professor from the first day of medical school rang in my head. But it was no good. This *was* bloody murder.

And that's when I began to scream.

I wasn't hysterical, but I needed help. Even in my daze I could see that the blood was spilling rapidly and it wouldn't be too long before I passed out. I tried to assess the situation medically, but I couldn't. Searing pain. Cascading blood. The thought crossed my mind that if someone didn't come soon, I could die. I tried to lift my head, raise my body up, but it was as if I were made out of Play-Doh. Whatever signals my brain was sending were cut off well before they got to the nerve endings in my feet or hands. I couldn't move myself.

A scream got caught in my throat as I started to choke on saliva and blood. And suddenly it occurred to me that what had sounded like screams in my own head were probably feeble yelps. Nobody could have heard me.

My eyes started to close and I wanted to let them. Maybe I was going to die, right here on the sidewalk. That crumpled thought was enough to make me hold my eyes open and keep struggling. I thought of all the people in emergency rooms whom I'd urged as a young resident to keep fighting. I believed then that you couldn't die if you wouldn't let yourself, that the heart had to stop in an emotional, giving way before the beating would cease. *Keep fighting*! Now I understood how it happened that you didn't want to fight anymore. That blood and exhaustion overcame you. Maybe I could just rest for a moment before I was saved, close my eyes briefly, sleep for a moment to regain my strength.

"SARABETH! Oh my God!"

A blur again, and I opened my eyes, saw Paco kneeling next to me.

"Sarabeth, can you hear me? Oh my God, don't die. Can you hear me?"

I wanted to tell him yes, but all that came out was a groan.

"If you can hear me, I'm going inside to call 911. Hang on, honey. Hang on. I'll be right back."

Then silence. Hang on. I was hanging on. Hanging on for me. Hanging from a tree. Would someone hang for

doing this to me? Hang. Hang. Hang it all. I didn't want
to die. I didn't want to cry. I was going to try. No,
maybe I should sleep, sleep, sleep . . . Hang on! Someone wanted me to die. I wasn't going to die. That
wouldn't be right. This was just a fright. I was going to
be all right. I'd make it through the night. . . .

"Sarabeth, Sarabeth."

Paco again, this time sobbing and holding my pain,
lying on top of the blood. I told him I'd be all right but
he couldn't hear me. Then voices. Voices other than my
own. Many hands touching me and Paco saying, "It's
okay, Sarabeth. You're going to be okay. Help is here.
I love you."

Then other voices, many voices.

"She's trying to say something."

"We don't have time. Gotta make sure there's an air
passage."

"Let her talk first. Maybe she can ID the attacker."

"Officer, if she's not getting any air, she could die."

"Damn, you know who this is? That woman doctor
who was indicted!"

"She's got to talk!"

"She's got to breathe! Get the hell out of my way!"

Paco's face. I still saw Paco's face. Then a pair of
gloved hands coming at me. Good. Relief. Somebody
else could breathe for me. But first I found Paco's face
again.

"I'm telling you she's trying to talk!" That officer's
voice. He tried to get near, but I wouldn't talk to him.
Not a cop. Not ever. Then finally Paco's face. That's
what I wanted. That's why I needed to talk. Closer,
closer. I tried to whisper.

"Don't let me die."

And then everything went black.

III

THE WRONG SIDE of a hospital.

I was in a bed, looking up, and Paco was stroking my forehead.

Something hurt, but I couldn't place what it was. Something between my head and my toes. I narrowed the options, and considered each organ, muscle group, and body part, one by one. The mental checklist was easy to fill in. Yes, yes, yes. Everything hurt.

"What happened?" I asked Paco.

"That you'll have to tell me." He tried to smile as he said it, but worry lines creased his forehead.

"Jeez." I tried to sit up or move, but nothing was working. "I mean medically. What happened?"

"A six-inch stab wound. Deep but clean, the doctors tell me. You have a partially collapsed lung but it doesn't look like any permanent damage."

I guess that was good news, but every breath felt as if I were sucking rocks, and when I tried to move, my back screamed its searing pain.

"I feel like dirt," I said.

"Forty-two stitches," Paco said. "As doctors always seem to say in these situations, another inch and you wouldn't be here. They managed to stop the internal bleeding without surgery, which I guess is a good thing. I wasn't paying attention to the details. All I cared about was the prognosis, which is apparently good. Your buddy Eric said you were going to be hurting like hell but to call him as soon as you were awake, and he'd come by and explain the whole thing to you. Much as I hate to admit it, he was amazing.''

The events that had brought me here suddenly swarmed back like a pack of bees. Eric's name stung its warning and I looked around. "Eric was here? Where am I?"

"The hospital, honey." Paco's voice was soothing. "You came here in an ambulance. Do you remember?"

"No," I said impatiently. "I don't remember that at all. I remember being stabbed. I remember seeing your face and not wanting to die. But that's it. I wasn't awake to give the ambulance driver directions, and these rooms all kind of look alike. So—which hospital are we at?"

"P&S. The ambulance driver did me a special favor bringing you to your own hospital. We drove right past Mass General, but I figured—" He stopped, because pain or not, I was doing everything I could to sit up. And my face was contorted like a baby eating her first lemon.

"I've got to get out of here, Paco." I looked at the IV dripping into my arm and began picking at the bandages holding the needle in place. "Jeez, I've got to get out."

Paco looked at me helplessly. "You've got an IV. And a chest tube."

My hand flew to my chest, and there it was. Like a hundred-pound anchor tying me to the bed. The thing about collapsed lungs was that they leaked. Air built up in the chest cavity, which meant the lung couldn't inflate unless there was a chest tube to get rid of it. Medically, it was good to have it there, but my case was different.

The tube might help my breathing but not my life.

"Look," I said, panting more in anxiety than pain. "I have one question. Personal effects. Did you find any after I was stabbed?"

"What do you mean?"

"My tote bag. My pocketbook. Were they on the sidewalk?" I had to stay awake, figure this out.

"Your pocketbook, yes." Paco pointed to it, lying on the dresser near my bed. "The police brought it. They made a point of saying that it didn't seem like a robbery with a purse left three feet away from you. Your wallet's still inside."

"How about the tote bag?"

Paco shrugged. "I didn't hear anything about it. Or see it. I could be wrong, of course. I didn't know to look."

I started to cry. I couldn't help it. I'd been through too much and I hurt too badly and now I was lying in pain in the last place in the whole world where I should be. The crying made everything hurt more, and a helpless expression crossed Paco's face. He stroked my hair and wiped at my tears and even tried to hug me, but the damn chest tube was in the way.

There was no place I could go, but I had to get out.

I sniffled and it hurt. Paco gave me a tissue, and I blew my nose, which made the pain worse. "I have to leave," I said. "They got the copies that were in the tote bag and they'll come back to get me. I know it. Whoever's doing this isn't letting it drop. I have to get out."

It must have sounded like gibberish to Paco, but for an artist, he was practical. And he wasn't going to try to make sense of it. "Let me get Eric," Paco said briskly. "He can give you the medical report, and we'll figure it out from there."

"Good." I nodded to the phone, but Paco said, "The phone's not working, for some reason. Can't get it hooked up until tomorrow. I'll go down and call him."

Terrified, I grabbed Paco's hand. "Don't leave me. Please."

"I'm not leaving you. I hear you that this isn't a good place for you to stay. So let's get you out. But right now, you've got a twenty-four-hour armed guard outside your door. Courtesy of the police department. Nobody's coming in." He stood up. "Just rest. I'll be back in a very few minutes."

I closed my eyes briefly and realized that the conversation had done me in—I was exhausted and still groggy. I heard the door open and close, then a moment later, open and close again. Paco back so soon? But my eyes opened to see a slim, shapely nurse standing by the IV pole. She was mostly turned away from me, but there was something familiar about her.

"Who are you?" I asked sharply. "What are you doing?"

"Just your nurse—Patsy." Her jet-black hair glimmered in a dagger of sunlight. "Some pain medicine the doctor ordered. I'll just be a moment."

She swung toward me, her face partially hidden by her flowing hair; her thick-lensed glasses distorted her eyes, distracting from her features, but I noticed a large brown mole on her left cheek. She reached across the bed for my arm.

"Go away. I'll talk to my doctor about medicine," I said.

But instead of responding, she took my arm and expertly wrapped a tourniquet above the elbow, exposing a vein in the soft, fleshy underside. "Just relax, it'll be okay," she said.

I tried to fight the grogginess. Something was wrong. I tried to swat her hand away, but her grip was tight and I was too weak to struggle. She turned away to get the needle.

"What's the medicine?"

"Whatever the doctor ordered."

"Why don't you put it in the IV bag?"

"It has to be an injection. The doctor said."

I looked blearily at the tourniquet. If the pain medicine hadn't been ordered as an intravenous drip, it would come as an intramuscular injection. Not an injection into the vein. No reason to inject into the vein when I had an IV in place. So why would I have a tourniquet?

The nurse turned back from the table and I noticed her French manicured fingernails as they dug into my arm. The unsheathed hypodermic needle gleamed at me like a sword.

I understood. And I began to scream.

The first holler curdled into her ear, startling her enough that she loosened her grip, and I twisted and struggled until I could pull my arm back. Still, she tried jabbing me with the needle, catching the air, the bedsheet, and the edge of my hospital gown. My screams, almost hysterical now, were a background noise to the circling needle.

"You need this. It won't hurt. The doctor ordered it."

She spit out each word through gritted teeth. Persistence. The needle continued searching for its mark. For a moment I wondered if I were screaming out loud—or if it was only in my head. It sounded loud but she wouldn't go away. I watched a drop of the liquid from her needle fall to the floor—just as the door came flying open and the police guard charged in.

"What's going on?" he called.

The dark-haired nurse, slim and agile, ducked under his arm. "This patient's hysterical!" she called. "I'm going for the doctor!" and she was out the door, disappearing into the hallway as Paco raced back into the room.

"Are you okay?" Paco was at my side, leaning over me anxiously, while the guard hovered at the door.

"I'm—she—" My heaving chest felt as if it were being torn apart by talons. "The nurse," I gasped. "She had a needle. She wanted to kill me."

Paco looked toward the policeman—middle-aged, unshaven, and overweight.

"What'd she do?" the cop asked, coming forward.

"The needle." I was panting. "It was what killed Hollis. I know it. Hollis. And now they wanted me."

The cop looked at Paco and shrugged. "The nurse had a written order from the doctor. Otherwise I wouldn't have let her in."

I was crying again, and shaking, the chest tube jumping up and down like the stylus on an old, scratched 45 r.p.m. record.

"What doctor?" I asked in a thin voice. "Who's my doctor?"

"I am."

Eric. His voice pierced through my terror and he materialized at my bedside, taking my hand and squeezing it tightly.

"I just chased out a nurse," I whispered, weak and shaken, not sure if I should be embarrassed or scared. "Intravenous injection. It doesn't make sense. Had you ordered a pain injection?"

"For you? No. Definitely no."

"Can anybody else sign orders for me?"

"They shouldn't."

I didn't have to say any more. Eric turned to the cop, who shrugged his beefy shoulders and said laconically, "The nurse had identification and a written order."

"Whose name was on it?" Eric asked.

"A doctor's," said the cop stubbornly. "Can't read any of your handwriting. But it was official. I know the forms."

"They're not hard to get," Eric said, then added, "Look, sir, I don't want to tell you your job, but it sounds like that order might have been a fake. A forgery. Shouldn't we talk to the nurse?"

"I was going to do that." The cop sauntered to the door, his nightstick slapping against his fat thighs, then stopped. "I can't leave this post. I'll call for some backup."

"Maybe grab the nurse first, before she disappears."

"Nurses don't disappear."

"She said her name was Patsy," I whispered. "You need to find her." The guard looked over at me, then closed the door firmly behind him, without bothering to respond.

Silence.

Eric and Paco flanked my bed. So they'd finally met. "You have to believe me," I said, looking from one face to the other, the panic refusing to subside. "That nurse had a look in her eye. She wanted me dead." Tears were streaming down my face, and Eric handed me a tissue. I blotted at my eyes, but I knew enough not to try blowing my nose again—my lungs would probably explode.

"I don't know what's going on," Eric said soothingly, "but we'll find out. And all I care about at the moment is getting you well."

"There was something familiar about her," I said, sniffling, my chest screaming at each inhaled breath. "But I can't place it."

The guard came back in. "No nurse named Patsy on this floor," he said. "No Patricia or anything like it. That's what they say at the nurses' desk." He walked out again, as if that settled the matter.

I didn't have the energy to fight. Not yet. Eric was right—I had to get well and get out of here. I unwrapped the tourniquet from my arm and tucked it under my pillow.

"I need to know what happened to me," I said. "Medically. Give me the details. And tell me how you ended up as my doctor."

"Collapsed lung," Eric said, becoming the surgeon. "Paco brought you here by ambulance and Lasordi was on in the ER. When he saw it was you, he ignored the call list and just paged me. We stopped the bleeders and I got Rita Daley in as a pulmonary consult." The names didn't mean much to me, but they were Eric's colleagues. People he trusted. Something to make me safe.

Eric continued: ''Once we'd established the collapsed lung, I let Rita do the chest tube. But I sewed you up, babe. Forty-two stitches—did Paco tell you? And they're gorgeous.''

''I'm glad you did them,'' I said, trying to sound calm. ''But being here could kill me. They're out to get me.''

Paco and Eric exchanged a look across my bed. Indicted, stabbed, and hurting, they seemed to be telling each other. Let her rave. I shut my eyes again, and replayed the scene with the nurse on the screen of my closed eyelids. I shook my head and opened my eyes slightly, willing the images away. I shivered involuntarily, and Paco pulled the sheet closer around me. Outside, I knew there was the heat of a July day, but in here the air conditioner droned and I felt a dangerous chill. I was suddenly too exhausted to move. I stared at the floor, noticing how the filtered sunlight played against the linoleum floor, making luminescent spots where—

I grabbed Paco's arm. ''Don't move,'' I said.

''Why?''

I looked up into his startled face. ''There's a drop of liquid about eight inches from your left foot. It dropped out of the syringe—I swear it did—when the nurse was in here.''

Paco looked down, then squatted in front of the spot. ''There is a drop. You're right. I don't know what it is.''

''TPA,'' I whispered hoarsely to Eric. ''Your theory. Our theory about Hollis. If you're right, I'll bet that's what was in the syringe. Think about it. TPA and a stab wound.'' I squeezed my eyes shut, blocking out the image of myself choking on the blood filling my lungs, the doctors unable to control it . . .

Paco stood up. "TPA?" He asked. "What's that?"

"A drug that would have no place in this room," Eric said. He looked from the drop on the floor to me, and the same image must have been in his head, too. "This is one time I'd hate to be right," he said. He turned quickly and walked out of the room, hollering to the guard, "Nobody comes in! Nobody! Under any circumstances!" and slammed the door.

There was silence for a brief moment, then Paco said, "Want to tell me what's going on?"

"A theory Eric had about what killed Hollis," I said cryptically. "It's starting to make sense."

Paco seemed on the verge of losing patience. "Look, I'm not a medical genius like he is, but it would help if you filled me in a little."

Before I could respond, Eric burst back into the room, holding a fresh 3-cc syringe. "Where is it?" he asked.

Paco pointed, and they both leaned over. Eric drew back the syringe and carefully pulled up the drop of liquid, then capped the syringe and straightened up.

"I'll take it to the lab, Sarabeth. See if they can analyze it. That will give us a better idea of what's going on." He dropped the syringe into a plastic bag. "I have orders to let the police know as soon as you're able to talk."

"I can't," I said.

"I know." He stroked my forehead. "Our idiot guard outside hasn't figured out that you're lucid yet, so we can stall a little. Meanwhile, want to tell me what happened before you got stabbed?"

"I visited Ginny," I said weakly. "Just like you and I talked about. She knew of a secret file in Gus Ardsley's office that she thought had some information on Sloane Brewster. So we broke into it late last night."

Paco uttered a cry of surprise, but Eric ignored him and nodded for me to go on.

"We found files. Papers. Reports. I made copies of all the information and put them in my tote bag. I hadn't read them yet, but at first glance I couldn't figure out what they were about. Now I realize they must implicate him. Or somebody."

"Because . . ."

"Because Paco found my wallet after I was stabbed but not my tote bag. That makes it pretty clear, doesn't it? Maybe somebody followed me home from the hospital. Maybe Ginny blew the whistle, though I really don't think so. One way or another, somebody knew I was in Ardsley's office last night and wanted to get the papers away from me quickly."

"Are the originals still in the office?"

"Unless Ardsley—or whoever it was—took care of those, too."

"You think someone from the hospital attacked you to get the papers," Paco said quietly, finally understanding. "Now I know why you're so terrified. I never would have brought you here if I'd known. Obviously."

"Not your fault," Eric said, and I was surprised to see him offer Paco a look of friendly sympathy. "Doesn't sound like she's told you a lot." He leaned over the bed and kissed me on the cheek. "Here's my plan. Paco will stay with you, and I'll take this to the lab and see what they can do. Then I'll call Alicia and get her over here. Pronto.''

''Good,'' I said tremulously. Under the sheet, I felt myself shaking.

''You in pain?''

''A little.''

''Can I get you something for it?''

I shuddered. ''Answers. Is that too trite to say? That's about the only thing that will make me feel better now.''

I must have fallen asleep, with Paco holding my hand. When I woke up, he didn't seem to have moved. But Alicia was next to him, dressed impeccably as always. She was wearing taupe-colored linen pants and a beige linen shirt, both so wrinkle-free she might have been airlifted to my bedside from the dry cleaner. But her face was soft, not starchy, and there was real concern in her eyes when she asked how I was.

''I'm not sure yet.'' I tried to move and felt a throbbing pain in my back. Probably a good sign—maybe the wound was starting to heal.

Alicia wanted details. I repeated what I'd told Eric and Paco, but she knew all that—knew about the nurse and the injection and the break-in last night.

''There's a step before this that I'm missing,'' she said. ''The very basic one—what were you looking for in the office when you broke in?''

''Evidence to connect Ardsley with Sloane Brewster,'' I said. ''Because from the medical end of things, I can't come up with a natural scenario for Hollis's death that makes sense.'' I paused, my voice dry, and Alicia handed me the ice chips that someone—probably Eric—

had left by the side of my bed. Somewhat soothed, I asked, "Did Eric tell you our TPA hypothesis?"

"Yes, he did as a matter of fact."

"And what did you think?"

Alicia shrugged. "As you say, it's a hypothesis. You could probably come up with ten others."

"I couldn't. I haven't been able to come up with anything else that makes sense."

But Alicia wasn't interested in debating medical hypotheses now. Her mind was focused elsewhere. "Let's talk about those papers you got last night. Anything at all stick in your mind?"

"I wasn't paying much attention to them," I said, groaning, more from despair than pain. "I was in a hurry to get out of there, so I just Xeroxed and ran. I was planning to study them later."

Alicia allowed herself a small smile, then said, "There are a couple of ways we could go. First is to march up to Ardsley's office and ask for his cooperation. Maybe he had nothing to do with Hollis or with the stabbing, and whatever dealings he had with Sloane Brewster seemed harmless. When he sees what happened to you, he might reconsider. We talk to him and get him to share the files."

"Oh, please." I reached for more ice chips. "Ardsley hasn't wanted to give me the time of day in six months. Even if he's not involved, he wouldn't help us out. He'd wait until we leave and review the files himself. He won't help. Forget it. Next possibility."

"I call Judge Snow and get a search warrant. Or, more exactly, convince an assistant D.A.—like Justin Bryant—to get one."

"He's on the other team," I said hollowly. "Didn't he call me an 'outrage to society' in court? Didn't he ask for bail to be set at five hundred thousand dollars?"

"I told you that's all posturing," Alicia said, removing an imaginary piece of lint from her pants. "Don't tell me it got to you."

"Of course not," I said bitterly. "I love games. You should see me at Jeopardy."

"Well, good," she said, ignoring my obvious irony. "The point is that Bryant would never have brought this case himself. He got direct orders from the D.A. to prosecute—and he's had hints that the D.A. is taking *his* orders from the governor."

"How do you know that?"

"We had a drink together a couple of days after we were in court."

I must have looked startled, because Alicia smiled coyly and said, "Games, as I told you. All games. Anyway, according to Justin, Sloane Brewster is a huge supporter of Governor Boggs. Major money for his last campaign. So when Brewster's wife dies, Boggs has to do something dramatic, be the hero. What might have passed as a mistake—your mistake—in other circumstances and resulted in a malpractice suit, turns into the state galloping in and calling it murder."

It didn't feel right. Something was missing. But I said, "Okay, you get a search warrant by saying where I was last night. Then I get charged with breaking in."

"You're already charged with a lot worse."

"But Bryant knows and he makes sure a jury knows, too. How does that look?"

"Nothing's looking great, Sarabeth. But you're lying

in bed after a narrow brush with death, and the papers
that might explain why could be sitting upstairs.''

"Then let's do it."

Alicia left my room, and when she came back a short
time later, two uniformed officers were with her. Cops.
It seemed like my life was filled with policemen. I offered a silent prayer to the soul of my father, hoping
he'd forgive me.

At Alicia's direction, I told the officers exactly what
had happened the night before, and one of them pon-
derously wrote it all down in a notebook. Couldn't the
Boston police force afford tape recorders? They left and
came back; there was buzzing around my bed, and I tried
to stay awake for it, but I was overwhelmed with fatigue.
The body healing itself, I thought. I need sleep.

But I had to get up.

Alicia was sitting on my bed, and so were Paco and
Eric.

"Wake up, Sarabeth—we have the search warrant,''
Alicia said.

"Then go search."

"We need you with us. The warrant is very specific
to the files you looked at last night. Nothing else can be
touched."

I tried to focus and saw a wheelchair an arm's length
away.

"You can do it," Eric said.

"How? I can't even sit up."

What followed were enough maneuvers to launch a
military operation. Alicia stood at the IV pole. Eric laced
his fingers under me and ordered Paco to hold onto my
legs. There was tugging and yanking and Eric yelling at

Alicia to move the IV when he moved and then I was in the wheelchair, sitting up, and feeling like I'd just run the marathon and made it over Heartbreak Hill.

We were an odd parade going to the elevator—the cops, the lawyer, Eric, Alicia, and Paco, and me in a wheelchair. Somewhere along the way, Justin Bryant joined us. His suit was the same olive-green one he'd worn in court, and he looked even more scraggly. I wasn't sure why he was here or whose side he was on today.

We got off the elevator on seven, and as Paco pushed the wheelchair over the thick carpet, I decided I could get used to the seventh floor. Maybe someday this nightmare would be over, Ardsley would be out, and I'd become chairman of the department.

Maybe pigs would fly.

Another temp was sitting in Ginny's seat when we got there, and when one of the cops flashed the warrant, she looked like she'd faint.

"I'll see if he's in," she said, her voice breaking in panic, but as she reached for the phone, the cop said, "No need," and turning to the usually well-protected door, pushed it open.

I suppose all the pain of being moved in a wheelchair with forty-two sitches, an IV drip, and a chest tube were worth it to see the look on Ardsley's face when we walked in. Cops. Me in a wheelchair. People he didn't know. He was like a hibernating bear whose cave is suddenly invaded. You could almost smell the fear and rage.

The cops explained the situation and once Ardsley understood my involvement, he half rose from his chair and seemed so threatening that Paco stepped in front of me, as if to shield me with his slim body and delicate artist's hands.

The cop went to the oak cabinet and asked Ardsley to open it.

"You have the search warrant," he said testily.

"Fine," the cop said calmly. "If you don't want to open it, I can break the lock. You're correct. I have every right."

Ardsley opened his top drawer, dug inside, and pulled out the box I'd come to know last night. We'd put the key back in the right place, and he had no reaction as he tossed it onto his desk.

The cop unlocked the cabinet and turned to me. "Second drawer," I said weakly. "The red folders."

Paco pushed me closer, and the cop flipped through the file just as I had done last night. Green folders. Purple. Orange.

No red.

"Maybe Ginny put them back in the wrong place," I said hoarsely, but didn't actually mean it. I just wanted to ward off my defeat for another couple of minutes. The cop went through the drawer again slowly.

"Should I try the top drawer?" he asked.

"You can," I said, but it was useless. Ginny would have put the files back carefully last night so Ardsley wouldn't notice anything amiss.

The cop opened the top drawer and went through it, file by file. Still no red folders.

"I'm afraid there's nothing here that would match the description in the warrant," he said finally, looking from

Bryant to Alicia. "That's the extent of my authorization. I can't search further."

"Be assured there's nothing to search for," Ardsley said.

"Of course not," I said, near tears. "Someone wanted my copies badly enough to stab me, so I guess it's not a surprise that he got rid of the originals, too."

Ardsley's eyes flashed as if he were about to start screaming wildly, but instead he turned icy cold.

"The woman is pathological," he said. "There are no red folders. I couldn't tell you what unfortunate activities she's involved in that put her in this condition"—he looked me over, as if the stitches and tubes were somehow all my fault—"but it has nothing to do with anything she found in this office."

Nobody said anything.

Finally Justin Bryant asked, "Did you notice anything disturbed when you came in this morning?"

"Nothing. And my office is always locked at night."

"Anybody have a key?"

"Not anymore. My old secretary, Ginny Degley, used to, but she turned in her keys when she left. I discovered she has a drug habit and couldn't allow her to stay. Access is too easy in this position."

I made a point of not looking up, afraid I'd start to scream. *Liar, liar, liar.*

"Do you have any files pertaining to Hollis Brewster in that cabinet?"

"Of course, Mr. Byrant," Ardsley said smoothly, "and the defense lawyer has no doubt seen them, too." He went to the cabinet and pulled out an orange folder with a red label that said HOLLIS TAFT BREWSTER. "A

red label,'' he said. ''Maybe that's what started her tale
of the red folder.'' He laughed derisively. ''What's that
saying about the best defense being a good offense? I
suppose that's what the defense is trying here.''

''You'll have to forgive me, Doctor,'' Bryant said.
''Dr. Love *is* involved in a murder case that you know
about and she *was* stabbed last night. When her lawyer
told me of these claims about red folders and financial
statements and links between you and Sloane Brewster,
I didn't want to stand in the way of a search warrant.
Otherwise, her statements in court about this incident
could deflect attention from the facts we do have—con-
cerning the death of Mrs. Brewster.''

Pompous ass. Did he always talk as if he were in
court?

''I understand. I was just surprised to see all of you.''

''You had no indications about this?''

''None. I'd frankly doubt that she''—he gestured
vaguely at me, another patient in a wheelchair, not worth
naming—''was in my office last night. And if I'm
wrong about that, believe me, there's nothing she could
have found that would result in a stabbing.'' He chuck-
led, completely at ease.

Well, he'd recovered from the shock, all right. Now
I wondered if I would.

Bryant turned to Alicia. ''So much for joining you in
a search for the truth,'' he said, and walked out of the
room, as if he had settled the matter once and for all.

Our little band prepared to retreat, but at the last moment, Alicia seemed to change her mind and sauntered
back to Ardsley. She paused at his desk, then walked
around it so there was nothing between the seated doctor

and the standing lawyer, and she was peering directly down at him.

"Excuse me, Doctor, but before we came in, did you know that Dr. Love was in the hospital?"

"I—um—" He paused. "She's not on my floor."

"I understand that. I just wondered if you knew she'd been brought in last night with stab wounds."

"Word travels."

"So you knew."

"I heard something about it. No details."

"And you didn't bother to get the details?"

"No. I've been busy today."

"You wouldn't have ordered an injection for her, would you?"

A dark shadow of venom mixed with fear and anger crossed his face. "That's a ludicrous question, and I believe you've exceeded the limits of your search order." He stood up abruptly, as if ready to strike, but Alicia wasn't moving. She was tall, and they were almost eye to eye now, just inches apart.

"A nurse named Patsy," Alicia said coolly. "You should be on the lookout for her."

"Get out," he said, his eyes narrowing, his voice shaking in fury.

"And if you find her," Alicia went on pleasantly, "tell her she missed her chance. Blew it. I have a private detective outside Dr. Love's door now. I have every intention of getting her out of here alive."

IV

PACO WANTED TO stay with me for the night, but I

didn't need him. Alicia's guard outside the door made me feel safe—he was big and burly with a friendly smile, but it was pretty obvious that he got the message: Nobody coming in meant nobody. Strangers weren't the danger here—it was nurses and doctors. As far as I was concerned, the better I knew them, the more dangerous they might be to me. Paco, Eric, and Alicia were the only exceptions.

We talked about my transferring to another hospital, but Eric was against it and Alicia agreed. "We don't really know who we're fighting against or why," Eric said. "We transfer you to Mass General and who knows? Maybe there's a conspiracy that goes well beyond this hospital. Maybe Ardsley or whoever's behind this has buddies on the take there. As long as you're at P&S, I can take care of you. Period."

That word again. Conspiracy. But who were the conspirators and why were they out to get me?

Paco finally agreed to go home. He hadn't gotten any sleep the night before, rushing me to the hospital, and he seemed shaken to the bone. He gave me a soulful kiss, moved the now-working phone closer to my bed, and made me promise to call if anything at all happened.

Five minutes after he was gone, Eric came back, wheeling in a cot.

"What are you doing? Paco left."

"Yes, but I'm here."

"I thought you were sleeping in the on-call room."

"I changed my mind. You're still a sick puppy, you know. If there aren't going to be any nurses—real ones—checking on you all night, I think someone should be close."

"Great." I closed my eyes. I couldn't remember ever being in this much pain before. "If we decide to have wild sex during the night, watch out for the chest tube."

"I'll bear that in mind. Or should I call Paco and see if he'd like to come back?"

"At least you can do something about all this pain," I said, grumbling. "Paco only holds my hand and looks at me with those pathetic eyes."

Eric sat down on the edge of the cot. "I know you're in pain and I know you're cranky. But don't be so hard on the guy. He loves you very much."

"Oh, really?"

"Really. Think about it. He finds the woman he loves stabbed on the front steps of their house. He rushes her to the hospital, then discovers that she thinks people there are trying to kill her. Not easy on a guy."

"Poor Paco. And it's been such a lovely day for me."

"No, it's been a rotten day for you—I get that. I'm just saying that maybe you need to let Paco into your life a little more. He spent half the day in a daze because you hadn't been telling him what was going on. He had to play catch-up the whole day."

"Defending Paco suddenly? What, did you two bond in the ER?"

"Yeh, I suppose you could say that. I saw how concerned he was about you. He so badly wanted to do the right thing. And I thought—yup, that's what I want my best friend to have in life—someone who loves her that way, no strings attached."

"You used to refer to him as my, quote—big dick of a lover—endquote."

"Well, I hope he's still that."

"I wouldn't know." The damn chest tube was hurting so much that the very thought of moving around on a bed with or without a lover was painful.

Eric came over to the bed and checked the various tubes that were protruding from my body. I groaned in pain. "Maybe I should have let Nurse Patsy give me that injection after all," I said. "Dying sounds like a pretty good alternative right now."

"A week and you'll be bounding out of here," Eric said. "You'll forget how uncomfortable you were."

"I swear on my holy chest tube that I'll never again tell a patient that she may feel 'uncomfortable' during a procedure," I said. "What a doctor's phrase. From the patient's end, trust me, it's more like an inferno of pain."

"Lovely," said Eric, stroking my forehead. "Now get some sleep, Dante."

In the morning, Eric wanted me to eat something. He left just as I was waking up, then came waltzing back in with a tray. "Clear broth, Jello, and tea," he said. "Just what the doctor ordered."

He helped me sit up, and I stared glumly at the food. I wasn't hungry.

"If you eat, you get strong, and if you get strong, you get out of here," Eric cajoled.

"How To Get Strong on Clear Liquids," I said. "Maybe you should write a book."

"You want pudding instead? I can sneak in pudding."

"You're wonderful," I said sarcastically.

"Ah, sarcasm returns. That's a sign of healing."

My chest felt like the Brewster Tower had collapsed

on top of it. And in a way, I suppose it had.

"Paco called to see how you are. He'll be by in a little while. Alicia also called and is coming over."

"So early? What time is it?"

"Ten-thirty."

"How did I sleep so long? Right through two phone calls." I stared at him. "What did you put in my IV?"

"A Demerol drip—5 cc. You needed it. You're being brave, Sarabeth, but a collapsed lung is miserable. A little relief from the suffering seemed to be in order."

I couldn't argue. Going to sleep for five days until the chest tube was removed didn't seem like a bad idea, either.

By the time Alicia came in, twenty minutes later, I'd had two bites of jello and a sip of tea. I wasn't exactly revived, but I was ready to talk. Alicia's crisp seersucker suit—a dark green-and-gray plaid that she wore with a sleeveless, emerald-green shell—made me wish briefly that I'd been able to take off my hospital gown and put on a real robe. But it was useless. Moving that much would leave me screaming in agony.

Eric left while Alicia and I made hospital talk for a few minutes and she told me how hot it was outside. A new record high. Well I was certainly lucky to be trapped inside. "Eric says you're well enough for me to torment you with questions," she said finally.

"About?"

"The papers you Xeroxed. Something about them has to have stuck in your mind."

"I've been through kind of a lot since then."

"Let's go back over it step by step. From the first time you opened the file. Something caught your eye and made you decide to copy the pages. Maybe if you re-create the scene, you can see it again.''

I tried: *Ardsley's office at night. The lights dim, Ginny standing at the door as if half-afraid to come in. My heart beating with trepidation—wanting to find answers, but not sure what I'm seeking. And for all my bravado with Ginny, desperately not wanting to get caught. I open the file marked "Sloane Brewster," feel the excitement of having hit on something important.*

"The first sheets looked important, but I wasn't sure why," I said slowly. "There were pages and pages with numbers. They didn't seem to be budget sheets—just vertical rows of numbers added together on plain white paper. With the sums circled.''

"How big were the sums?''

"Usually in the hundreds of thousands, I think. A few well into the millions. I didn't look that closely, but that's the impression I had. On several pages, each number in the row seemed to have a two-letter code next to it. Lowercase *mc* and *ed* stand out in my mind, for some reason.''

"Initials?''

"Could be. My plan was to go home and make sense of it.''

"I know. But you didn't have the chance. What else did you see? Think of yourself back in the office. You've turned past the pages with the numbers. What then?''

"Insurance forms. The kind most doctors fill out every day.''

"What were the names on them?''

I tried to summon them up, but I couldn't. Some new

pain in my chest was getting in the way. "Lots of different names, I guess." And then taking the next step, I added, "Whether or not they corresponded with the initials on the numbers pages, I couldn't say."

"Okay, so you flipped past the insurance papers. You see those every day, so it's nothing to get excited about. But now something catches your eye . . ."

"The checks!" I exclaimed, pleased to retrieve the memory. "Actually copies of checks. Three of them. Made out from Brewster Insurance to Dr. Archibald Ardsley. One was two hundred fifty thousand dollars. I remember, because that one gave me pause. The others were less. Fifty thousand and seventy-five thousand, I think."

"Isn't that . . . shocking?"

"Not really. Doctors get checks from insurance companies, remember? That's how it works. Ardsley probably charges fifteen thousand for a C-section delivery. Three of those, and you have a check for close to fifty thousand."

"Three and a third, actually."

"Meaning what?"

She shrugged. "Do doctors typically hold on to their bills and submit them all at once to the insurance company? Or do they send them along as they get them?"

"Depends how competent their secretary is. Ginny would have been efficient enough to submit charges quickly, I suppose."

"Two hundred fifty thousand is a lot of charges to be gathering dust," Alicia mused. "Okay, let's try another possibility that would explain a big-bucks check. Ardsley's chairman of the department. Could his office be responsible for billing insurance companies for patients' hospital stays?''

"No way. There's a main billing office for in-hospital charges.''

"Okay, so let me understand this: Ardsley's office bills just his personal charges. Probably to a lot of different insurance companies. He has to keep a record of them somewhere—probably in the computer, I'd guess. But you find a folder where he collects the payments received from Brewster Insurance, and there are copies of exactly three checks, each for a very large sum. Does it sound like fee-for-service to you?''

I unwittingly took a deep breath, and the sharp intake of air made me feel as if someone were skewering my chest for a Fourth of July barbecue. "Not fee-for-service, no,'' I said. "I don't know why I didn't get that before.''

"No reason you should have. In my DiSalvo days, I learned that large, unexplained checks can mean one of three things. Bribery. Blackmail. Or hush money.''

My breathing was getting more and more labored, and whether it was from anxiety or the collapsed lung, I couldn't decide. Alicia suddenly leaned forward.

"Are you okay?''

I couldn't answer. I started wheezing, but no air came in. The room was spinning and black spots began dancing in front of my eyes. My chest was being crushed, held in a vise. I heard Alicia open the door and scream "Eric! Has anyone seen Eric!''

He must have been sitting at the nurses' station, because he was at my bed in seconds; I felt his hands and stethoscope examining me, then he was pushing my head down, and giving a sharp blow to my back, which was so horribly painful that I felt as if he were ripping out my lungs with his bare hands. I was rendered speechless, any trace of a scream caught unarticulated in my throat. The black spots turned to stars—as vivid as those in an animated cartoon when a cat runs into a tree and reels in rainbow color from the pain. I felt as flattened and airless as that cat, but then there was a loud noise, a humming, and the animators must have drawn me back to life, because I could breathe again, and the oxygen coursing back into my body seemed as lovely as champagne.

"Sarabeth, can you hear me?"

I nodded as vigorously as I could, but from Eric's reaction, the motion was barely visible.

"Sarabeth, you're okay. The danger's past. You're able to breathe. If you're in a lot of pain, just raise your index finger for me."

My hands were curled lightly into fists, and I tried to remember which was my index finger. The second! I wanted to move it, but my fingers seemed glued together, and separating one was just too hard. Anyway, I'm not in a lot of pain, I thought, as I drifted off into unconscious rest.

"Did I upset her too much?" I heard Alicia asking. "Was it the shock of what I was saying?"

"I think she could handle that. But the chest tube got clogged and the leak hasn't healed. The cavity was filling with air. Which meant neither lung could expand." So the sharp blow must have been a needle, shot to its deep mark, an emergency procedure to extract the air collecting against the chest wall. It was a procedure I had never done and probably never would. Eric, all alone, had been prepared for it and handled it in seconds.

"We need a private nurse in here," Alicia was saying to him. "You can't deal with all this by yourself anymore."

"I don't mind. She'd do the same for me."

"Of course, but a private nurse doesn't detract from that. Just another human being here for emergencies."

"Nice thought, Alicia, but no. If she wakes up and sees a nurse, she'll freak out."

Sleep and air. Sleep and air. All I needed. Whoever thought of air as being so dangerous, or so valuable? When I was well again, I would drink it by the gallon.

"Could she have died this morning?" It was Paco's voice, his face leaning over me.

"It wasn't good."

"You saved her life, didn't you?"

"I wouldn't put it that way. It was just a medical procedure that needed to be done. It's my job. I know how to do that."

"No wonder she confides in you. You're her lifeline."

"Maybe today, but not always. That's your job."

"One crisis after another, and I realize how precious she is to me. Don't let me lose her, Doc. Medically or emotionally."

"I can guarantee the medically."

"You think her emotions have drifted?"

"She's got a lot to cope with right now, and she needs practical help. I give her medical advice. Alicia gives her legal advice. From you, she gets love. Something for the spirit. In the end, I think people need that more than anything. Don't you?''

''I don't think she has any idea how much I love her.''

Breathing. I could do it. It wasn't that hard. Opening my eyes and breathing. The chest tube remained, but my lungs weren't screaming anymore. Eric smiling at me, telling me I was okay, but that I didn't need to be a hero about the pain, and he was continuing to give me Demerol. Or morphine. It didn't matter anymore. Sleep was good. Very good.

''I wanted Sarabeth to hear this, too, but I don't think she's completely conscious.'' Eric was peering over at me, looking for signs of awareness. I wanted to offer one, but nothing would come. I seemed to be swimming in gelatin.

''You got the results back from the lab?'' Alicia asked.

''Yup. It was a tiny sample, and contaminated from the floor. They're sending it out for further analysis. But it looks like it contained TPA.''

''That's the drug you two thought might have killed Hollis.''

''Yup. And it would have done the same here. With compromised clotting her chest cavity would have filled up with blood.''

''What would you have been able to do?''

''Probably nothing. Anything I tried would have been too late.''

•   •   •

Bribery. Blackmail. Hush money. No matter how many times I drifted in and out of consciousness, the words came back to me. Bribery. Blackmail. Hush money. Alicia was right that Ardsley was getting one of them. I had to figure out which.

V

A DOZEN TIMES a day in the hospital I tried playing Alicia's memory game—closing my eyes, imagining I was in Ardsley's office, seeing myself flipping through the pages in the red folder. I tried to re-create things I knew I'd seen—the memos from Doheny, the note from the governor—but they hadn't made sense to me at the time, so my brain hadn't known how to store them. The stabbing hadn't exactly helped my memory, either. Between the pain and the IV drip of 100 mg Demerol, I was lucky I remembered my own name. But Eric insisted I wouldn't get better without some relief from the pain, and I didn't disagree.

My fourth day in the hospital, Eric dropped the dosage of Demerol to 75 mg and I was disappointed.

"How about keeping it up for one more day?" I asked. "I like feeling blurry."

"No way," Eric said, smiling. "In fact, tomorrow, you're off altogether. The IV comes out and you're getting Percoset tablets. You'll probably also go home."

"I'd like to take the Demerol drip with me."

"Terrific. I've created a Demerol addict."

I stiffened, squeezed my eyes shut, then covered my face with my hands. Something was playing at the edge of my mind, but I couldn't quite grab it. "What did you say?" I whispered.

He stroked my forehead. "It was only a joke. You're fine."

"No, I mean it. Say what you said again."

"That I've created a Demerol addict."

And then I had it. I took my hands away from my face. "That happens in hospitals."

Eric looked at me quizzically, not following what I was saying.

"One of the memos in Ardsley's file. I swear, it just came back to me. I saw it and then Ginny took it to copy and I never noticed it again. But it was handwritten from Sloane Brewster to Ardsley, and it might be important."

Eric sat down on the edge of my bed, and I filled him in on what I remembered. He raised an eyebrow as I spoke, asked a question or two, and then said, "You're right. It's interesting. I should call Alicia and let her get one of her private eyes on it. See if they can dig up more information."

"I can call Alicia. You don't have to bother."

"It's not a bother. I want to help."

I slithered into the pillows, trying to get comfortable. "What do you think of her?" I asked.

"Alicia? Smart and dynamic but a real person. I'm glad she's on our side. She reminds me a lot of you, but without the drawbacks of a chest tube."

"She dresses better than I do."

"Much better. Green hospital gowns don't do anything for you."

I reached out for his hand. "Have I told you how

much I appreciate you this week? You saved my life, you lifted my spirits, you never left me. It'll take me half a lifetime to pay you back. And if I go to jail, make that a whole lifetime.''

"You don't need to pay me back. We just need to get this solved.''

"You solve it,'' I said, closing my eyes again, and enjoying the last drops of Demerol.

I left the hospital the next day, which Eric said was a new record for a collapsed lung. I wasn't going to run any marathons, but I had survived. Paco came in the morning to take me home. He drove carefully, trying to avoid bumps, and apologized every time there was an unexpected jolt. I didn't like being treated like a china doll, but he was right—each bump hurt.

I looked out the car window at the bustle of downtown Boston—people strolling, business going on, department stores opening. After five days it was hard to remember that the world was bigger than my hospital room, but life apparently was continuing and there were people who didn't know and didn't care that I'd been stabbed.

We parked, and I leaned heavily against Paco as we walked slowly toward our townhouse; he had his hand gently at my waist, not holding me up, just offering support. At the steps to the front door, I paused for breath, holding on to the curved iron railing before going up. My eye was drawn to a large, odd-shaped stain on the sidewalk; I stared at it without much thought, and then suddenly it penetrated.

"Is that—" I stopped and tried again. "Was I right there when I was stabbed?"

Paco nodded. "There was a lot of blood. I hosed it down but that little memento remains."

"You should paint it," I said, trying to sound light-hearted, but the joke fell flat and I clutched Paco's arm to go inside. My blood on the sidewalk, a few steps from my own front door. Somehow, that was the scariest image of all.

The house looked bright and neat inside and Paco kissed me at the threshold, saying, "Welcome home." The first floor seemed to be throbbing with energy, and it took me a moment to realize that his painting "A Day in the Hospital" was propped up against the far wall, dominating the entranceway and living room. Finished, the work was a masterpiece, commanding attention. I looked from the painting to Paco and back again. "You really did it," I said, meaning it this time. "It's incredibly good. Can we hang it?"

"No." Paco smiled. "I sent a Polaroid of it to the Fifty-seventh Street gallery and they're going to add it to the show next month."

"Then I'll hope it doesn't sell. I like it." I sat down, staring at it, my eye following the complex patterns and powerful colors from the red in the middle to the sun bursting through at the edges. I imagined it hanging in the chic New York gallery where rich clients would measure it and talk about colors and try to decide if it fit in with their decorating schemes. Or maybe someone would appreciate it as a true work of art. I fiddled with the ring on my finger. His show was next month. Just in time for my trial. Maybe my notoriety would help bring a good price for his pictures.

Paco went off to get me some iced tea, and I leaned over to the phone to dial Ginny's number. Both Alicia and the police had been trying to locate her since the day after I was stabbed, but she seemed to have disappeared. Now the phone rang three times, and an answering machine clicked on.

"This is Ginny Depley. I'm on vacation and won't be back until the end of the summer. No need to leave a message because I won't get it, so call back in September."

Paco came back into the room, and I hit the button for the speakerphone and redialed. "Listen to this," I said. "Tell me what you think." The phone rang again, the message picked up. It was definitely her, no doubt about that. The voice was a little shakier than usual, maybe not quite as lusty, but definitely Ginny.

". . . so call back in September."

I hit the button and broke the connection.

"Not too worried about burglars, is she?" Paco commented. "Usually you don't advertise that you'll be away for two months."

"Exactly. So you have to figure her concern isn't burglars—it's people with knives who might be looking for her. I wonder if she saw something that night in Ardsley's office that scared her, or if it was just what happened to me."

"What happened to you was enough," Paco said, stroking my hair. "Do you need some rest?"

I nodded, and he pulled down the shades in the living room, leaving me to stretch out on the couch. But I wasn't going to sleep because my mind was too busy with what lay ahead of me. In a way, the stabbing had been a distraction from the even grimmer truth—I was going on trial for murder. Alicia was requesting a postponement of the trial, but she wasn't optimistic. It was pretty obvious to me that my stabbing was somehow connected to Hollis's death, but Alicia didn't see how she was going to convince the judge of that. So we had to get back on track, preparing the defense. Break-ins at my computer and a stabbing on the street might seem relevant to me, but the real defense was simpler than that—what happened in the hospital to Hollis.

While I was in my Demerol haze, Alicia had kept busy interviewing witnesses—including the resident and intern on the floor the night that Hollis died. The intern, brand new, was terrified and clearly didn't know a thing. Jay Tucker, the resident on call, wanted to be helpful, but he hadn't been needed on the floor at all that night. He'd delivered a baby, gone to the residents' room to sleep, and then been awakened around 6 A.M. when he heard the code. He rushed to Hollis's bedside, but Ardsley was already there, in charge; a cardiologist was trying to shock Hollis's heart back into beating, two other residents were pounding her chest, and Jay was told to start an IV and get a blood transfusion going fast. They'd worked on her for an hour, but there were no signs of life.

Next on the list was Blanche Dolton, and I'd told Alicia that I wanted to be part of that conversation. She agreed. Propriety would have advised we meet in Alicia's office, but pain counted for something, so Dolton was coming to the house this afternoon at three-thirty, after her seven to three shift ended.

Alicia arrived slightly earlier, fussed about how I felt, and talked cheerfully with Paco, who eventually excused himself, saying he'd go upstairs to paint. I raised an eyebrow, knowing he wasn't working on anything at the moment, but he just looked away. This wasn't a meeting he wanted to attend.

The doorbell rang just as the grandfather clock in the living room was striking the half hour, and Alicia got up to answer it. Blanche Dolton came in, still in her nurse's uniform, her features pinched as she nodded a curt greeting. I figured she was in her mid-fifties; her eyes were dull, and deep lines ran from her nose to her mouth, giving her the look of a ferocious animal. In the hospital I'd always thought of her as tall—perhaps because she was usually shouting and commanding attention—but here in my living room, I realized she was shorter than I, and squat. Her face was sweaty from being out in the July sun, and her skin was splotchy, white patches that suggested vitiligo, mixed with heat-induced red blotches. Alicia waved her to a chair, and she sat down stiffly, running her fingers through her short, iron-gray hair.

Blanche Dolton looked around the room, taking in Paco's painting propped against the wall and our eclectic furnishings. The room was modern, creative, original. Not Blanche's style at all. She shifted uneasily in her chair, probably wishing she'd insisted on holding this meeting on some more neutral ground.

"We appreciate your coming," Alicia began pleasantly, reaching for the legal pad and notebook she'd left on a side table. "As you know, we'll be taking depositions later this week for Dr. Love's trial. What we're doing today is a more casual conversation that's not on any formal record. However, if we ask the same questions at the deposition, those are public records."

Blanche Dolton nodded again. "I said I'd talk to you, but I don't have anything to say that the police don't already know. I gave my statement about Mrs. Brewster's death the first day."

"I understand that." Alicia opened up a notebook. "Let's just run through a few things and make sure I have the facts right. First off, you were working the overnight shift that July fourth weekend. Not your usual shift, but several people were out on vacation and you were filling in. Working a double shift, I believe."

"That's correct."

"It was a light night, and you were getting by with just you and a student nurse on the floor. I know you've gone through this before, but would you mind repeating to me what occurred on the floor Sunday night, July fourth, before you found Mrs. Brewster?"

"As you say, I've already told it."

Blanche Dolton could make me mad just by being in the room and now I wanted to spit and ask her why she'd come if she wasn't talking. But Alicia, ever cool, just said, "Okay, let me run through it." She looked down at her notes. "You explained to the police that when maternity patients have rooming-in, you don't typically check on them during the night unless they ring a call button, correct?"

"Correct."

"And Mrs. Brewster had rooming-in—that is, she had her baby in the room with her."

"Correct."

"So after Dr. Love left that night, you went in just once."

"Correct."

"What did you say to her?"

Blanche started to answer "Correct," then must have realized it wasn't going to work this time, so she paused. "It's been some time, of course, but I seem to remember that I asked her if she'd like me to take the baby to the nursery for the night. She'd had a long day, and I thought she could use some sleep. I'm not a great fan of this rooming-in. The new mothers go home fast enough these days. Let them rest the one night they have nurses to help them."

"And what was her reaction?"

"She wanted her baby with her. In fact, she asked me to push the bassinet closer to the bed, which I did."

"Did you offer her anything in the way of food? Drink? Pain medicine?"

"No. We're not running a restaurant, you know. And her doctor"—Blanche looked at me but apparently couldn't bring herself to say my name—"hadn't ordered anything for pain."

"Something else you disagree with?" Alicia asked.

"Pain medicine has its place," Blanche said. "All this concern about being natural and not using drugs during a delivery may not be the best thing for the mother, in my opinion. Afterwards, you take something if you need it. A lot of doctors forget to prescribe for the women who need it, and then there's nothing I can do.''

"Did you have the feeling that something should have been prescribed for Mrs. Brewster?"

"Not really. She seemed comfortable."

"In good spirits?"

"That's not something I judge."

What a relief, I thought. Blanche Dolton wouldn't recognize good spirits if they hit her in the face.

"Did you take her temperature and blood pressure when you went in?"

"No."

"What time would you say you checked on Mrs. Brewster?"

"Just after eleven, when I first came on duty. The doctor''—again she nodded at me—''had left before I arrived. I couldn't say when she left.''

Alicia flipped a few pages in her notebook. "Dr. Love left the hospital about quarter of eleven. The senior nurse on the previous shift says she checked Mrs. Brewster as soon as the doctor left to make sure she was comfortable and settled. Were you aware of that?''

The red blotches on Blanche's face deepened. "I don't remember.''

"Do nurses leave notes for each other when the shifts change?''

"Of course."

"Do you talk to each other?"

"Yes."

"So I'm going to draw the conclusion that when you went in to Mrs. Brewster you knew that the nurse on the previous shift had been in there about twenty to thirty minutes earlier. That would explain why you didn't take her temperature or blood pressure. But I still don't understand the reason you had for going in the room in the first place.''

''I was going to be on the floor for two shifts. That's sixteen hours. I wanted to make sure everything was under control. I believe in having a controlled, well-run floor.''

''That's good.'' Alicia offered the slightest trace of a smile. ''So rather than just trusting the previous nurse, you made sure Mrs. Brewster was well yourself, but you didn't administer anything to her?''

''Correct.''

Alicia sighed and studied her notes. ''According to the police report, you didn't have any reason to go into the room again during the night. You probably wouldn't have gone in until about seven, but an hour before that you heard a baby crying.''

''The student nurse heard the baby,'' Blanche said, correcting Alicia. ''She came to me at about six A.M. to say that the baby in Room 501—Mrs. Brewster's room—had been crying for a long time and perhaps we should see if the mother needed some help. So I went in, and that's when we found Mrs. Brewster dead.''

''Let's back up a second. Why would the student nurse come to you, the head nurse, if she heard a baby crying? Wouldn't it be her job to poke her head in and check for a problem?''

Blanche seemed momentarily nonplused. ''Mrs. Brewster was a very well-known woman and a large contributor to the hospital. The student nurse didn't want to do anything incorrect around her.''

"Had you warned the nurses not to go in there? Or at very least to check with you before they disturbed Mrs. Brewster?"

"Perhaps. I don't recall."

"Well, I'm sure one of the other nurses will recall," Alicia said, the first note of testiness creeping into her voice. "Now, another fine point I want to clear up. The student nurse tells you a baby is crying, and instead of having her check on it, you go running to the room yourself. Is that unusual?"

"I've already told you that Mrs. Brewster was an important woman."

"So she got special treatment."

"Everybody on my floor gets special treatment. In this case, we weren't terribly busy and I thought I'd see for myself."

Alicia fiddled with her pen, jotting a note on her copy of the police report. "Okay, so we have a baby crying. A student nurse who doesn't want to—or has been directed not to—check on the problem herself. You march with her to Room 501, and open the door. Can you describe what you found?"

Blanche Dolton shuddered slightly, but this time didn't suggest Alicia read it herself from the police report. "Mrs. Brewster was lying in blood-soaked sheets, clearly unconscious. I stood at the door for a moment, stunned, and then tried to assess the situation; I tried for a pulse and didn't feel anything, so I immediately called a code four."

Alicia looked down again, and the silence in the room was palpable. The grandfather clock ticked loudly; the only other sound was my too-labored breathing. Blanche

Dolton didn't seem nervous. If this had been a lie-detector test, she would have passed so far. But Alicia wasn't done.

"Let's back up a step again. Did you see anybody go into Mrs. Brewster's room at any time during the night? That is, at any time between eleven o'clock or so when you left her and the early morning hour when you saw her again?"

"No." She crossed and recrossed her legs.

"Did you leave the floor at any time during that shift?"

"No."

"Is it possible that anybody went into her room without your noticing?"

This time she seemed to take a breath. "Possible, but not likely."

"When you called the code, who arrived?"

"Dr. Ardsley was the first one there. He happened to be on the floor. Several residents and interns came after that. I had my nurses available, but there was very little we could do. The code continued for about an hour. I suspect they realized that it was futile long before that, but with a young person, doctors don't want to give up."

"After it was over, did Dr. Ardsley give you any instructions? Tell you what you should say about the events that had just occurred?"

Again the deep breath. "No. He only said that he was taking the chart and would handle any investigations and questions."

"You've known Dr. Ardsley a long time."

"He's been at the hospital for twenty-five years, I

believe. I've been here just over twenty. I have the
greatest respect for him.''

"Enough to lie for him?"

"Of course not."

Alicia leaned forward, caught Blanche's eye, and
wouldn't look away. "Part of Dr. Love's defense will
be determining what happened during the night that Mrs.
Brewster died. A woman bleeds to death in a hospital,
fifty feet from a nurse's station, and nobody knows until
it's too late. How likely is that? Why didn't she ring her
call bell? Why did nobody go in? These are among the
questions we're looking to answer. Let's say—just hypothetically—that somebody didn't want you to go in.
Had ordered you to ignore all signs of trouble. Now let's
say—again hypothetically—that person was Dr.
Ardsley. How long would you be willing to protect
him?''

"This is ridiculous.'' Blanche stood up abruptly.
"I'm a nurse. A professional. Doctors like to think they
have nurses under their thumb, but that's not the case. I
do what's right and nobody could tell me to do otherwise.''

"Even if he were blackmailing you? By threatening
to expose your Demerol addiction?''

"What?'' It was more a shocked gasp than a question.
Blanche reached back for the arm of her chair, steadying
herself, then slowly sank back down.

"We have records here from the Newton-Wellesley
Hospital,'' Alicia said quietly. "You were taken to the
ER there three months ago. Your roommate, Lydia
Valen, brought you in, unconscious, and said you'd suf-
fered a seizure. The emergency room doctors did a CAT
scan for a brain tumor and checked for metabolic ab-

normalities. Nothing. Also no trauma or stroke. But when they ran a routine toxicology screen, they came up with high levels of meperidine circulating in the blood stream. They concluded the seizure was a Demerol overdose. Probably a sign of a serious addiction."

"The tests were wrong," Blanche said, choking on her words. "Toxicology makes mistakes. It's not a good hospital."

"But that's where your roommate took you. Strange, since you live five minutes from P&S. But maybe she knew, and she didn't want any records turning up at your own hospital. Unfortunately, you signed the insurance form that had the diagnosis on it."

"I'm not discussing this," Blanche said.

"Let me explain this again, Ms. Dolton," Alicia said quietly. "If we don't get satisfactory answers today, we'll be bringing this up again at the deposition. You're under oath there, and the answers are public record."

"My lawyer will object to the questions, then. They have nothing to do with Mrs. Brewster's death."

"Quite the contrary. You've been at the hospital over twenty years. You must be near retirement. But as at all hospitals, there are strict rules about drug use at P&S. Stealing or abusing a prescription drug is grounds for immediate dismissal. You'd probably lose your pension. If somebody at the hospital knew, they'd be holding a mighty sword over your head."

Blanche got up again and this time walked over to the window her back turned to us.

"We can settle this before the deposition," Alicia said again.

Blanche turned back around. "Nobody at the hospital

knew. Dr. Ardsley didn't know and he never tried to
blackmail me or anything like you're saying. Your
whole premise is wrong, so there's no need to bring it
up again."

"Unless we have some better answers, I'm afraid we
will."

"Now that certainly sounds like blackmail."

Alicia shrugged. Her warm, understanding demeanor
was gone. "A woman is dead, and you may know something about it. I'm just pointing out that if you have
personal reasons for not talking, you can forget them.
The Demerol addiction is going to become very public
knowledge as we make our case. If Ardsley wasn't holding it over you, you'd better come up with some better
explanations for what happened that night."

Blanche suddenly laughed, a nasty, angry sound.
"I'm not the one on trial here and I didn't do a single
thing wrong that night. Your client killed Mrs. Brewster
with her arrogance—thinking she knows better than all
the other doctors. That's it. That's why she's on trial for
murder."

"No, she's been framed for this murder. Someone entered Hollis Taft Brewster's room during the night. On
your shift. And gave her an injection that killed her.
Either you saw someone go in or you did it yourself."

"You sound awfully sure about that."

"I am."

"You don't have a shred of proof."

"But you're going to tell us the truth at some point—
I know it. Not out of any great affection for Dr. Love—
because you don't have any. But because you don't want
the real murderer to get off. You're a nurse, and you've

had the right values for twenty years. So you made a mistake and you got hooked on Demerol. It happens to nurses and it happens to doctors and it happens to all sorts of people. That's not a reason to blow everything you've always stood for.''

Blanche's squat body was seething with anger and fear. ''Tell me why you think Dr. Ardsley knows about the Demerol.''

Alicia took a moment, obviously trying to decide whether or not to answer. ''I'm asking you to be truthful, so I'll do the same. We found a note to him.''

''From who?''

''That I can't say.''

''Now I think you're lying.''

''I'm not,'' Alicia said. ''He knows. Think it over and call me when you want to talk. You have a week.''

''I'll remember that,'' Blanche said, storming toward the front door. ''And I'll also let myself out.''

The door slammed behind her, and Alicia casually checked the front window to make sure Blanche was really leaving, and then locked and bolted the door.

''So what do you think?'' she asked, turning back to me.

''You have good detectives,'' I said. Blanche's anger had penetrated my skin and left me quivering. For the moment, I couldn't talk about the woman herself, and sidestepped Alicia's question. ''I don't know how much we're paying these private eyes, but they're good. I liked the facts you had about the Demerol addiction.''

''They are good, but this one wasn't too hard. We traced it through the hospital insurance policy. The whole staff is covered by Brewster Managed Care, and

those records are easier to get than you'd think." She
smiled, then sat down next to me. "But tell me your
take on Blanche."

I sighed, realizing I couldn't avoid the conversation.
"Ardsley didn't set her up or use her to kill Hollis," I
said. "I'm pretty sure of that now. Blanche was stunned
to think he might know about the Demerol problem. On
the other hand, I'd bet anything that she saw someone
go into Hollis's room. She gave you a flat 'no' when
you asked, but she sure looked uncomfortable."

"Agreed. She's a dominating control freak, and probably a lesbian, not that it matters. But I can't see her
being willing to give a lethal injection, no matter how
much she's been threatened. Covering up for somebody—yes, she'd do that."

"Now we just have to find out who went into that
room. Only other person who might know is that student
nurse."

"I've tried that route, but somehow all the nursing
records from July fourth are missing, and nobody knows
who was on the floor with Blanche. I've asked for police
cooperation, but they say it's not relevant. The case
against you doesn't have anything to do with there being
other people on the floor."

"Maybe Eric can find out," I said, going over to the
phone to call him. "One of his great strengths is honing
in on nurses."

Alicia laughed as I dialed, but I was right. When I
filled Eric in on the conversation with Blanche Dolton,
he took on the student-nurse job with enthusiasm. In less
than twenty minutes, he called me back.

"The student nurse's name is Lori Meadows," he

said, when I picked up the phone. "I have her home number, and I already called it. Her mother answered and said she's working at Hyannis Hospital for the rest of the summer."

"Hyannis Hospital? On Cape Cod?"

"Yup. It was kind of unexpected, but it's part of the school program, too, and they transferred her there on July sixth for a twelve-week stint. She's doing the three to eleven P.M. shift this week." He paused. "How are you feeling?"

"Not bad. Worry seems to be overriding the pain at the moment."

"If you can handle a car ride, I'll come by within the hour. We'll drive down there and talk to her when she gets off her shift."

"I'll see you in an hour. And just curious—how'd you get her number?"

"Jay Tucker." He laughed. "I know you think I'm bad, but Jay's the real specialist. Never met a nurse he didn't like. I was worried that a student nurse might have been too young for him, but not to worry. He knew exactly who I meant and had her name and number in his Wizard."

I hung up and repeated the conversation to Alicia, asking if she wanted to come with us.

"I can't tonight—I have a big business meeting that I shouldn't miss. But maybe we should send one of the private eyes down instead. Save you the trip."

"Eric and I will get more out of her," I said. "Two docs just casually talking won't be as intimidating."

"It's all right with me," Alicia said, "but can you handle it?"

I just shrugged. I was handling a lot of things I'd never thought I could.

By the time Eric arrived, I'd taken a brief nap, washed my face, and swallowed two Percosets. I wasn't going to worry about how I felt. There'd be time to recover later, when this was all over.

Eric drove a Yugo, which was cheaper than my Honda and just about as uncomfortable.

"This is enough to make me wish I were old and rich," Eric said as we cruised down Route 3 and I clenched my teeth to keep from crying out in pain. "I need a Lexus. Or a Cadillac."

"Not your style," I said. "Maybe a Humvee."

Traffic was relatively light until we hit the Sagamore Bridge going into the Cape and finally swung onto Route 6, the Mid-Cape highway. It was midweek, but everyone in Massachusetts must have been vacationing on the Cape. Some vacation. We sat in bumper-to-bumper traffic, barely moving, listening to horns blowing. I knew there was an ocean somewhere around, but all I could see were fast-food restaurants and miniature golf courses. Eric apologized for not taking 6A, the winding country road that ran parallel to the highway and was much prettier, but usually slower. It didn't matter. I wasn't much in the mood for meandering through old New England towns, either. We finally turned off Route 6, heading south to Hyannis, and the traffic eased a little. We stopped at a nondescript seafood restaurant for dinner, jostled our way through a big crowd of vacationers drinking beer and frothy drinks with cherries at the bar, and sat down at a table by the window, overlooking the parking lot. The clam chowder, at least, was good—

thick and creamy, and actually tasting like it contained
something other than potatoes. Eric followed his soup
with fish and chips, which he covered with tartar sauce
and devoured quickly. I decided to play it safe, ordering
another cup of soup and calling it dinner.

It was only about nine-thirty when we arrived at
Hyannis Hospital, but I was so tired that I would have
gladly crawled into one of the hospital beds and spent
the night. Eric installed me in a reasonably comfortable
chair in the lobby while he went in search of Lori Meadows. I picked up the nearest magazine which happened
to be a *Vogue*, and flipping through the pages, wondered
why all the models were wearing winter clothes. I turned
back to the cover and saw it was the February issue.
February. If only I could relive the last six months of
my life, from the very first day I met Hollis. I was more
convinced than ever that someone had killed her. But
who? And why? In all our visits together, there had to
be a hint of what was to come. There was the secret deal
she'd mentioned, between Brewster Managed Care and
P&S. I still hadn't heard anything about it. But even if
it took place, what could that have to do with Hollis?
Beautiful, rich Hollis who always seemed vaguely troubled. Yet she had never seemed happier than the day she
came with me to the clinic in Roxbury. Hollis was looking for something, but I was never quite sure what.

"Sarabeth?" Startled out of my reverie, I jumped in
my seat and realized Eric was back, along with a sweet-
looking young nurse whose nametag said LORI MEAD-
OWS. So he'd found her. No wonder Jay Tucker had
taken her phone number. She was small and slender,
with peaches-and-cream skin set off by curly black hair

cut to just below her chin. She had huge brown eyes and her smile was warm and friendly.

I stood up and introduced myself, shaking her hand.

"Lori said we don't have to wait until eleven to talk," Eric said. "She can take a break now."

"Let's go to the nurses' lounge," she suggested, and we followed her across the lobby to an unmarked door that she opened with a key. Stepping inside, I immediately decided that the nuns were right, and I should have been a nurse, after all. The walls were painted pale pink, and there was a thick carpet on the floor; pastel-colored sofas and white wicker tables and chairs made the room look more like the lobby of a fancy Cape Cod hotel than a spot for nurses to gather. I thought of the rows of lockers and benches in the doctors' lounge at P&S and noticed that here there were private dressing rooms in the back, separated by ruffled chintz curtains.

"Nice place," Eric said. "Good hospital?"

"Probably not the same caliber as P&S, but I like it," Lori reported, sitting down on one of the pastel sofas. "The nurses seem much gentler. Not quite as rough with the patients as they are at P&S."

"They're not all as bad as Blanche Dolton," I promised her.

Lori blushed slightly. "I don't have anything against Nurse Dolton. It just happens that a lot of obstetrics nurses have been around forever and don't like anything to change. You learn that. I didn't challenge anything Nurse Dolton told me to do, even when I thought she was wrong."

Eric had already filled her in on why we had come, so it didn't require much explanation to bring the conversation around to the night of July 4. Lori confirmed that just she and Nurse Dolton had been together on the maternity floor that night, and she didn't have any trouble remembering what the directives had been.

"I was absolutely not to go into Mrs. Brewster's room," Lori said. "That wasn't too surprising, though. Whenever there's an important patient, the head nurse likes to do everything. I've seen it before." She had the air of a young woman who understands that she's a lot wiser than many of her elders.

She confirmed the story of hearing the baby crying in Room 501 and going to Nurse Dolton to ask what to do. As she remembered it, the head nurse had gone ahead, then hollered for her just moments after she opened the door. When Lori started to run toward the room, she'd been told to call for help and put out a code alert.

"What an awful experience for you," Eric said compassionately.

"I just wish I could have done something," Lori said. "I felt kind of useless. I stood around the room during the code, waiting for somebody to need me, but nobody did. Then I started to wonder if it was my fault. I was supposed to be watching for call buttons during the night. While I was standing in the room, I happened to notice that Mrs. Brewster's button was disconnected—and not up at the head of the bed, which is where they usually get unplugged, but at the outlet way under the bed. I don't know how that could have happened. Maybe one of the doctors stepped on it during the code. But I don't think so. It was probably like that all night. So if she'd tried to ring it, I wouldn't have known, anyway."

Eric and I exchanged a glance, which Lori misread.

"I'm not trying to excuse myself, I'm really not. I just really don't think there was anything I could have done."

"Of course not," Eric said quickly. "I hope nobody chastised you about that night."

"No," Lori said. "Nobody's said a word. In fact, you're the first people who've even asked to talk to me. But I kind of thought that my transfer had something to do with it. The Cape's nice and all that, and it is summertime, but it's a little like being sent off to the boonies." She smiled sweetly and I saw Eric looking at her with a gleam in his eye. Damn. If Jay Tucker didn't call Lori soon, Eric was going to move right in. Lori seemed to pick up his interest, because she turned vaguely flirtatious, smiling a little more than the occasion warranted. I wanted to scream at them to cut it out, but then I realized it was okay—trying to please would just turn Lori more voluble.

"I have a very important question for you," Eric said, leaning close to the young nurse, and looking at her as if she were the fountain of all knowledge. "Did you see Nurse Dolton going into Mrs. Brewster's room any time during the night—before you told her about the crying baby?"

Lori squinted her eyes and seemed to think about it hard. "I really don't think so. She went to a couple of rooms where people called, and she took one baby that was supposed to be rooming-in back to the nursery. But I think the only person who went into Mrs. Brewster's room was the private nurse."

"The private nurse?" It was all I could do not to scream.

"Yes. I thought it was kind of strange because usually a private nurse is on for a whole shift. But she came and went pretty quickly."

"Can you describe her?" I could tell that Eric was trying not to sound too excited.

"I didn't really pay that much attention. She was about my size, I guess, with dark hair like me, only it was very straight. And very dramatic. She had a mole on her cheek kind of like Cindy Crawford and really thick glasses. I remember thinking that she'd probably be really pretty if she got contact lenses."

Eric looked at me again and I nodded. It was the same description I'd given of the woman who had come into my room in the hospital. The same "nurse." The same injection. I felt a surge of adrenalin. We were on to something.

"Did you talk to this private nurse?" I asked.

"No."

"Did Nurse Dolton see her?"

"I guess so." Lori looked confused, not sure why her report of the visitor had generated so much interest.

"Have you ever seen her before or since?" I asked.

"I don't think so. She was kind of distinctive. I'd probably recognize her if I saw her again." Lori looked at her watch, then at Eric. "I really like talking to you, but I have to get back to my floor. We could continue this at eleven, if you want."

Eric clearly wanted to. "It would be nice," he said slowly, "but Dr. Love is just out of the hospital and needs to get some rest. Maybe you could give me a number where I could reach you down here?"

"Sure." When Eric proffered a pen and a scrap of

paper from his pocket, she scribbled down a number. "I'm staying at a nurses' residence for the hospital. It's really nice, too. From the top floor you can see the Kennedy compound in Hyannisport. If you're down for a weekend, I'd love to show you around."

Eric would have taken her up on it immediately, but my presence seemed to be putting a damper on his lust. He gave her his phone number, and told her to call immediately if she thought of anything else about that night that might be relevant.

She giggled. "I'll try, but I've already told you everything I know. And Nurse Dolton wouldn't be happy. Right before I was leaving that morning, she grabbed me and said, 'Nurse Meadows!' " Lori imitated Blanche's low, gruff voice to perfection. "She said, 'Nurse Meadows! Don't forget the nurse's code. "What you see here, what you hear here, when you leave here, let it stay here." ' And I said, 'Nurse Dolton, I've known that since I was a fourteen-year-old candy striper.' " Lori laughed, a sweet, ringing sound. "I'm not sure what she was afraid of my saying. I didn't really see anything that could be very helpful to you. I'm sorry."

I resisted telling Lori that she was the first person who had given us any important information. I figured that Eric would give her all the praise she needed when he escorted her back to the floor.

VI

WE DROVE BACK to Cambridge that night, Eric insisting that he wasn't tired and didn't need to stop at one of the endless motels that lined Route 6.

"Besides, what would Paco say if we shacked up for the night?" he asked.

"He'd know you were only using me until little Lori went out with you," I retorted.

"Hey," Eric said lustily. "You've got to admit she was terrific."

"Big brown eyes, nice body, and a sweet smile," I said. "Is that your definition of terrific?"

"I meant her information was terrific," Eric said, pretending I misunderstood him.

Now there I couldn't disagree, but I was also too tired to talk about it. An unplugged call button. A visit from a private "nurse." The thoughts went around and around in my head, humming along with the highway.

"If we're not going to stop at a motel, I'm going to fall asleep right here," I said. "I can't keep my eyes open any longer."

"Want to go in the back and lie down?"

"No. This is fine." I reclined the seat as much as I could, which wasn't very much, but it didn't matter, because we were still on Route 6 and Eric was still talking about Lori when my eyes started to close.

It was one or two in the morning when Eric dropped me off, literally handing me over to Paco, who came outside in cut-off jeans and a bare chest to meet us, and half carried me up the stairs and into the house. "A message from Alicia," he whispered, as I fell asleep for the second time that night. "The hearing on the trial postponement is tomorrow morning at eleven."

"You'll have to wake me up," I groaned.

But in fact I was up by eight, feeling better than I ever thought I would. My back was sore from four hours in the car, but Lori's information had energized me. We were on the right track. That realization carried me through my preparations for the morning's court session. Remembering Alicia's advice, I tied my hair back and put on a navy linen dress with white piping that I found in the back of my closet. The last time I'd worn it was to my college graduation. I stared at myself in the mirror, trying not to get depressed. I was looking for answers, but I had to spend a morning in court, playing more games.

Alicia had offered to pick me up in her BMW, and I agreed. As we drove to the courthouse, I told her about the meeting with Lori, and she said only, "Interesting. Good work."

"Do you think it's worth mentioning today?" I asked, thinking of the closed-session hearing with Judge Snow.

"Absolutely not. It has no relevance."

"What do you mean? Isn't it more proof that there might have been something strange going on that night?"

"It won't sell. Look, I'm going to be arguing that the attack on you proves there's more evidence to be unearthed. I'm asking for a two-month delay so detectives can examine hospital records. But the D.A. is going to make mincemeat out of it. I don't have any way of proving that there's a link between the trial and the stabbing."

We went to the judge's chambers, where I'd been expecting dark-wood paneling and brocade draperies. I was wrong. The office was in the basement of the courthouse and looked like it was made of cinder blocks. The one window had bars over it, suggesting that Judge Snow

understood what it was to send someone to jail. A half
worn-out Oriental rug was thrown over the floor, and
some effort had been made to put the most threadbare
parts under the desk. If Judge Snow had any personal
life, it wasn't obvious. There wasn't a family picture in
sight, and the only decorations on the wall were diplomas from Boston University and Harvard Law School.
A bookcase filled with leather-bound law treatises
loomed over one end of the room, and stuck in a corner
of one shelf were two framed photos—one showing a
much younger, robed Judge Snow shaking hands with
Mayor Ray Flynn, and the other, snapped more recently,
showing the judge in street clothes smiling alongside
Governor Boggs.

There was no casual chatter to break the ice, no back-
room bantering. Judge Snow invited us in, then sat silently at her desk working on an opinion until Justin
Bryant came in. He looked sallower and sallower each
time we met. His tie was a sickly yellow and the suit he
was wearing today was nominally khaki but had a green-
ish tinge that cast an ugly pallor over his skin. Maybe
sitting in the sun was bad for your health, but he needed
those ultraviolet rays badly.

Alicia, competent and forceful as ever, outlined our
position. The night I was knifed outside our home, I was
in possession of sensitive papers which had since disappeared. Common sense suggested that the attackers
had been after those papers.

"And there's more," Alicia said, standing very close
to the judge's desk, her voice hushed. "Information I'm
afraid the prosecutor doesn't yet have." She nodded at
Bryant. "A lab is currently analyzing the substance that

an unidentified nurse tried to inject in my client her first day in the hospital. From the early reports we have, it's a substance that could have resulted in her death.''

She paused for effect, but there was nobody to appreciate the dramatics. And it all sounded so correct and legal the way she said it that I wanted to scream out Eric's view: That the syringe wielded by ''Nurse Patsy'' had contained TPA. That I was targeted for a gruesome death. And that Hollis had died that way, too.

Judge Snow, taking notes on a legal pad, looked up over the top of her reading glasses. ''How do these attacks bear on the charges for which Dr. Love has been indicted?'' she asked. ''What is the bearing on the trial date?''

''Dr. Love has been falsely accused,'' said Alicia. ''The individuals who were truly responsible for the death of Hollis Taft Brewster are frightened. That's why they're violently attacking my client. We need time to find them and prove their involvement.''

Justin Bryant, looking as if he'd just discovered dog excrement on his shoe, half rose. ''Your Honor, may I respond?''

''Go ahead, Counselor.''

''Let me say first that I'm sorry that Dr. Love was stabbed.'' He glanced at me with contempt, not looking sorry at all. ''Unfortunately, such things happen when a single woman is walking alone on the streets of Boston at two in the morning. As is appropriate, the police are investigating the incident. When they find someone to charge, we will go forward.'' Dismissing me, he took a step toward Judge Snow.

''A few days ago, at the defense's request—and with

my agreement—you issued a search warrant for Dr. Archibald Ardsley's office. You issued the warrant because Dr. Love claimed she had seen certain papers in the esteemed chairman's office the night of the attack on her. So we went in—and found nothing. Nothing even close to what Dr. Love described.'' He paused to scratch the bridge of his nose, squeezing his eyes shut as if reliving the embarrassment of that moment. ''Now she believes a nurse tried to kill her. But we don't know why. And she'd like two months to find out.'' He offered a long, unpleasant-sounding snort. ''Your Honor, I believe this is what is known as a fishing expedition. I haven't heard a shred of evidence to support any of these allegations. This is a straightforward case in which a doctor has been accused of wrongdoing. It's not an episode of Perry Mason. Postponing the trial would be a mockery.''

I looked helplessly at Alicia. Did everything get distorted once you entered a courtroom? But Alicia, used to all this, was looking at the judge.

''Your Honor?''

Judge Snow nodded at her. ''Please.''

''Coincidence is always a possibility, Judge Snow. But when you take these events together, a very clear pattern emerges. We can't ignore that.''

''A pattern?'' Bryant retorted. ''The only pattern is fantastical allegations that don't stand up to any serious scrutiny.''

''No,'' said Alicia, not raising her voice. ''The pattern is a concerted effort to make Dr. Love a scapegoat, at any cost.''

''Don't try to turn this into organized crime, Counselor." Bryant spit the word. "I know you won that case, but this one's different. We're talking about a single incompetent doctor who's been charged with killing a patient."

"You're wrong, Counselor." Alicia spit right back. "This was a very organized crime. If we dig deeply enough, we're going to find Dr. Love framed by an entire hospital that's spinning out of control. As for your reference, I thought you might have learned something from that case."

Judge Snow didn't have a gavel handy, but she pounded her fist on the desk. "Ms. Rice, Mr. Bryant. You are not permitted to make personal attacks on each other in these chambers. If either of you have any further evidence to present to me, please do so. Otherwise, this session is over."

It was over.

After we left Judge Snow's chambers, Alicia drove me home, steering her BMW competently through the winding streets of Boston. We spent five minutes analyzing the meeting with Judge Snow, but there wasn't much to say.

"One thing you learn as a lawyer is that everything is subject to interpretation," Alicia said, making a quick right turn at a red light. "It's pretty clear to us that someone is trying to hurt you and get you to shut up. But there's no hard evidence. Bryant was right about that. So it ends up being all posturing, as I've told you before."

"All that posturing is why doctors hate lawyers, you

know. We like things black and white. Either it works or it doesn't. Either it's true or it's not.''

"But life is endless shades of gray," Alicia said. She was briefly silent as she negotiated an intersection where cars coming from five different directions all converged. "Only in Boston," she muttered.

"So what's our next step?" I asked, when she was safely back on a main road that went in only one direction.

"You did a good job with Lori. We obviously need to find that dark-haired nurse you both saw, but I don't know where to begin on that, do you?"

I didn't, and it was frustrating, because I was the one who had seen her, and that meant I should be able to identify her. I had the feeling I could—if only I could get on the right track. I needed a hint, but there was nobody who could supply one.

"While we're working on that, I'd say the most important thing is to find Ginny," Alicia said. "That woman knows something, which is why she's scared to death. But it's odd that she's disappeared."

I thought about the message on Ginny's machine and realized that she wouldn't be leaving any obvious trails to follow. "She still hasn't turned up?" I asked, knowing the answer.

"No. The police say they're looking, but who knows? The private detective I put on it says her apartment is orderly and looks like she intended to leave. No evidence of violence. He's turned up one sister in New Hampshire who says she hasn't heard from Ginny in weeks. He wasn't convinced, though, so I told him to take a trip up and talk to her."

My mental calculator began ticking off the bucks. A two-hour drive to New Hampshire, an hour investigating once he was there, two hours driving back. How much did these private eyes cost, anyway? Fifty bucks an hour? Maybe we'd find out the truth in the end and I'd be free—but I'd also be broke.

"Anyone you know who might be in touch with Ginny?" Alicia asked.

I thought about it for a minute. "Ardsley, of course. But my guess is that he's the reason she's hiding." I paused, running through other people I knew at the hospital. Everyone liked Ginny and confided in her. But to whom would she tell her own secrets? Not the doctors. Maybe one of the other secretaries.

"Ginny once mentioned a happy group of adulterous couples who would go on trips together. Ginny had Ardsley and they'd slip away with John Franklin—my partner—and Juliette. One of his nurses. I got the feeling that Ginny and Juliette talked a lot together. About their men, at least."

"Good. I'll have one of the private detectives go talk to her."

"She's not going to tell him anything."

"I'll have them send a woman detective."

"It doesn't matter." I tried to picture the ever-controlling Juliette revealing a secret to a detective. "Juliette's coy and plays her cards very close to the vest. Even with me, she'd say exactly what John Franklin told her to, and nothing more."

"So what do you suggest?" An edge of impatience crept into Alicia's voice. "Ginny saw the same things you did. We have to find her."

"Okay, let's try this. Your hotshot detectives can follow people? Have phone lines tapped?"

"Of course."

"Good. Tell them to put a tap on Juliette's line—at home and at our office. I'll go see her tomorrow and talk about Ginny. I'll casually tell her you think you've located her and that you're going there. If Juliette's in touch with her, she'll probably call her or go there to warn her."

"Not bad," said Alicia, the impatience gone. "But will you be comfortable confronting her?"

"I won't confront her. It's my office, remember? I still work there. I'll go in to collect my mail. Tomorrow afternoon? Can the detectives set up taps and tails that fast?"

Alicia pulled up in front of my townhouse and stopped the car.

"Honey, that's child's play." She pulled out a notepad. "What's Juliette's last name?"

"Martin. M-A-R-T-I-N. You have the office address and phone. I believe she lives in Brookline. Coolidge Corner, actually. I can find the phone number if they have any trouble."

"They won't." She made some more quick notes and then ticked them off as she said, "A tail on Juliette for twenty-four hours. Phone taps on the office lines and her home line. With tracers on both. Think that should do it?"

"Sounds good. Unless I hear from you otherwise, I'll go tomorrow afternoon."

"Need me to drive you?"

"Paco can do it."

"He's a nice man," Alicia said, leaning over the steering wheel and smiling at me. "You're lucky. He was falling all over himself in the hospital wanting to help and take care of you. He loves you a lot."

"So I hear," I said, and got out of the car.

Going back to the Beacon Hill office was strange. I was still officially working there—nobody had called to say otherwise—but the moment Paco pulled the car up in front of the door, I realized that I didn't belong. Whatever happened with my trial, my life, and my career, I wouldn't be staying with Franklin and Pierce.

"I should be about a half hour," I said to Paco. "Definitely not more than an hour. Where should I meet you?"

"Right here. I'm not leaving."

I started to tell him that was silly—why would he just sit in the car—but then stopped. Maybe this was one of his ways of showing he loved me. I had to start recognizing those.

The waiting room was surprisingly empty—only one very pregnant woman sitting there reading a magazine. Delores, the receptionist, greeted me as casually as if I'd been coming in every day.

"Seems very quiet in here," I said.

"It's late," she said, glancing at the wall clock. "Four thirty-five."

"Don't office hours go until five thirty today?"

"Not today. Dr. Franklin's away. Dr. Pierce had been handling the office this week, but he was in emergency surgery today, so I had to cancel almost all the patients. Juliette has been taking care of some of the routine pregnancy visits. We need you badly. When will you be coming back?''

I looked at her, wondering if it was possible that she didn't know. Had she been in a cave for the last couple of weeks, not reading a newspaper or watching the local news? That still wouldn't explain it. She had to hear people talking about me in the office.

"Um, I'm not sure," I said. "I just came in today to open my mail and get my messages."

"There are a stack of messages. Some mail. I put everything on the desk in your consultation room."

I went down the hall to my office and tentatively turned the handle. It opened a crack and then stopped, hitting some kind of barrier. A wave of heat rushed out at me, and a stale, sickly sweet odor assailed my nostrils. I pushed harder, and as the door swung open farther, my mouth dropped open. Every surface, including much of the floor, was covered with baskets of overripe fruit and wilting bouquets of every description from elaborate florists' arrangements to bunches of homegrown lilacs, nasturtiums, and daisies. The air conditioning had been shut off in the room and it was sweltering; the scent of decaying flowers in the humid, still air made it feel like a funeral parlor. I knelt down to look at one bouquet, a long-past-its-prime mix of exquisite orchids and roses, and opened the card that was stuck on a plastic vine. *Get well soon. We believe in you and know you're innocent. Love, Mona and Rick Simpkin.* I left it and moved to the next. *We heard about the horrible attack. Our thoughts are with you, Katie and Steve O'Rourke.* Card after card, almost all of them from patients whose babies I'd delivered. A few from college and medical school friends. *Affection. Best wishes. We want to help however we can. Don't let the bastards get you down.*

I went back down the hall to Delores. "Where did all those come from?" I asked.

"They were sent to you at the hospital," she said, without looking up, "but nothing was being allowed in your room, so somebody sent them here."

"I wish I'd known."

"Now you do."

I looked out into the waiting room; the pregnant woman was no longer in her seat.

"Is Juliette still here?"

"She's seeing a final patient."

"Would you ask her to stop into my consulting room when she's done?"

"Sure."

I went back to my office, turned on the air conditioner, and started sorting through the flowers, taking the cards from each and putting them in a stack. I kept looking around in amazement. I wasn't alone. People still liked me. I'd been a good doctor once, and maybe I would be again.

I glanced through a pile of pink While You Were Out message slips and noticed one from Mona Simpkin, dated the day before Hollis died. A lifetime had passed since then. But looking over at Mona's flowers, I dialed the number.

"Hello." The voice was almost drowned out by the wailing of a baby.

"Mona? This is Dr. Love. Sarabeth Love. How are you?"

"Dr. Love! How great to hear from you." More baby

wails, and then shushing noises from Mona, trying to comfort her. "Are you well?"

"Much better, thanks. I'm just out of the hospital and wanted to thank you for the flowers. It meant a lot to hear from you." Even if I hadn't heard until today. The baby started in again, and I said, "I'd love to catch up, but it sounds like it's not a great time."

"Little Rose has a cold and doesn't like it." There was a lilt to Mona's voice that suggested she was cooing at the baby, not talking to me.

"Then I won't keep you. But I'm back in my office today, and going through a stack of mail, I saw an old message from you. Wanted to make sure everything was okay."

"Wow, that was ages ago. As I remember, I was calling with an insurance question. I got a statement from BMC—my insurance company—about how much my hospital stay had been. P&S was reimbursed for something like one hundred twenty-three thousand dollars. I know I had complications, but that seemed like a lot."

"It is. Want to send me the statement, and I'll take a look at it?"

"Oh gosh, it's not important now. You have other things to think about."

"No, really. I'd be curious." The baby started her protestations again. "Listen, I won't keep you. Give Rose a kiss for me. And put that statement in the mail if you get a chance."

"I will. And Sarabeth, you're so sweet to call. I'm the one who should have called. Because I meant what I said on the card—I think you're the best, and I refuse to believe the things I've been hearing."

I felt my eyes fill with tears. "Thanks, Mona," I said, just as we clicked off.

I started going through the mail, but there wasn't much. There never was. It suddenly occurred to me that in six months of working at Franklin and Pierce, I'd never seen an insurance form. Not that I'd wanted to. I was getting a salary, and the business side of medicine never held much interest for me.

I went back down the hall to Delores.

"What happens to all the insurance forms that come in for me?" I asked. "You know, notifications of re-imbursements to patients. Or checks when I'm paid directly."

"Dr. Franklin gets them. Anything from an insurance company goes directly to him." She looked at me as if this was perfectly obvious. "After he's sorted through them, I record all the payments in the computer."

I eyed the terminal at her desk, but I knew it wouldn't do me any good. Mona's odd bill had been a payment to the hospital, so there wouldn't be a record of it at the office. But there would be other payments. Lots of them. "I suppose a lot collects when Dr. Franklin's out," I said, trying to sound casual.

Delores rolled her eyes. "Too much. I'll be busy when he comes back."

I looked around her desk, which was neatly organized: an appointment book and a message pad, a few desk supplies and a glass of iced tea. No overflowing stack of payments. She must keep them elsewhere.

The phone rang, and when Delores went to answer it, I slipped away. Halfway down the hall, I looked back. She had her head down, talking. Nobody else was

around. With hardly a second thought, I kept going—
past my office, down to the next. Breaking into offices
was becoming my new specialty. I opened the heavy
wooden door and went inside.

Dr. Franklin's consulting room was cool; the sunlight
filtering through the shades cast a gentle glow on the
highly polished wood desk. Everything felt rich, comfortable, and in place—even the foxes in the hunting
prints seemed less gruesome than usual. And someone
had been keeping everything neat. Pencils were lined up,
messages neatly stacked, and there wasn't a trace of
dust.

Or a trace of mail.

I looked around carefully, trying to figure out where
Delores could store the mail. Not on the desk, that was
clear, and not on the long, low cabinet behind it, either,
which was loaded with expensively framed photos of Dr.
Franklin and his children—hiking a trail in Yosemite,
whitewater rafting, horseback riding, and lazing on a
beach at what looked like a Caribbean resort. Funny, I
didn't remember family pictures in his office before, but
from the changing ages of the children, it looked like
the photos spanned a lot of years. I shrugged. No time
to figure it out now. I looked under the desk and even
opened a file cabinet or two. Nothing. I was about to
leave when I noticed a flat brass ring set into the wood
paneling. I pulled it—and a door opened, revealing a
closet I hadn't seen before. My heart began to beat hard.
It wasn't exactly a secret compartment—the handle was
right out in the open—but you could sit in this office
forever and not realize it was here.

The closet was large and mostly empty. A single tan

raincoat hung from the clothes bar. On the shelf above
were several thick black ring-binders, piled one on top
of the other. Curious, I tried to take the top two down,
but they were heavy, and I wasn't in any shape for
reaching and straining. I glanced around the office and
noticed two Mies van der Rohe–style chairs—tubular
steel with a burgundy leather seat and backrest—that
were meant for patients. They looked horribly uncomfortable to sit in for any length of time—maybe that was
how Franklin kept his consultations brief—but they also
looked light. I dragged one across the carpet to the
closet, kicked off my shoes, and tested the leather seat
with my bare foot and half my weight. It wasn't strong,
but it could hold me.

I climbed up on the chair, holding on tightly to the
shelf so that I wouldn't fall. Once I was balanced, I
reached over to examine the ring binders. There were
five of them, each labeled by year. I pulled down the
top one and glanced through it, feeling like I had the
night I was riffling through Dr. Ardsley's office. But
maybe this time I wouldn't be so naive. The binder was
packed with computerized financial statements, put together month by month. Within each month were pages
marked JF, OP, or SL. Now there was a code I could
crack—John Franklin, Oliver Pierce, and Sarabeth Love.
At the end of each month's report was a page labeled
"D," with more names and dollar amounts. Why would
Dr. Franklin keep these records in here when all the
other financials were in a storage area in the back? Then
it struck me. Could it be that he kept two sets of books?
Were these, in his private closet, for his eyes only?

I was still holding the binder when I glimpsed a box

tucked into the back of the closet. I climbed down from
the chair, still holding on to the binder, and opened the
top flap of the box. Eureka. I fell to my knees in front
of it, as if I'd just stumbled upon a sacred altar. Mail.
Lots of it. I went through it quickly. Most of the envelopes had my name on them, but there were a fair number for Dr. Franklin and a sprinkling for Dr. Pierce. I
put the ring binder down and began pulling out all the
mail addressed to me. In a minute, the pile outside the
box was bigger than the one in it. There must have been
more than a hundred envelopes with my name.

I was eager to open them, but it wouldn't do to sit
here and go through the pile—someone, surely, would
walk in. Without giving it a second thought, I took all
the envelopes that were addressed to Franklin or Pierce
out of the box and shoved them into the closet, then put
the ones with my name back in. Taking my own mail
wasn't stealing, I told myself. I should know what was
inside envelopes that were addressed to me. I contem-
plated the binder for a minute, then quickly popped open
the rings, extracted a handful of pages from the back,
and put them into the box, too. Jumping back on the
chair, I returned the binder to its place. Then it was a
matter of cleaning up. I was feeling sore and tired, but
I had to keep going. I returned the chair to its place, put
on my shoes, and pulled the box out of the closet. It
was bulky, though not particularly heavy, but my back
still screamed in protest. The severed muscles might
have been well-stitched, but they weren't ready to do
any work. I stopped for a breath and convinced myself
that I could make it to my office.

I opened Franklin's door slowly and looked out. Nobody around. And what if Delores or Juliette saw me with the box? I didn't have any excuse, but I didn't care.

I dragged the box across to my own office, then shut the door. Alone, I stared at the envelopes, wondering what secrets I was hoping to find inside. A plastic letter opener advertising an antifungal vaginal cream was sitting on my desk, and I cautiously began slitting the tops of the envelopes and pulling out the insurance forms inside. As "medical provider"—was that what doctors had become?—my name peeked through the window on the envelope, but the checks were made out to the practice. Reasonable enough. I kept opening one insurance form after another, hoping to see a pattern that would explain the papers I'd so casually ignored in Ardsley's office. But my brain felt dulled. I didn't understand insurance and managed care and group plans. I'd never really wanted to understand it, either. I wanted to practice medicine, not finance.

And then something stopped me—a form with a patient's name I didn't recognize. I sighed and went on. Maybe that's what happened in private practice—you saw so many people you forgot their names.

No, that wasn't like me. Even in the clinic, I remembered my patients.

More reimbusements for patients I knew, then several more I didn't. The forms had names and dates and ID numbers, and my name listed as provider.

I didn't get it.

I went back over the insurance forms, sorting them by company. Within a few minutes, there were forms spread everywhere, often with only one or two in a pile; it made sense since there were a lot of insurance com-

panies in Boston, fighting for attention and money. But
the stack for Brewster Managed Care dominated the
room, rising like a wobbly tower with some sixty or
seventy pages.

And that was only the accumulation from the week
or so in which Franklin was gone. I generally saw a lot
of patients in the office, but this was crazy.

I put my head in my hands, thinking about Franklin.
Had he hired me back on New Year's Day with this in
mind—to use me as a front for stealing money from
Brewster Managed Care? And how much did the others
in the office know about it? Delores was probably just
doing what she was told—piling mail into a box in a
closet, never thinking that there was anything unusual
about it. But Juliette was different. She'd been having
an affair with Franklin, even if, according to Ginny, that
had ended a while ago. If Franklin was involved with
something messy in the office, she knew about it.

I pulled out the computer pages I'd taken from the
ring binder in the closet and began pouring over them.
The fact that Franklin was keeping two sets of books
was pretty obvious. There were pages for the patients
that each of us saw and billed for. The page marked
''D''—whatever that stood for—was for Franklin's own
information. I gathered they were the patients listed in
this log—but who had never actually been treated. There
also were various flow charts and graphs, which seemed
to be following the path of his illegal money.

There was a knock on the door.

I called ''Just a minute'' and started to scoop the envelopes and insurance forms back into the box, but who-

ever was outside wasn't waiting even a second, and the door swung open.

"Something you needed?" Juliette stood in the doorway, slightly disheveled, her uniform clinging even more than usual to her voluptuous body. Something in her pose made her look like a porn queen, starring in a triple-X version of *The Nurses*.

I stuffed the forms deep into the box, covering them with unopened envelopes. "Come on in. I'm just catching up on mail."

"Doesn't look like there's a lot of room to come in." She remained in the doorway. "Does Dr. Franklin know you're here?"

"I work here, remember?"

"Still?"

The word hung between us in the air. She'd never liked me, that I knew, but now there was open hostility.

The intercom on my desk beeped, and I pushed the speaker button. "Is Juliette in there?" Delores asked.

"Yes, she is."

"Ask her to pick up line two. A patient is on the phone who's eight weeks pregnant and starting to spot. She's nervous and needs to be calmed down. And if it's okay with you two, I'm leaving. Juliette can lock up."

I backed away from the phone and Juliette came forward, carefully stepping over the profusion of flowers and gift baskets. She picked up the receiver and I retreated, giving her space. A wave of fatigue swept over me and I realized it had been a long day. You can't rush healing, I always told my patients. But now I was the one who wanted the healing to be done. I took a floral arrangement off a chair opposite the desk and sat down, waiting for Juliette to finish. Standing in profile against the window, she was all blond hair and big breasts. She held the receiver in the crook of her neck, listening to the patient describe her symptoms, and stared at the well-manicured nails on her hands.

"Spotting is perfectly normal in the first trimester," Juliette said into the phone, when the patient finally stopped talking. "As long as you're not experiencing any cramping or heavy bleeding, you don't have to worry."

But the woman evidently launched into another round of nervous questions, and Juliette was getting impatient. She glanced over at me, clearly eager to get out of the office, wondering, perhaps, why I was watching her instead of busying myself with some other office work.

She shifted the phone to her other ear, turning her back more toward me. Then into the phone, she said. "I know you're concerned, but just relax. It'll be okay."

She hung up and turned quickly to me. "What's in the box?" she asked.

"Insurance forms," I said. "Do you know anything about them?"

"What would I know?"

"Dr. Franklin seems to be ripping off Brewster Managed Care, using my name." I said it casually, as if this were the kind of discovery I made every day.

"I doubt it." She didn't seem too worked up by the possibility. "These things have a way of working themselves out, Sarabeth. Just leave it alone. It will all shake out, I'm sure."

"I'm wondering if it has anything to do with Hollis,"

I said, suddenly remembering why I had come here in the first place. "And I'm also concerned about Ginny. She seems to be on the run, but my lawyer thinks she's located her. She's going to see her tomorrow."

"About what?"

"Oh, the things we know about Hollis. And Ardsley. Ginny knows some things that have got her scared, too, but it's okay. We'll talk to her about it."

I was vamping, with no place to go, offering meaningless blather, but Juliette looked ready to pounce on me. Suddenly, I was scared. Delores had left; I was alone with Juliette, and I had just told her that I knew about the insurance rip-off. I edged toward the window and saw Paco, standing against the car door, glancing at his watch. He looked up and down the building, then noticed me in the window. I made a small motion for him to come in.

At my desk, I tossed the message slips into the box, on top of the insurance forms, then noticed the Steuben elephant Hollis had given me. It hadn't provided much good luck for either of us, but I took that, too, and pulled the box toward me, making it clear that I was about to leave.

"What are you going to do with those?" Juliette asked.

"They're more evidence to help me figure out what's been going on."

I picked up the box, and she lunged at me, but the office was crowded and half-a-dozen baskets of flowers stood between us. I swung around, trying to escape, but the shooting pains in my back paralyzed me. I dropped the box—just as Paco came up behind me.

"Need me to take that?" he asked quietly. Bending over, he retrieved the forms that had fallen to the floor, rescued the crystal elephant, which had tumbled out and broken cleanly in two, then scooped up the box.

"You're stealing!" Juliette hollered.

But we were gone, down the hall and out the front door. I had the feeling that I'd just ended my association with Franklin and Pierce.

VII

I WOKE UP early the next morning, pulled myself out of bed, and told Paco that I was going to the Roxbury clinic.

"What for?" he asked.

"Life has to go on. Everything that's been happening doesn't change the fact that I'm a doctor. It's what I spent the last nine years learning how to do. I'm not giving it up."

Paco looked worried, but he didn't try to dissuade me, except to say mildly, "It's not your regular day."

"I know. But when people see I'm there, they'll come. Trust me."

I got tentatively into my own car, drove down to the Memorial Bridge, across the expressway, and into Roxbury. On this hot day it was like driving into another world: Mothers and children were sitting out on their stoops to avoid the heat inside their cramped apartments; clusters of men were barbecuing pork ribs in the middle of one street, and a gang of scruffy-looking seven- or eight-year-olds were gathered around an open hydrant at a corner, cooling themselves off as hundreds of gallons of water spilled into the street.

I parked in the first space I saw, and even though I had to walk several blocks to the clinic, I realized that these streets held no terrors for me anymore. I'd been stabbed in front of my own home in an upscale section of Cambridge. Hollis Taft Brewster had died by an unknown hand at the elite P&S Hospital in Boston. By contrast, the sordid, crowded, noisy streets of Roxbury seemed almost appealing.

A block away, I began fumbling in my pocketbook for the key to the front door of the clinic, but I couldn't find it. I dug deeper—it had to be there someplace. By the time I got to the clinic, I still hadn't located it, and I was wondering if I would have to go home again, when I realized that the front door was flung wide open and a new sign saying "WELCOME! PLEASE COME IN!" was hanging out front. I stepped in and saw the waiting room crowded with patients and the clinic administrator, Ruby, sitting at the front desk.

"Hi," I said to her. "What's going on?"

"Dr. Love!" She jumped up and gave me a small kiss on the cheek. "How wonderful to see you. Are you well? Is life okay?"

"Life is life," I said, smiling. "You know that. You do what you can when it's gloomy. But I wasn't expecting to see you here—or even find the clinic open."

"I've been wanting to tell you all about it," she said. "But with what's happened to you, the time never seemed right. What a blessing you're here."

"So tell me now," I said. The waiting room seemed

spiffier than I remembered; the carpet was clean, and I thought a couple of the chairs were new.

"That fine woman you brought with you last time you were here, Hollis Taft Brewster, God rest her soul. The day after she came, she sent me a check for fifty thousand dollars with instructions that half of it be used to fix up the clinic and try to increase operating hours. So that's what I've done. It means paying a little something to some of the doctors to come extra hours, but it's worth it. And I'd be glad to pay you, too."

"Wow. That's wonderful. And the other half of the money?"

"She was very specific. It was to shelter women being abused by their husbands. She wanted me to call it the All-Women's Center, and I'm just getting it started. She said it needed to be for all women, rich or poor. Because when it comes to suffering abuse, we all suffer the same. That's what she said, Dr. Love, and that's the kind of woman she was. She insisted she didn't want any publicity about this, that I should do it quietly, just in the community. So even in all the hullabaloo that's been going on since her death, I didn't say a word."

"I'm so pleased. I'm sure she didn't plan on its being a legacy, but that's what she's left, isn't it?"

"She said she learned an awful lot the day she was here. And that's thanks to you for bringing her. Whoever would have thought to bring Hollis Taft Brewster to Roxbury? She said she understood how hard it was for women to leave their husbands when they're being treated bad, because she'd been in the same situation and knew what they were going through. Of course, she didn't really mean that, but it shows what a woman she was. Trying to make everybody feel comfortable. A fine, fine woman she was. I'm sorry she died and I think it's awful that they're blaming you for it. I know it wasn't your fault.''

"Thank you, Ruby." I'd forgotten just how much Ruby could talk, and she still wanted to tell me exactly what she'd added to the clinic so far and what she planned to do—how much money was going for doctors, how much for supplies, and how much for sprucing up the physical plant.

"You've done quite a job, Ruby," I said. "I'm sure this is exactly how Hollis would have wanted it."

A nurse-practitioner was already seeing patients this morning, and there wasn't space in the clinic for two of us to be working at once. So I told Ruby to let me know what days she needed help—and that I'd be there.

"You're just too good, Dr. Love. That's what Mrs. Brewster said about you, too. The best doctor she'd ever met. She had absolute faith in you."

Faith, hope, and charity. Hollis believed in them all. It didn't seem fair.

Paco listened carefully to my story about Ruby and the clinic, but didn't immediately jump to the same conclusion I did. "I think Ruby might be right," Paco said. "Hollis was just being charitable, and trying to walk in another person's shoes. I can't imagine Sloane Brewster abusing his wife."

"Why not? Because rich men aren't abusive? Maybe it wasn't physical—he just ignored her and demeaned her. I'd always had the feeling that Hollis wanted to tell me something. That there was a secret she had about

Sloane but was too embarrassed to share. Maybe that was it.''

''And how does it fit in with her death?''

''Hollis was getting emotionally stronger during this pregnancy. I had the sense that she was getting ready to take a big step in her life. Maybe it was to leave Sloane. He sensed it and couldn't take it. So he killed her.''

''By having somebody sneak in with an injection of TPA?''

''It could be. Sloane's insurance company had just made a huge payment to the family of the man who died from a TPA overdose at Mass General. He knew how it could happen accidentally—so maybe he decided to have it happen on purpose.''

''And he hired that Nurse Patsy to administer it.''

''Right. So all we have to do is find her and get her to admit that he hired her.'' I rolled my eyes, realizing how difficult, if not impossible, that would be.

''Of course, there's still the possibility that Ardsley hired her. Or Franklin. Because Hollis knew they were ripping off BMC and threatened to expose them.''

''Which would have destroyed their fancy careers,'' I added. Then I sighed. ''We're right on one of these, Paco, I know we are. We just need some proof.'' I put my hand to the back of my neck, trying to release some of the tension that was building up there.

''Need a back rub?'' Paco asked.

''A neck rub. And very gentle. I'm still sore.''

I slid closer to Paco, and his long fingers began delicately probing my tight neck muscles. ''Some way to identify Nurse Patsy,'' I murmured. ''There must be some way.'' And then suddenly it struck me. After

Nurse Patsy had been in the room trying to give me an injection, hadn't I taken the tourniquet—

Paco's fingers hit a particularly tender spot of bunched muscles near my neck and I yelped in pain.

"Sorry, honey." He stopped massaging and draped his fingers over my shoulders. "The tourniquet. What about it?"

I hadn't even realized that I'd said the word out loud.

Now I turned to face Paco, the neck rub over. "I was just thinking about when Patsy was in my room. She wrapped a tourniquet around my arm, and after she left, I took it off and stuck it under my pillow. Any idea what might have happened to it?"

Paco looked momentarily bewildered, then said, "Would that be a long, stretchy rubber tube?"

"Exactly. It's called a Penrose drain, but it's also used as a tourniquet."

He shrugged at the medical term, but said, "I think I saw it one day at the hospital when I was changing your pillowcases. I might have stuffed it into your duffle bag."

"I didn't notice it when I was unpacking."

"Let me check." He got up, unwinding his long legs from the sofa and strode over to the stairs. I watched him disappear, marveling, for the first time in a long time, at the slim hips and broad shoulders that fit together on him like the pieces of some perfect, bronze sculpture by Rodin.

When he was changing my pillowcases? What was that about? I tried to think back to the hospitalization, but it was a blur. The only thing I knew was that every time I awoke, Paco was there, or Eric, giving me ice chips, wiping my forehead, fluffing my pillows. With nobody else allowed in my room, maybe Paco had played nurse even more than I knew. I felt a surge of humility.

Paco came back down, holding the blue Land's End duffle bag that he had brought to the hospital for me. He'd stuffed it with pretty robes and books and my favorite chocolates—most of which I saw for the first time when I got home and emptied it out. Now I zipped open the main compartment. Empty. There was a pocket in the front, and I checked that, too. Also empty.

"Maybe you just threw it out," I said, disappointed, but still feeling generous toward him. "That would have been the reasonable thing to do."

"I really don't think I did." He began digging through the bag, running his hands inside the pocket and along the soft fabric of the bottom. "Damn," he said. Then suddenly he seemed to feel something, and looking down, tugged at an inside zipper. "A lot of pockets in these bags," he said. A moment later, he pulled out the tourniquet.

I gasped slightly. "That's it."

"I knew it." He seemed to be following my train of thought now, because he held the rubber tube gingerly, then returned it to the zippered compartment in the bag. "We'll know it's here," he said.

"Fingerprints," I said hoarsely, feeling my voice crack from the tension. "The nurse was holding the tourniquet when she came in, and she had her fingers pressed against it when she wrapped it around me. We can find out who it was. Rubber must hold fingerprints well."

"Unless they've been obscured. You and I both touched it."

"Not all over. Besides, they can separate them out, can't they? Mine are already on file," I added.

Paco laughed. Finding the tourniquet seemed to bring a new spirit into the room.

The phone rang, and we both jumped. Paco answered it, then handed it to me, mouthing that it was Alicia.

"I have news," she said grimly, when I took the phone. "The private eye who went up to New Hampshire met with Ginny's sister. His instinct was right. Ginny *had* gone up there to stay for a few days but she told her not to tell anyone. But now the sister's panicking, because Ginny apparently went out to the store for milk this morning and hasn't returned. When our detective showed up, she was hysterical and ready to talk."

"Does she know anything?"

"I don't think so. But Ginny had put the fear of God into her sister, so she was afraid to notify the police. Mike—the private eye—felt pretty strongly that the police should be called, and I concurred. That was about an hour ago, so we'll see if anything turns up."

"Make sure they don't forget about Juliette," I said. "As planned, I told her you knew where Ginny was. But a few other things happened at the office, too."

I filled her in quickly on my discovery of the insurance forms in Franklin's office. She groaned audibly.

"We've got to get that box out of your house," she said. "Don't you understand, Sarabeth? Somebody's playing a very nasty game here. Can you have Paco bring the box to my office immediately?"

I covered the phone and repeated the request to Paco,

who nodded. "He'll be there," I said into the phone.

When Paco left, I went to my study, deciding to sort through my papers. I turned on the radio for company, listening to the endless chatter of an all-news station. It remained as a gentle hum in the background until a report in the business news caught my attention and made me sit up straight. Brewster Managed Care, the large health-insurance concern, was rumored to be planning an exclusive deal with P&S Hospital. Nobody had thought it would be approved because it meant such obvious fee-fixing, but the governor's office was considering giving the go-ahead very soon. More details would soon be forthcoming.

I got up from my desk and began pacing around my study. Hollis had told me about that deal weeks ago— but it hadn't meant very much to me. Could it be important? I tried to imagine somebody killing Hollis in order to make a deal go through, but my mind wouldn't accept that premise in the same way that it wouldn't allow me to seriously consider the possibility that Ardsley or Franklin had done it to keep an insurance scam going. Sure, exposure of the insurance fraud might finish off their careers in a baby's heartbeat. But murder was a big deal. Maybe I was an innocent and Alicia would just laugh at me, but I couldn't believe anyone would kill Hollis for financial gain.

I ran through my conversaton with Ruby again and tried to put that in perspective. If a man was abusive, he didn't end up killing his wife subtly, with an injection, administered by a nurse in a hospital room. He exploded and killed publicly and violently. And that's not what had happened.

I sat down again at my computer and sighed. Many

strands, but none of them formed the knot. Something
was missing. I hadn't killed Hollis, but she was dead,
and somebody had made very sure that I would take the
rap.

Fraud. Deals. Abuse. Power. Nurses. Injections. It all
had to add up somehow. I picked up the phone, dialing
the main number for Brewster Insurance and asking for
Sloane Brewster's office. I was put through to a grav-
elly-voiced assistant who, when I asked to speak to Mr.
Brewster, informed me that her boss had left for the day.
Glancing at my watch, I realized it was almost six
o'clock, so I asked if I could have his home number.
No, I could not. It was private and unlisted. I hung up.
I had called Hollis at home many times during the
months we knew each other; I tried to picture the number on my office Rolodex, but it eluded me. I didn't want
to get in my car again, so without quite thinking about
what I was doing, I called Cambridge Taxi and asked
how soon they could be over. When asked my destina-
tion, I said, "Downtown. The Brewster Building."

VIII

THE CAB PULLED up to the Brewster Building and I
said, "I need the private entrance to the Tower, please."
The cab driver, muttering, made a wide-U turn and
stopped in front of the elaborate, limestone entrance. I
gave him an excessive tip and jumped out before a door-
man could hop to my aid. Strolling to the glass doors of
the Tower lobby, I saw at least three uniformed guards
and doormen at the ready, so I stayed on the sidewalk
and kept going to the private-garage entrance where I'd

entered last time with Paco. The attendant must have been off parking a car, so the entrance gate was down. But there was enough room to the left of the gate to slip by; I did that, looked around to make sure nobody had noticed, and sauntered into the back lobby, where, I remembered, the elevator to the penthouse was located.

"Good evening, Morgan," I said, smiling at the seated elevator attendant, pleased that his name had popped, effortlessly, into my head. "How nice to see you. I'm here for Mr. Brewster, of course."

He stood up, obviously recognizing me. I just hoped it was from the last time I was here and not from some newspaper photo. At least I was a familiar face, and maybe he wouldn't remember the source, either.

"Good evening." He looked around, obviously wondering why I had arrived, unescorted, from the garage.

"Your colleague over there got busy," I said, nodding toward the garage. "I told him I'd come ahead."

"Oh. Fine." He closed the elevator door, and we began moving upward, slowly and smoothly. "Everyone wants to see Mr. Brewster since the tragedy," Morgan said, making conversation, just as he had the first time. "Not so busy tonight as usual, but always people here."

"I guess you meet them all."

"Oh, yes, ma'am. Whoever thought I'd meet the governor? Now he's been here three times. Stood right where you're standing. When he came in tonight I finally got up my courage. I told him, I said, 'Governor Boggs, I know a lot of working-class people didn't support you, but you had my vote. And you'll have it again.' That's what I told him. And he said, 'Thank you, sir.' Wasn't that nice? 'Sir.' He's a real gentleman."

"Sure," I said, not mentioning that I wouldn't have voted for him for dogcatcher, and that as far as I could tell, Governor Boggs was the most corrupt politician in the state of Massachusetts.

"And what will you and Mr. Brewster be speaking to the governor about tonight?"

I didn't say anything, and from behind, I saw Morgan's ears grow red.

"I'm sorry, ma'am. I shouldn't be asking that. Mr. Brewster has told me a hundred times not to have conversations with the guests." He turned around and smiled sheepishly. "Don't tell him I spoke to the governor, would you?"

I nodded, wondering how likely it was that I would have a chance to tell him anything at all.

The elevator stopped and for a moment I looked up, praying to the angels dancing on the painted mural of the vaulted ceiling. What would Morgan say when, standing by in the elevator, waiting for me to be admitted to the Brewsters, he found that I was thrown out on my ear?

I stepped into the private lobby, wondering briefly why the elevator didn't open directly into the Brewster home. After all, nobody else lived on the floor. Maybe it was that extra bit of security—exactly what I didn't need right now. I rang the gentle chimes at the door and looked over at Morgan, who stood at attention in the elevator, his arms folded. A uniformed maid opened the door and I smiled brightly. "Hi, how are you? I'm here to see Mr. Brewster and the governor. Sarabeth Love."

She looked at me coldly. "I'll tell them you're here."

"No need, really. I know where to find them." I

brushed past her, knocking slightly into the Picasso on
the near wall, but it was well anchored and didn't move.
I heard the elevator door closing, Morgan pulling away,
and then I walked across the foyer with as much assur-
ance as I could muster, my heels clicking on the marble
like tiny hammers. The apartment was as breathtaking
as I remembered it, but now it was also flooded with
summer sunlight, still pouring in despite the evening
hour. There was a soft pattering of feet—I thought it
might be the maid following me—but the sound went
off in the other direction. I looked around the vast room.
Hollis's room. Decorated with that cross between old
money and new pride that made her so appealing. Thirty
feet away, I noticed the heirloom tortoise-shell chairs
that had embarrassed Hollis the day she gave me a tour,
and I paused, thinking I heard her sweet laugh, her explanation that hiding them away ''wouldn't bring the
tortoises back to life.'' Death was final—it didn't take
four years of medical school to know that—but in this
room it was impossible to imagine Hollis not returning.
Her family, her home, her budding self. Pregnant, she
seemed to be growing confidence along with her baby,
and I'd felt sure that once Kristin was born, Hollis would
strike out to a brave new future. What was that next
stage of her life going to be? She'd never told me what
she had in mind or why it was that she needed courage.
Toward the end, though, I'd had the sense that she'd
found herself and was ready to take what she wanted.

But then she'd lost it all.

Stepping closer to the high-backed tortoise-shell
chairs, I realized that there were two men sitting in them,
their heads bent close as if they were sharing some se-

cret, and then jerking apart. Raucous laughter ripped
through the room. A joke, I thought bitterly, recognizing
one of the men as Sloane, his well-groomed sandy-
brown hair unmistakable in the light. Hollis was just
weeks gone, and he was able to tell a joke.

Sloane stood up, as did the man next to him, and I
recognized him now as Governor Boggs. I was barely
ten feet away from them, and as Sloane turned slightly,
he saw me and a look of confusion crossed his face.

He could have shouted for help, pushed a button for
the security guards, or demanded to know how I had
gotten in. Instead, he looked briefly at the governor and
then extended a hand to me, as if he'd been expecting
me.

"Dr. Love," he said. "I haven't seen you since . . ."
The sentence trailed off; there was no place for it to go.
He didn't ask how I'd gotten in.

The governor looked startled at hearing my name,
then turned to Sloane, who just shrugged.

"We still have a few formalities to finish with," the
governor said to Sloane, obviously deciding that ignoring me was the best option. "Are those papers ready?"
His question was directed toward another seating area
by the window. I turned and saw two men sprawled in
Louis XIV chairs; one had his long legs stretched out in
front of him. At the governor's words both men straightened up and rose to come forward. I felt my jaw drop
open when I recognized them—John Doheny and Peter
Vicente, the investigators who had been in Ardsley's
office with me, the day or two after Hollis's death.

They strode toward us, and long-legged Doheny
looked me over with an expression of distaste that sug-

gested he had just come across a large cockroach in the Brewster living room. "Is there a reason Dr. Love is here?" he asked curtly, of nobody in particular.

"It might be best if you left, Sarabeth," Sloane said mildly. "If you need to speak to me, you can make an appointment to see me in my office."

"It's quick," I said, feeling the urgency of the moment, not wanting to let it pass. "Some information you should have about doctors at P&S."

"Oh, well, you'd better tell all of us," Doheny said, his voice dripping with nastiness. "That's what we're here to talk about."

I looked at Sloane, who said coldly, "Go right ahead, Dr. Love. If it was so important that you barged in here, these gentlemen can hear it."

And suddenly I felt foolish. The great powers of business and government were ranged in front of me, and I wanted to discuss some insurance forms I'd stolen from a closet. Really, I wanted Sloane to understand from it that I hadn't hurt his wife, and that some other forces, evil forces, had been behind her death.

"It's complicated," I said, fumbling for words, figuring I had just one chance to get it right. "But I have proof that certain doctors have been using my name to fraudulently submit claims to BMC. I don't know how much has been stolen, but surely it's well into the thousands of dollars."

"Oh." Sloane sounded as unexcited as if I'd told him that the sun would set tonight. The other men in the room didn't bother responding at all. I looked over at Vicente. D.A.'s office. Governor's liaison. Shouldn't he care about this? "I was stabbed about a week ago," I said, looking at Vicente, "after I found some sensitive papers in the office of Dr. Archibald Ardsley. There's a good chance he's part of the same scheme." Vicente didn't even bother to shrug.

Doheny sighed, then tugged at his pants leg. "Dr. Love, you've been charged with a murder, as I recall. I'd recommend that you concentrate on defending yourself against that charge, rather than making things up about everyone else."

"Could we cut through this, please?" The governor's voice rang out. "The papers, John. If you have them, we're almost done with the deal."

"What's the deal?" I asked, remembering the report I'd heard on the radio.

Doheny was too arrogant not to answer that one. He wanted to brag. "The governor will be announcing an exclusive affiliation between P&S and Brewster Managed Care," he said. "All patients under BMC who need hospitalization can be admitted only to P&S. It's a model for cost containment that the governor is very proud to be encouraging."

"Good for the hospital, good for the insurance company, but lousy for the patients," I said, remembering Hollis's take on the deal. I turned to Sloane. "Is that why you were bribing Ardsley? To get the deal through? And I suppose you were bribing Franklin, too. You knew he was submitting fraudulent claims, but you didn't care. Or maybe you even gave him the names and ID numbers. Another bribe, just subtler. How many doctors did you have to bribe to get the deal through?"

"Sloane, would you like this woman removed?" Doheny interrupted. "She's raving."

I looked at him. "Special investigations," I said to

him. "I'm beginning to understand what that means. You make sure that everything goes the way the governor wants it. And in this case, that meant however Mr. Brewster wanted it. How much money did Mr. Brewster contribute to the governor's campaign, anyway? Gosh, is there anyone in this city he hasn't bought?"

"Raving," Doheny repeated.

And maybe I was. But I didn't care. "There are a lot of *other* things I know, too," I said, turning to Sloane. "Like about how you treated Hollis. We've never spoken, you and I. It's time we did. But we should talk privately. And right away. Tonight. I can't wait any longer."

The three other men were staring at him, but Sloane refused to meet their eyes. He looked out his window, at the city that he had at his feet. "Dr. Love, could you wait in my study, please? I *will* talk to you. But I have to finish here first, and get these papers signed before tomorrow. If you would please follow Isadora, I'll find you in a few minutes."

From nowhere, the maid appeared, and I was ushered out, back across the football field of a living room. I glimpsed the dining room and noticed that the table was bare. The antique brass candlesticks that had graced the table the last time I was here were lined up on a sideboard. The maid opened the door to a room that I hadn't been in before and said, "This is Mr. Brewster's study. Why don't you sit down." She motioned to a chair covered in what looked like zebra hide, and remembering Hollis's laughing comment that she'd put all the evidence of endangered species in Sloane's study, I shuddered and turned away. A fur rug tossed over the arm of a green leather couch also looked too real—lynx, perhaps, or jaguar. But the maid wasn't moving until I sat down, so I chose a spot at the opposite end of the sofa, far away from the suspect fur. That settled, the maid asked, "Would you like something to drink?"

"Iced tea, please," I said.

She looked around somewhat uneasily, as if worried about leaving me alone, then went out a door at the other end of the room. I didn't budge from the sofa—I was exhausted and the pain in my lungs had returned. But it didn't matter. All I had to do right now was think.

I had some of the pieces. But too many were still missing.

The first part was easy now. P&S wanted that exclusive contract with Brewster Managed Care. Sloane Brewster wanted a lot of money to make it happen. Too much. But Brewster had a hold on any number of the doctors making decisions, including Franklin and Ardsley. Sloane let them know they could make lots of extra change as long as the deal went through, with the hospital giving BMC a huge guarantee. The governor sent Doheny in to make sure it all went however Sloane wanted it to. Everybody benefited. Sloane got his money. Franklin and Ardsley got their payoffs. The governor kept Sloane happy.

And then Hollis died.

That was the part I still didn't understand. And Doheny was right. That was the only part that I should be thinking about. How could Hollis have interfered with the plan they had all carefully put together?

Even if Hollis knew exactly what was going on, why would that have worried somebody enough to want her

dead? And the next steps didn't fit, either. That somebody would have had to wield enough power to get
Nurse Patsy—whoever she was—to sneak in with a syringe of TPA and make sure Hollis bled to death. If
Ardsley or Franklin had been involved, they would have
done it themselves, without involving a nurse. Always
safer to keep the circle as small as possible. Ardsley had
something on Nurse Dolton, but she wasn't Nurse
Patsy—that much I knew.

I got up and went over to Sloane's desk and almost
instinctively tried the drawers. Locked. The desktop was
clear except for an antique carriage clock and a Steuben
paperweight that Hollis must have given him.

The door behind me opened and closed, and I turned
around, expecting to see the maid returning with my iced
tea. Instead, walking in with a silver drink tray was a
stunning woman in a tight red dress and stiletto heels;
her makeup was perfect, her cleavage well-bared, and
her hair swept up—making her look like a younger version of Ivana Trump. It was a long moment before I
realized that I was looking at Juliette.

"Your tea," she hissed, holding the tray inches from
my face. Her eyes were blazing and fury seeped from
every pore. I could see that under the makeup, her skin
was chalky white, and I sensed that if I didn't take the
glass, she would smash it into my nose without a moment's hesitation. Too stunned to do anything else, I
reached for the frosted glass, and its iciness seemed to
penetrate my blood. Juliette deposited the tray on an
onyx side table and as she adjusted the red silk purse
that was tucked under her arm, I hastily put the glass
down next to the tray, sloshing a little of the liquid onto

the table's smooth surface in my eagerness to get it out of my hands.

"It's not poisoned," she said mockingly. "Drink it."

"What are you doing here?" I asked hoarsely, too dumbfounded to know whether or not to be scared.

"You don't know that? I thought you knew everything." She laughed evilly. "I'm here every night, Doctor. I help Sloane with the children, since you killed their mother. They're asleep now, thinking about how much they hate you. When I came downstairs and heard you come in, I told Isadora I'd bring your tea. So drink it."

We both stared at the amber liquid in the glass. "You're pretty dressed-up for a babysitter," I said, not moving.

"This is how Sloane likes me to look." Juliette smoothed the dress over her hips, a slinky movement that might have been practiced in front of a mirror but seemed instinctual now. She tossed her head, and there was something about her style, her gestures, that seemed oddly familiar. She glanced at the well-manicured nails on her hands. French manicure.

I turned to go back to the couch, afraid that I couldn't stand up much longer. I picked up the iced tea, thinking I might take a sip after all, try to calm down, but my hands were trembling, and the glass slipped from them and fell to the carpet. It didn't break, but the liquid spilled, and I yelped.

Juliette laughed, then bent down to retrieve the glass. "You're awfully nervous. Just relax, it'll be okay."

I couldn't breathe.

The pain that shot through my chest was solid terror at what I had just figured out, a sucker punch of reality striking me more brutally than any knife. I put my head down, trying to stop the dizziness and keep myself from fainting. It couldn't be. I had to be imagining this. Other people had French manicures and used that same phrase. It was a common phrase. A meaningless one. Nurses used it all the time.

Just relax, it'll be okay.

That was what the nurse said in the hospital when she came at me with her deadly syringe. And that's what Juliette had just said now, in the same mocking voice. But it wasn't simply the words. Everything had suddenly snapped into place. The vague sense I'd had in the hospital of knowing the nurse. The way she looked at me with the sullen contempt Juliette always displayed whenever there wasn't a man around.

Nurse Patsy as Juliette. Juliette as Nurse Patsy.

Juliette's blond hair and shapely figure were her most obvious assets. Hide them, and she disappeared. But not completely. There were certain mannerisms, and a tone of voice, that were a dead giveaway.

A black wig. Thick glasses. A mole on the cheek. How easy to be deceived.

"Nurse Patsy," I said.

Juliette froze in the middle of taking a step forward, her foot poised above the floor a fraction of a second too long. But she recovered almost immediately, the foot coming down gracefully as she looked at me insouciantly.

"Who's that?" she asked.

"The nurse who tried to kill me. The nurse who killed Hollis."

"Oh? Did she look like me?" Blond and buxom Ju-

liette, with her smooth skin and clear blue eyes, gazed
at me.

"No," I said. "Nurse Patsy had thick dark hair, coke-
bottle eyeglasses, and a mole on her cheek. A pretty
obvious disguise."

She laughed. "Nobody in a million years would believe that. I'm the exact opposite of the woman you described to the police."

I pictured trying to make the point about the disguise
to Judge Snow, and realized how ridiculous it would
sound.

But I knew.

I sank down into the green couch, and the move
seemed to ignite Juliette. "Don't sit down," she
snapped. "You can think what you want, but you're all
wrong. And what matters right now is that Mr. Brewster
wants to talk to you. He's not meeting you here. He told
me to bring you to him upstairs for your little chat."
She walked to the same door where the maid had exited
and held it open for me. I didn't want to go, but there
wasn't much choice. I followed her out, then stayed a
few feet behind her as she walked quickly through another study, past the dining room, into a hall. I expected
her to mince, but she didn't. The dress was short enough
not to interfere with her stride; the stiletto-heeled shoes,
strapped around her ankles, landed purposefully with
each step.

Juliette the babysitter in a red dress. Juliette in a black
wig. Juliette who had ended her affair with John Franklin—because she was now the mistress of a very rich
man.

She didn't say a word, just approached the staircase

to the family quarters and marched up confidently, as if she had lived there all her life. Upstairs, there were more rooms than I could count, and only a few of them were inaccessible, the doors shut tight. The children's bedrooms no doubt. Beyond them, I caught a glimpse of a child's playroom, and then a music room, with toy xylophones and a child-sized piano. An arched entrance led to another wing, probably where the master bedroom suite was located along with exercise rooms and what had been Hollis's study. Juliette turned sharply, down another hallway, through a set of French doors, into a wing that seemed to be maids' rooms. Without pausing, she went to the end of that wing and through another, less formal set of double doors, then on to one more narrow hallway, this one darker and smaller with an ominous steel door at the far end, restricting further passage. But Juliette punched a code into the inset keypad, and when a click indicated the door had unlatched, she swung it open. In contrast to the endless opulence of the apartment, the stairwell in front of us seemed like a fire exit, with steps leading upward and fluorescent lights along the walls.

I took a step inside, then hesitated. The door slammed shut behind me. "Sloane isn't up there," I said.

"Just go up," she said.

"No, I think I won't."

"I think you will." From her shiny red purse, Juliette took out a tiny pearl-handled revolver. "Go, or I'll use it. You know I will."

I knew. I took the stairs slowly; partly biding my time, partly because my chest was throbbing. Step after step,

two flights to the top, and another heavy steel door that
warned FIRE EXIT ONLY.

"Just push it," she demanded, and when I didn't, she
slammed past me to push against the steel herself, grab-
bing my arm as she did so, and tossing us both to the
other side of the door. A burst of sticky heat and noise
overwhelmed me, and it took me a moment to realize
that the compressors for the building's air-conditioning
system were roaring at us, spewing heat and condensa-
tion. Above, I saw wispy clouds and sky still twinkling
blue even though the sun was gone from view, hidden
on the other side of the building as it began to set in the
west. So we were on the roof of the Brewster Tower, I
thought, wondering how I was going to escape.

"Move!" Juliette shouted over the noise, waving her
gun and coming at me like a red dragon. I stepped backwards, wanting to run but not having any place to go,
until a sign caught my eye that said "Fire/Emergency
Helicopter Evacuation" with an arrow pointing to a
roped-off area a football field away. I charged in the
direction of the arrow, as if a helicopter might just be
waiting to swoop me away from this emergency, but
Juliette yelled, "Other direction," and pointed to a side
of the roof that seemed unfinished and dangerous.

"What's going on, Juliette?" I asked, calling loudly
to her, hoping to get her talking, thinking she might not
try to kill me if I could engage her in conversation. But
there was too much noise for her to bother answering;
it was easier to just wave the gun menacingly and keep
me stepping briskly on the forced march. Half stum-
bling, half walking, I kept going until we were far
enough across that the roar of the compressors settled

into a background din, a terrifying clatter. This part of
the roof was a jumble of jagged concrete with odd pieces
of small machinery left around from some unfinished
construction. Elsewhere, a ten-foot ledge encircled the
roof, but here there was merely a rocky border, not more
than four feet high. I stopped and we were face to face.

"You're going to jump off the roof," she said, her
face contorted in the same odd mask of evil that I had
seen briefly when she came at me as Patsy. "Get up
there." She motioned to the rocky ledge with her gun,
and even from here, I could see that there was nothing
on the other side but sky and air—and seventy stories
below, a concrete sidewalk. My mouth filled with bile,
the acrid taste of nausea and fear.

"I won't." It was barely audible, hardly the ringing
testament to my courage that I intended.

"Oh, yes you will. Because otherwise I'll kill you
slowly. Torture you. A bullet here and a bullet there. I
like to watch people bleed to death, remember? Especially doctors and rich ladies who think they're too good
for the rest of us." The gun was in her hand firmly, the
muzzle pointed at me.

"Then Sloane will know it was you," I said. "And
that you killed Hollis. That's not what he wanted."

"He wanted me and he still does!" she screamed.
"He hated that prissy bitch of a wife! I'm the woman
he wants and now he has me! So get up there and
jump!"

"It won't do any good if I'm gone," I said. "I swear,
Juliette, I won't get in your way ever again."

"That's because you're going to be dead! And everyone is going to think that you killed yourself over what

you did to Hollis. You came here to tell Sloane how sorry you are. To beg his forgiveness. And once you did that, you couldn't take it anymore. The guilt was too overwhelming, so you came up here and jumped.''

"You think quickly," I said. "But my lawyer knows everything about the fraud and the deals and why you had to get Hollis out of the way. It will all get traced back to you. Was it Ardsley who made you kill her? Or Sloane?''

Her manic laugh rang out across the roof. "If you'd just shut up, you wouldn't keep getting yourself in trouble,'' she said. "Because you don't know anything. And neither does your lawyer.''

In the setting sun, Juliette's hair shone golden, making her look like some deranged fairy princess with a gun. But the makeup and tight dress and stiletto heels changed the image from princess to whore, a fashion magazine's notion of a woman trying to get her man.

And then I got it.

Nobody had controlled Juliette. Nobody had told her what to do. She had killed Hollis all by herself, and not for money, but for love.

"How long had you and Sloane been having an affair?'' I asked.

"It wasn't an affair. He loves me. He's going to marry me. And you're not going to get in the way.''

"He was abusing Hollis,'' I said. "He's going to do the same to you.''

"She deserved it. She's a bitch and I'm not. He wanted her gone, and now he's going to be grateful to me. You almost ruined it, but you can't.''

"You had to know I'd defend myself,'' I said. "You

had to know I wouldn't just say I was responsible and go to jail.''

She snorted, a coarse sound that clashed with the rest of her smooth, rich style. ''I didn't know you'd be charged with murder. That was the governor's idea. It almost fouled things up, because it turned you into such a damned busybody. But it's over now. It's over.'' She took a step toward me and said, ''We're not talking anymore, so shut up. Get up on that ledge. Now. Get moving.'' And when I didn't move, she leaned forward, firing the gun so that a bullet whizzed through my upper arm, taking a chunk of flesh and splattering it against the parapet. I screamed in pain and grabbed at the thick river of blood that formed on my arm; then I staggered a few steps forward.

''Juliette, you don't have to do this,'' I said. ''We can work it out. You'll marry Sloane.''

''You've already told him too many stupid things. I heard you. And I can imagine what you were going to tell him in private about me. But you never will. Not now.'' She raised the gun again, and this time I did move toward the ledge. Close enough so that she wouldn't shoot me again. Not so close that she would push me over.

I tried to catch my beath, knowing that the only choice was to try to break away, make a run for my life. But there was no way I could do that. She fired again and the bullet whizzed by my ear, missing me, but I fell to the ground, screaming, rolling closer to the parapet and landing on one of the loose pieces of concrete. The sharp edge of a rock lodged in my knee, and I reached to pull it out; suddenly I was holding my only possible weapon—a hunk of concrete, sharp-edged as a sword.

"Get up!" Juliette screamed at me. "Die with dignity. Jumping is the death you deserve!"

I was shrieking on the ground but not moving, so she rushed toward me, ready to pounce, overflowing with the energy she needed to send me flying over the edge. I reared back with my unbloodied arm, and as she leaned forward, sent the concrete slab smashing into her face. She screamed and fell back in shock; her hand flew to her face and the gun went clattering backwards. I tried to scramble for it, but she was too quick and dove for it; the gun disappeared into her hand, and then I heard a *crack* as one stiletto heel lodged in a crevice of the jagged concrete and sent her smacking into the ground. I was up now, dashing to hide behind one of the pieces of machinery, stockpiling more concrete. She couldn't shoot through the metal machine, and if she came around, after me, I could attack again.

Suddenly I heard footsteps running across the roof, a man's voice shouting "Juliette!"

Then with an edge of hysteria, she was screaming, "I'm going to kill her, darling! I'm going to kill her! She'll never say anything about you! I won't let her ruin your life, darling! Get out of the way!"

Then more footsteps pounded on the roof from another direction, and a man's voice I hadn't heard before called, "Drop it!" and a gun, Juliette's, was fired. Again the order came, "Drop it or I'll shoot!" and after the small retort of the revolver, I heard the roar of mightier artillery launching across the roof. I stepped out from my shelter and there were Alicia and Paco and a heavily armed man I didn't know, racing toward me. Twenty feet away, Juliette was on her back, bent at the waist in a pool of blood with her legs sticking straight up, the stiletto heels looking as if they would poke holes in the sky. And at the other end of the roof, screaming in horror, was her darling, Sloane.

four

AND LIFE GOES ON

I

I WAS SITTING in Hollis's bedroom, dripping blood from my arm onto her peach moire bedspread, and I didn't care. The thing was, I didn't think she'd care, either. We'd come downstairs from the roof, Juliette slung over the shoulders of the man with the gun—one of Alicia's private detectives, it turned out—and Paco carrying me in his arms, like a baby. Alicia began barking orders, her yellow linen dress smeared with blood from the moment on the roof when she grabbed me to her and said, "Thank God you're alive!"

Ambulance attendants had arrived almost immediately, strapping Juliette onto a stretcher and carting her away, while Sloane dashed after her. A second ambulance crew arrived and wanted me to go to the hospital, too, but I wouldn't. I'd had quite enough of hospitals. Instead, I marched into one of the Brewsters' bathrooms, followed by Paco, who gently bathed my arm in the sink while blood ran over the brass faucets and down the white granite countertop. The crisply pressed white Pratesi guest towels were immediately soaked with blood, but I could see that the injury wasn't severe, just a flesh wound, and we took the two towels that were left to wrap tightly around my arm until the bleeding would stop. "Not an emergency," I promised Paco, and he put his arms around my waist then, kissing my hair, my forehead, and my lips. "Don't do this to me again," he whispered. "Seeing you up there, bleeding, I thought my heart would close down forever. I can't lose you."

"You won't," I said, looking into his anguished blue eyes. "You have me forever. That is, if you want me."

"I've always wanted you. But it's been pretty hard lately to get anywhere near you."

I started to cry then, softly, and Paco took a tissue to wipe my eyes and catch the tears rolling down my cheeks. "I hate for you to see me the way I've been lately," I said. "Weak and attacked and vulnerable and scared. It's not why you're with me. You fell in love with a competent, tough doctor, not this needy, frightened girl."

"I fell in love with you. With Sarabeth. Not some doctor. If there's a time you need help, I want to help. That's what people do when they love each other." He adjusted the towels around my arm. "Don't push me away when things are rough. I don't know that I've ever loved you more than I did swooping you up from the roof."

"Rescuing me."

"Being there when you needed me," he corrected.

"I never needed you more," I said, crying harder.

For an answer, Paco kissed my salty cheeks, licking at the tears, hugging me tighter until my injured arm got in the way, and I yelped in pain, and we both laughed and kissed.

Alicia said the police were on their way, and Eric was, too—she'd called him to come check on my wound. Waiting, we all stumbled into Hollis's bedroom. Alicia fussed about my arm, then introduced me to Mike, the private detective.

"Nice to meet you," I said, the etiquette of the moment escaping me. "Thanks for shooting Juliette" didn't sound quite right, so I tried, "Thanks for saving my life."

"Part of the job."

"How did you find me?" I asked, looking from one face to another.

"Easy," Alicia said. "Mike was tailing Juliette, as you'd suggested. He followed her to Sloane's apartment and was waiting for her to come out when he saw you going in. Since he hadn't heard that was supposed to happen, he called to tell me right away. Paco was at my office and we came over together to check it out."

"But the roof," I said. "What made you go up there?"

"We were standing at the lobby security desk when an alarm sounded and an electronic voice said, 'Penthouse fire door has been opened.' It's a pretty high-tech security system. The guard flashed to a video monitor, and Paco swore he saw you just before the door closed. Mike, meanwhile, had been chatting up an elevator operator named Morgan."

"I met him," I said.

"Right. And when we rushed over and said it was an emergency, and that your life was in danger, he took us up to another roof access. He kept muttering that he'd probably get fired for this, but that you'd seemed like such a nice lady, he wanted to help. We got out on the roof, and Mike spotted you and saw Sloane standing there and Juliette waving the gun, and the rest you know.''

A beeper on Mike's belt went off and he walked out of the room to make a phone call.

''How did you figure out that Juliette had killed Hollis?'' Alicia asked. ''And that she was having an affair with Sloane.''

''I didn't,'' I admitted. ''The pieces weren't fitting together, and I came here to talk to Sloane. Juliette saw me here and went over the edge. I guess she figured that everything she'd so carefully planned was going to fall apart. Then I saw her again and there were a couple of things—her manicure, an expression she uses—that clicked, and I realized that she was Nurse Patsy. I don't know why it took me this long to make the connection. I think I realized it yesterday, in the office, but my mind just wouldn't accept it.''

''Did Sloane know Juliette killed his wife?'' Paco asked.

''No, that was the whole point. She did it on her own. She hated Hollis because she desperately wanted to be Mrs. Sloane Brewster. Meanwhile, Sloane treated Hollis like dirt—he was having an affair, he slapped her around, he didn't want her to have another baby. But I think that during this pregnancy Hollis realized she didn't have to take all that. Isn't it funny? Rich Hollis Taft Brewster learned her lesson about dignity and self-esteem at the Roxbury clinic for poor women. So she told Sloane she was going to leave him, and that's when he realized he didn't want her to go. He fought to get her back. He promised to behave, and he probably ended his affair. But Juliette couldn't accept having her designs on Sloane thwarted. She took her revenge."

"I still don't understand why the death was pinned on you," Paco said, gently adjusting one of the towels on my arm, and watching another drop of blood spill on the bedspread.

"That's the part I *do* understand," Alicia said, getting up and coming over to check my arm. "Once Hollis was dead, very different forces kicked in—all the forces that surround a very rich man. The hospital wanted this exclusive deal with Brewster Managed Care, so everybody moved into protective mode. Blaming you seemed to be the best way to deflect attention."

"Ardsley and Franklin were getting money from Brewster and so was the governor," I said. "They wanted to keep Sloane happy and figured that 'solving' his wife's death, in a way that clearly had nothing to do with the hospital, was the safest thing." I sighed. "The only part I'm missing is what was in those files in Ardsley's office and who wanted them badly enough to stab me."

There was a sudden flurry at the door—Eric rushing in, and literally bumping into Mike, who was coming back from the other end of the hall.

"What have you done to yourself this time?" Eric asked, eyeing my arm, and putting his doctor's bag down on the floor.

"Just a bullet wound. Not nearly as painful as a stab wound, by the way."

"How wonderful that you have a basis for comparison," Eric said. "Maybe you can write a paper on it for the *New England Journal of Medicine*."

Mike, still standing at the door, smiled uncertainly, and I said, "Don't worry, Eric's always this way. It just takes a while to pick up his style."

Mike, whose style was obviously jocular, not wry, said, "I came back to tell you that the phone call was from Ginny's sister. They've found her. She'd cut out when she saw my car hanging around—she figured the same people who got Sarabeth were after her in New Hampshire."

"I'm so glad she's all right," I said. "Tell her I want to talk to her later. See if she remembers anything from those files."

"She remembers a lot," Mike said. "In fact, she knows where they are."

"What?"

"When you thought she was putting them back, she actually hid them in what used to be her desk. Then you got stabbed, and she never went back to get them."

"No wonder she was scared."

"I told her about Juliette and she'd already figured out that Juliette was dangerous. Apparently Ginny had mentioned to her—and only her—that she was going to Ardsley's office with you. Just a casual confidence to a good friend. But after the stabbing, she began to wonder."

Alicia and I exchanged glances. "You want to make the connection?" she asked.

"No, go ahead. I'm having trouble with this part."

"Let's assume Juliette mentioned the plan for the

break-in to Sloane, who knew you'd find dirty evidence about his deal in Ardsley's office. That wasn't going to look good for him or for the governor, so he also passed the information along.''

I tried to follow what she was saying. ''You think the *governor* ordered me followed and . . .'' I couldn't say the rest.

''Rotten, isn't it? We'll never prove it, but I wouldn't be surprised if Doheny was behind it. He didn't wield the knife himself, but he has plenty of hoods on the street who owe him favors. So he arranged for one of them to get you. As far as he knew, you were responsible for Sloane's wife's death, so you deserved it. I'd say that kind of thinking explains the break-in at your home computer, too.'' She sighed. ''I suspected that from the beginning, and I must say it's what got me caught up in this case. I started recognizing the dirty fingers of government.''

I was silent for a moment, not wanting to think about the high-level hideousness. Doheny was an obnoxious individual, but it never occurred to me that he could be involved in this kind of scheming. All at once, I missed my dad, who'd brought me up to trust authority. It was sad to realize that I never would again.

''Once the government had you in the hospital, Juliette, for her own reasons, wanted to finish the job,'' Alicia went on. ''She was starting to realize that you might be the one to expose her and make her lose Sloane. She didn't know where your poking around might lead.''

Eric, listening, shook his head, and picked up his doctor's bag. ''Where it's led,'' he said, ''is to a bullet wound, which I'd like to take care of. Do you think you could all wait while Sarabeth comes with me for a few minutes?''

''I could wait for her forever,'' Paco said, and after all we'd been through, and for reasons I'll never understand, I blushed.

II

ANOTHER DAY IN court, but this time I wasn't wearing a blue suit. I pulled on a long, pleated silk skirt, a pale pink cotton T-shirt, and espadrilles that tied around the ankle. My long hair spilled down over my shoulders.

''You look gorgeous,'' Paco said. ''But this isn't your Judge Snow look.''

''My Judge Snow look hasn't exactly gotten me any votes,'' I said. ''This time she might as well see the real me, since she's going to hear the real story.''

After the last hearing, Judge Snow had ruled that the trial date was not to be postponed. Now there was another hearing, since Alicia had petitioned that all charges be dropped.

The courthouse didn't seem as frightening today as it had in the past, maybe because when I walked in, Judge Snow's courtroom was filled with familiar faces. Eric was there and Lori Meadows, Ruby from the clinic, and Ginny with her sister. Justin Bryant came in and shook hands with Alicia. He'd managed to get the hint of a tan and some of his sallowness was gone.

Alicia made her case concisely. Hollis Taft Brewster had died from an injection of TPA, an anticoagulating drug that caused her to bleed profusely, with symptoms mimicking a postpartum uterine bleed. The drug had been given by a nurse who had sneaked into her room, disguised, during the night. A student nurse could substantiate that. She could also substantiate that the call button had been unplugged from the bedside outlet. Postmortem findings showed that morphine had been injected along with the TPA, so Hollis had been too dazed to get out of her bed and seek help.

As for the head nurse, who had told police that nobody had entered the room, she was suffering from Demerol addiction. An anonymous phone call—from the killer—threatened to expose her addiction if she mentioned anything.

I turned around slightly when Alicia got to that part and caught Ginny's eye. That had been her contribution. She had mentioned the note about Blanche Dolton to Juliette weeks earlier—mostly to point out how little confidentiality there was left in medical records. Juliette had used the information for her own purposes.

Alicia had more to say.

The description of the nurse who entered Hollis Taft Brewster's room matched the description of the nurse who entered Sarabeth Love's room when she was in the hospital. Fingerprints on a tourniquet identified that nurse as Juliette Martin.

Alicia paused, and I knew she had volumes more to offer. But Judge Snow turned to Justin Bryant.

"Does the prosecution have any response?"

"Yes." Bryant stood up and looked at Alicia. "The district attorney's office would like to congratulate the defense team for shedding new light on this case. We are willing to drop all charges against Dr. Sarabeth Love.''

I expected my friends in the visitors' seats to cheer, but they probably figured you didn't do that in Judge Snow's courtroom, because the prosecutor's statement was greeted with absolute silence. I turned around, though, and saw a row of grinning faces.

Judge Snow banged her gavel. ''This case is dismissed. All charges are dropped. Would the former defendant please rise.''

I looked in shock at Alicia, who just shrugged and motioned for me to stand. Judge Snow, as solemn as ever, turned her full attention toward me. ''Dr. Love, this court regrets the improper charges that were brought against you. I intend to order an investigation to see if they were brought maliciously, or simply in error. At this time, the court orders you only to take care of your wounds and get well.''

I grinned. ''Thank you, Your Honor.''

''This court is adjourned.''

''So that's it,'' Alicia said, hugging me, when we were all back outside, on the street. The day was cloudy but sweetly warm; a slight drizzle had made the air feel fresh. ''Judge Snow is no great fan of the governor. It will be interesting to see what her investigation turns up. I can at least guarantee that the deal between Brewster Managed Care and P&S won't go through.''

''Good,'' I said, then I realized that I didn't really care what happened to Brewster Managed Care or P&S.

''Alicia, you did an incredible job,'' Paco said. ''There's no way to thank you.''

"I should thank *you*. This case put me back on track in my career and reminded me of what I really like to do." She looked across the street, where Justin Bryant seemed to be waiting for her, then gave me a kiss on the cheek and said, "Call me."

When she was gone, I turned to Ruby, who was standing a little apart from our group. "What are you doing this afternoon?" I asked her.

"Back to the clinic, Dr. Love."

"May I come with you?"

"For what?"

"For a job. I can't go back to my private practice and I never want to see P&S hospital again."

Ruby laughed. "You always have a job with us. But even with our new funds, we can't pay you much."

"Well, then let's become partners in the clinic," I suggested, "and make it bigger than Hollis ever dreamed. We'll use her contribution as seed money to get other donations—then build the Taft Clinic and Shelter. A tribute to her. She deserves it."

Ruby's eyes shone. "I'm not going to stop you from that, Dr. Love. But you heard what the judge said. You have to get good and healed first."

"I'm good," I said, laughing.

"You've never been better," Paco said as he leaned over to kiss me. "I think it's the most wonderful idea I've heard."

The sun, struggling through the clouds, burst through just then, and I tilted my head upward to feel the warm rays. "From pain arises hope," I said, smiling at Paco and thinking of his hospital painting.

"Enough pain." He kissed me on the nose. "Let's go get some coffee and hope."